CHOICES

AN ANTHOLOGY OF REPRODUCTIVE HORROR

Edited by Dianna Gunn

Renaissance

Diverse Canadian Voices

PressesRenaissancePress.ca

First edition 2025

Cover art and design by Alexander Cuvelier and Nathan Fréchette.
Interior design by Éric Desmarais.
Edited by Dianna Gunn, and Bradley O'Neill.

Legal deposit, Library and Archives Canada, September 2025.

Paperback ISBN: 978-1-990086-91-5
Ebook ISBN: 978-1-990086-96-0

Renaissance Press - pressesrenaissancepress.ca

Renaissance acknowledges that it is hosted on the traditional, unceded land of the Anishinabek, the Kanien'kehá:ka, and the Omàmìwininìwag. We acknowledge the privileges and comforts that colonialism has granted us and vow to use this privilege to disrupt colonialism by lifting up the voices of marginalized humans who continue to suffer the effects of ongoing colonialism.

Printed in Gatineau at
Imprimerie Gauvin
Depuis 1892
gauvin.ca

Renaissance gratefully acknowledges the support of the Canada Council for the Arts

To every person who never had a choice, and every person who fought to give people like me the right to choose.

A Note for Readers

This book deals with many harrowing subjects, including domestic abuse, sexual assault and coerced reproduction. Some of these stories contain graphic depictions of mutilation, including self-mutilation, torture, death, and suicide. Each story has its own unique warnings placed underneath the title so you can choose the ones you want to read and avoid stories that may cause you significant psychological harm.

Please take care of yourself as you read and remember that it's okay to pause to take a breath, let out a scream, or take a nap. The stories will be here when you're ready to face them again.

TABLE OF CONTENTS

From the Editor

I was a surprise. Not an accident, my mother would say, because an accident implies something unwanted, something forced upon you. She wanted me to know she had a choice, that I was her choice.

Many years later, I had to make my own choice. I chose differently. I continue to choose differently, living a childfree life I cherish.

Other women—and uterus owners of various genders—aren't so lucky. Some live in places where they cannot easily access the appropriate care, even if it is technically legal. Others come from religious backgrounds where they are taught there is only one path, one they are pressured into taking for fear of abandonment, ostracization, or even murder. Others still cannot legally access an abortion or even birth control. The far right wants to force all of us into this final category, and they've had great success in the United States.

I am extremely aware of how different my life would be if I had been one of these people. If I hadn't had a supportive family who believed in reproductive rights, if I hadn't lived in a city with easy access to reproductive health clinics, if I hadn't lived in a country where abortion is legal. Any one of those changes could have forced me into motherhood— something I've never wanted—or into a back alley for a potentially life-ruining, or even life-ending, procedure.

The thought fills me with a dread that's difficult to express, a horror that tightens my chest and takes my breath away. A horror echoed every time I read the stories of the women I could have been: teen mothers who hate their children, hate their families, hate their lives. Uterus owners bleeding out from botched procedures and unable to seek treatment without implicating themselves in a crime. People stuck in abusive relationships, in poverty, in desperation because they have no time or energy for anything beyond the children they were forced to have.

I am not the only uterus owner who lives with this dread. It is a collective fear, one shared among millions of people carrying child-bearing organs, one growing every year as the far right—religious and otherwise—gains momentum around the world.

In October 2024, I called upon people of marginalized genders to turn this collective fear into stories, to show the world the terror so many of us live with every day through the power of fiction. More than 150 people answered the call. Their stories were beautiful, heartbreaking, horrifying. I ached to publish them all.

Sadly, a single book can only fit so many stories within its pages, so I had to make some difficult choices—though none so difficult as the choices made by the characters in these stories. I whittled the submissions down to nineteen incredible stories spanning the full range of emotions people of marginalized genders feel about the possibilities of reproduction, from abject terror to fierce joy.

Each one of these stories touched my soul. I hope they will touch yours, too.

FOREWARD: ON (RUNNING OUT OF) CHOICES

BY ALEX WOODROE

The first step in understanding any person, any problem, any situation, is listening.

Putting together an anthology is a work of both science and art; a complex puzzle of moving parts that have to come together just so. It's a gargantuan effort, and that means the engine needs a lot of fuel. Sometimes, they're fuelled by big press money or big names, but my favourite ones? The absolute best of them, they're fuelled by individual rage and the desire to make the world a slightly better place; to weave together a meaningful moment from the stories of artists with something to say.

And you can't do any better for that than Choices. Not only is it masterfully put together, but each of these individual authors mean business; you can read drive and purpose and heart in every piece. Every one is a winner at a gruesome competition nobody ever volunteered to take part in.

There's a near future in "Fireweed, Ferns and Moss," and a present-day in "The Referral," that'll have you itching to keep reading while wishing you could look away. You need to know, but you don't want to know. A raw hunger in "Infanticipation" that'll make you feel ashamed of yourself without fully knowing why. What you'll find in stories like "What is Asexuality in the Eyes of the Law," "Vessels of God," or "The Blood Mango Tree" is that they take all of ten seconds to drive a wedge of dread into your heart, and not through any descriptions of monsters and gore. No, the opening pages of those—and most of the other—stories horrify by promises, by hints, by suggestions that draw from our collective well of trauma and folklore, and understanding of what it means to be in a vulnerable body.

Because this is a showcase that will be perceived in varying degrees of horror depending on who is reading it, I have no doubt. Even though each of these stories is perfect in its own way, even though they're all loud and remorseless, it's as much about what you bring to the reading as it is about what they will offer you.

The highest impact will always, certainly be felt by the most vulnerable. There's so much to fear when you know exactly how far down the hill your situation can slip, and how quickly. So little needs to be said to understand the danger we're in. You'll spot it in one sentence, one line of dialogue, and sometimes in the turn of one word.

For those less vulnerable, it's going to be a journey. If they're paying attention, if they're really listening, the horror will increase as they go along. They might end this anthology on the final words of "The Watcher of the Wisps" a little breathless, thinking, "thank goodness that's over," except for many people, it's never over. They may pour through the whole volume in one sitting but then need respite, some Saturday morning cartoons and soothing music, and think, "it can't possibly be this fraught and dire constantly," except for many people, it can be, and it is.

It is this fraught, and this dire, and constantly.

For many people, these stories are hardly fiction at all; more of a unique way of looking at how other people view our daily horrors. A way to come together and laugh-cry-grief-rage as one shared body. And that's why it's so important to listen to, and honour, the struggles people of marginalized genders face: those struggles are the story of so many more people than you're imagining, they have ramifications that impact the entirety of our society, and frankly, we can't make positive changes unless we address them as a whole; as everyone's struggle, everyone's responsibility. Unless we listen as one and act as one.

When Dianna asked me to write this introduction, she asked me to touch on my part in bringing it to life, and it's only a modest part. I gave a little advice, a little support, and I listened. But I'm getting a lot in return; through being here and introducing you to this exceptional manuscript, I get to feel like I'm also adding my mouth and voice to this collective scream, like I'm also welcome and embraced in this shared body.

And we want to embrace you, too. We want you to feel with us and rage with us and grow with us. We believe you belong.

All you need to do is listen.

Infanticipation

by Kelli Etheridge

Content warnings: Graphic depiction of birth, captivity

Two Weeks Before Birth Day

Áine unlocked the door and entered the surrogate's spacious bedroom, carrying a tray with breakfast. Áine missed her own bed. She had given up the primary suite in her home to accommodate the pregnancy. Since Katherine would be sequestered to the home and, most often, the one room, it was a kindness to offer her the capacious bedroom and ensuite.

"Here, Katherine, a smoothie and two soft-boiled eggs, just like you prefer."

"Thank you. I don't have much appetite, though." Katherine was pallid and more gaunt than at the time of conception eight months ago. She had access to a patio furnished with a cushioned rattan couch for lounging, yet she had barely explored outside since autumn arrived. Áine wondered if pre-partum depression was a thing.

"You must eat, for both of you. Keep your strength up." Áine held the pink smoothie up to Katherine's face and maneuvered the straw to her lips. "Drink up."

Katherine sipped with reluctance. "I usually love strawberries, but it kinda tastes funny. A bit metallic."

"That's just the iron supplement. Gotta make sure you're not deficient." Áine couldn't tell her exactly what kind of iron supplement it was; she'd never agree to drink it. The fruit and copious addition of cinnamon should cover up the taste of raw liver well enough. She pushed the glass into Katherine's hand and sat down on a chair beside the bed.

"Ok, I'll get through it." She cringed with each of the small sips she managed to keep down.

Áine lifted Katherine's T-shirt and rested a hand on the surrogate's burgeoning belly. A crown of expanding stretchmarks peeked out from her underwear line. "I have some friends coming over for coffee this morning. I'll need you to stay in here and be quiet, okay? TV is fine, just keep the volume low."

"Sure, I know the drill. Quiet as a mouse."

"The walls are soundproof, so you don't need complete silence. No yelling though, obviously. If you need something, just text." She sauntered to the French doors and secured the lock.

It wasn't easy to find a surrogate who would agree to Aine's rather extreme terms. Katherine was a good fit, though. She was young and vibrant and she'd been a surrogate before, so Áine knew there was no concern she'd change her mind and want to keep the baby. In her surrogate CV, Katherine said she wanted to… "provide families who didn't have the privilege of pregnancy themselves with the opportunity to become parents. Everyone should experience the joy of becoming a mother or father. I'm grateful to offer the gift of surrogacy to others." Áine knew it wasn't an entirely selfless act; Áine offered her triple her going rate. Katherine couldn't resist. She told Áine she was going to use the money to start her own family after this pregnancy. Katherine intended for this one to be her final surrogacy.

So did Áine.

Áine had healthy eggs of her own, but refused to carry a baby to term. She couldn't confess to outsiders just *how* pregnancy was dangerous for her. She had practised multiple layers of protection as she went about a rather promiscuous youth. Oral birth control was an easy first defence, then condoms, of course. She followed her menses cycle closely. She knew her body intimately, its cycles, the ebb and flow of hormones. She recognized the sharp signal of ovulation, the mittelschmerz pain, as her eggs were released each month. She knew when it was safe to have sex and when it wasn't. She was terrified of becoming pregnant, which was the most effective prophylactic she had.

Áine returned with a tray of lunch after her friends departed. Her visits with Katherine focused almost exclusively around meals as of late. She used to spend more time with her, but over the months, a guilt had grown inside Áine that made her distance herself from the woman growing her baby.

She rested the tray on Katherine's lap. Tuna sandwiches, peppermint tea and a small glass dish with supplements.

"Thanks. Hey, Áine, I'd like to call my mom. It's been so long. Even though she knows I've been intentionally out of contact, I'm sure she's worried. I want to let her know I'll be home soon, with the birth so close now," she implored with a wisp of hope in her voice.

"Katherine, I know you've been lonely, but we're almost there. The NDA you signed states no outside contact. You agreed. It's binding. You can talk to her soon." She swallowed the lie with an uncomfortable gulp. She wished she could offer reassurance to both Katherine and her mom. It was a sin to cause a mother worry. "But at least you have a mother," Áine retorted.

A melancholy washed across her face. "I am lonely and bored, but I can make it a few more weeks, of course."

"I'm sorry. I know you can. Let me draw you a bath, help you relax, and pamper yourself. Then maybe we can play Scrabble, if you want."

"Sure. That'd be nice, Áine."

ONE WEEK BEFORE BIRTH DAY

"Will you tell me about the father? You never said much, other than he was a donor. How did you choose him?" Katherine inquired, picking at the makeshift vegetable platter that Áine had assembled for her.

Áine sat at the end of Katherine's bed, munching on pepperoni sticks and sipping on a glass of red wine. It was a rare, casual moment between the two women.

"Well, I knew what I wanted. That helped. He had to have red hair like me, like all of us." Others in the family had conceived through one-night stands with handsome redheads, but Áine loved the idea of sifting through a catalogue, searching for the perfect specimen. She couldn't check for important traits if she picked someone up in a bar. "I want her to have a deep sense of belonging, physically and emotionally. I made sure the donor was intelligent. Being attractive was a bonus. He's the kind of guy I'd marry if I wanted such a thing. I feel confident his DNA was the right choice, but our family genes are extremely strong. I know she'll have more of me in her, no matter who I chose."

"Well, I love your auburn hair. It's so unique. And your family all has red hair? Those must be some crazy, powerful heredity."

"Every one of us. Yeah, like I said, strong lineage. I'll show you. We're quite amazing. I think so, anyway." Áine left and returned, clutching a thick photo album. She opened it and showed Katherine her ancestors—her great-grandmother, her grandmother, her mother.

"This is my aunt Cara and my cousin Seren when she was little. They'll arrive closer to the delivery date. They're excited to meet you."

"And what about your mom? She is so beautiful. You definitely got a lot of her features."

Áine stared at her mother's image and refused to lift her head to make eye contact. "She died in childbirth. My birth. It's why I don't celebrate my birthday; it's her death day. I want my daughter's birthday to be a celebration. Anyway, I was raised by my aunt." Her matter-of-fact answer prevented Katherine from pursuing the mother topic further.

"Where is everyone else? Your dad and grandpa? The men in your family?"

"We have a solid history of single motherhood. Haven't had much luck with the men in our lives."

"I get that. I seem to pick some pretty awful dudes. I'm going to do better next time though. I want to find a good guy, dad material."

"Good luck. I think you'd have been a good mom. *Will* be a good mom, I mean, if you find the right guy."

"I hope so. One more thing…you keep calling her a girl. How do you know? Or is it wishful thinking? We never got an ultrasound or anything."

"We only ever have daughters in our family. Just how it's been for as long as our family tree goes back. Not sure why, but I'm good with it. Looking forward to raising a powerful female."

"Wow, that's weird. Interesting, for sure. Did you ever try to get pregnant, Áine? Or did you just know surrogacy was your best chance?"

"I would have loved to be pregnant. It's the birth that's the problem. My mom wasn't the only one in our lineage to die in childbirth. So, no. I didn't even try to get pregnant myself."

"No judgment from me, really. One of my other pregnancies was for a mom who didn't want to go through pregnancy at all. Wanted to keep her body intact, avoid stretch marks. She told me she couldn't live with a loose vagina from a natural birth and she didn't want a scar from a cesarean. By the end of the pregnancy, I wasn't sure if she'd even be a good mom. I thought I was doing something good. With you, it's different. You'll be a caring mom. I can tell you really want to be a mother. I want that for myself too one day."

Áine slammed the album closed. "Enough of that. Let's not talk about the past or the future. We'll focus on the now. Today. I'll see you when dinner's ready." She bolted out of the room.

Áine would have loved the chance to experience pregnancy if it weren't life-threatening. She longed to nurture life inside her, feeling her baby girl twist and kick within her own body, not limited to surface movements through a surrogate's skin. She wanted to nourish that life with what she consumed, knowing that every nutrient would be assimilated and shared with her unborn daughter. She wanted the primordial rite of passage—the pain, the pushing. She desired all of it. But it also terrified her. She didn't want her daughter burdened with the sense of culpability she sustained about her mother's death. Surrogacy was the only way to ensure that her daughter was not motherless.

Modernity, although it made it challenging for her family to stay shrouded, wasn't all bleak. It allowed her to have a biological heir through a sperm donor, in vitro fertilization and surrogacy. Her mother, Kyla, hadn't had that choice. Áine's birth destroyed her in a sanguinary sacrifice. Kyla knew the risks, but the biological imperative to reproduce was strong.

Kyla's sister, Cara, had decided for a premature cesarean to avoid labour. It was not without risks. Hospitalization was not an option; the c-section was performed at home under the most sterile conditions possible. Others in the family had attempted c-sections in this way with detrimental outcomes. Many of the children in the family were orphans and most were without siblings. Áine was both parentless and sisterless.

Day Before Birth Day

"This is Katherine, or Kiki if you prefer. Kiki, this is my aunt Cara and my cousin Seren."

"Very nice to meet you. I'm looking forward to being in the company of women for the birth. I had a male obstetrician for one of my pregnancies and he had the gentleness of a fisherman gutting his catch. Never warmed the speculum when I got pap tests, either."

"So true," Cara said, taking Katherine's hand. "This is women's work. We know our own bodies best." Cara gave Katherine's hand a gentle squeeze before letting go.

"Thank you. I totally agree, I…"

Áine interrupted, "I wanted to tell all of you now that we are together… I've decided to name her Kherington. It sounds like a strong name. It means *sprung from the fire*. And I love that it starts with K, an homage to my mother, and like Kherington's surrogate mother." She gazed at Katherine, whose eyes grew damp with tears.

"I love it. Hello, Kherington." Katherine circled her hands around her belly.

"Come sit on the rocker while we make the bed." Áine and Seren made the bed with a waterproof mattress cover and fresh sheets. They piled towels and facecloths up on the nightstand in preparation for the birth. "Births can get messy, as you know." Áine laughed.

"Áine, I'm sorta scared. I've never had a home birth. I know we agreed to it. But…" Katherine's face was gravid with unease.

"Women have been giving birth far longer than hospitals have existed. We will get through this." Áine didn't specify who *we* was in that scenario.

"Yeah, but a lot of women died in childbirth back then."

"Seriously? You think I don't know that, Kiki?" She barked at the girl, her face flushed with anger. Guilt crept in and commingled with her irritation. These feelings of sin and wrongdoing bewildered her now. They were unexpected emotions. She had actually thought she could avoid attachment after nine months of nurturing Katherine. She'd become more than a vessel, and Áine didn't appreciate it.

The room fell silent. Áine delivered her captive's dinner without another word and left her alone for the remainder of the evening.

BIRTH DAY

Áine placed the palms of her hands flat against Katherine's abdomen and caressed the taut skin. A confident kick from inside communicated readiness as the little one writhed in the amniotic pool. The biological imperative grew to a throbbing pain as Áine anticipated impending motherhood. *Soon, baby girl. We will meet soon.*

The arrival felt ancient, a primeval passage into the current modernity. It was getting more challenging each cycle to find shadowed corners of the world where they could remain unnoticed. They had to accept being visible in this society of selfies, surveillance and digital connectivity, but with a veil to blur who they truly were. It wasn't their appearance that would give them away; it was almost everything else.

Katherine pleaded, "Please, some painkillers. This doesn't feel normal, like last time or the first time. I need something to take the edge off." She rocked to and fro in her nest of pillows.

"Ah, sorry Kiki, drugs wouldn't be good for the baby. You're tough. You've done this twice before." Áine had grown to prefer using her nickname to Katherine. Calling her Kiki made her feel more inconsequential somehow. How could you take a Kiki seriously?

Katherine rolled onto her side in an awkward shuffle and sat up at the edge of the bed. "I'm not feeling right. I need to move around for a bit. If that doesn't help, I think we should get to the hospital."

"No, no, no. None of that. Lay back, rest. It'll be over soon. Don't worry."

Katherine rose and swirled with unsteadiness. She grabbed the bedpost for balance, the other hand circling her belly. "I need to walk around. I feel nauseous. Maybe some fresh air will help. Just on the patio even."

She shuffled towards the French doors that led out to the terrace. Áine blocked her path, put a gentle hand to her shoulder and eased a reluctant Katherine back into bed. "I'm going to bring in my aunt and cousin now to help with the birth."

"Is your aunt a midwife? I think we should have a doctor, or at least a trained midwife. I know we agreed to a home birth, but I think some sort of medical person would be best for the baby, for Kherington." She leaned back, closed her eyes, and breathed through her pain. "These contractions…they…they won't stop…they are continuous."

"My aunt has attended quite a few births. We have quite the birth history in my family." Áine opened the bedroom door and yelled, "Auntie Cara, can you both come in now? We're close!"

Her eyes still closed, Katherine rolled back and forth in the bed in a self-soothing rhythm. Aunt Cara and cousin Seren entered with a jovial energy. "Can you both help me with Kiki?" Áine passed them long pieces of cotton fabric and they took their places at the corners of the bed.

Áine and Cara each held one of Kiki's arms, caressing them until the muscles softened. They eased them out to the wooden headboard slats.

As the cotton circled her wrists, Katherine's eyes flashed open. She attempted to tuck her arms into her body, resisting the restraints. "What the hell, Áine? Áine! This is unnecessary. And cruel."

The woman yanked her arms back to the corners with a forceful tugging and tied them to the bed.

Seren's rope wrapped around the ankles, securing the legs in a closed position. Katherine kicked out in a desperate attempt at freedom, her heel striking Seren in the diaphragm. Seren fell back, gasping for air.

Cara grabbed the flailing limbs and leaned her weight onto them as Áine fastened the linked legs to the corners with more rope.

Seren regained her breath and stood over Katherine, who was thrashing in the bed like a wild animal caught in a trap.

Seren raised her arm to strike.

"Not nice!" Áine caught Seren's hand before she could slap the expectant mother. "Seriously, Seren. No! You can't blame her." Áine pushed Seren away from the bed with a firm nudge.

She leaned in and brushed the hair from Katherine's damp forehead with her fingertips. She whispered, "Try to calm yourself down. Deep breaths. It'll be okay." She hated lying, but necessity demanded mistruths.

Katherine stared into Áine's eyes, a silent pleading. Her breaths were heavy and rapid, despite Áine's demonstration of slow, deep breathing. They lingered there, breathing together, until Katherine's muscles relaxed in an exhausted acquiescence.

"How the hell am I supposed to give birth with my legs tied together?" Katherine's voice quivered.

"I know it seems strange. We have different births in our family. You won't have to do all the work."

"It doesn't make sense. I demand to go to the hospital." Katherine tugged on her restraints, then slumped back into the bed as the futility became clear.

"My dear," Aunt Cara said, "you are in no position to make demands. I do, however, appreciate your tenacity." She caressed Katherine's forehead, brushing away her damp bangs.

"Let's begin. Kherington is near." Áine nodded at her aunt and cousin.

Cara began lighting beeswax candles and dimmed the room lights to create a peaceful ambience. Áine lit an incense cone: frankincense, clary sage, and sweet orange.

"I made you a playlist, dear cousin, just for today. I thought this would be perfect for a birth. Can I put it on?" Seren held her hands up and rocked back and forth as if she was at a silent disco. "We can dance. You have that in your birth plan, right?" A quick nod from Áine, and Seren was connecting her phone to the Bluetooth speaker in the corner.

The songs penetrated the room, the volume louder than the softness of the candlelight would have suggested.

The three women danced around the room, spinning their long skirts until they billowed with air. At times, they held hands and whirled in a circle together. Their laughter, and occasional celebratory whoops, drowned out the moans of Katherine, who tossed her head back and forth on the pillow with eyes shut tight.

"Seren, these songs are perfect. Thank you," praised Áine as she swayed to the beat of Steppenwolf's Born to Be Wild.

"I thought you would enjoy the digital mixtape of classics. More to come. We still have Cindy Lauper's Girls Just Want to Have Fun, Sweet Child of Mine by your favourite band—Guns and Roses, Wild Child by The Doors, and We are Family by Sister Sledge." Seren bounced up and down, hands in the air, rock concert style.

A scream interrupted the family dance party. Seren paused the music with a scowl. Katherine lifted her head to speak to them through the sweaty, tangled mess of her hair. "Something's wrong. It hurts too much. Please, please can we go to the hospital? For your baby? It's what's best for her. Me too. But her, Áine. Think of Kherington."

Áine drew near and stroked Katherine's rigid skin, stretched from the pregnancy over time and pulled taut from within now. "I am thinking of her. What's best is to stay right here. She knows what to do."

"She? Who, your aunt? She's dancing around like she doesn't give a shit? I don't think she even knows what to do." Katherine's voice strained out the words between breaths. Her eyes bulged without blinking. The line between labour pain and terror blurred.

"No, Kiki. *She* knows what to do. My little one." Áine pointed at the undulating abdomen, nodded to Seren to turn the music back on, and resumed dancing as the wailing intertwined with the soundtrack.

Katherine's wailing shifted into a sharp scream as her abdomen heaved with rhythmic intention from within.

"Turn the music down a bit. She's coming." Áine rushed to the bed.

"Kiki, can you still hear me? I want to thank you for everything, for making me a mother, for nurturing my daughter for all these months."

Katherine tossed in agony, her pain-glazed eyes meeting Áine's.

Áine winced, wishing for an expedient end to the suffering. "Katherine, I'm sorry. I wish you had the chance to be a mother yourself, to hold your own baby in your arms, so see him or her grow up. You deserved that much. I've grown fond of you. I'm so, so sorry." Her voice trailed off at the end in hitching breaths.

Katherine's eyes closed in squinted agony.

Áine focused her attention on the belly, the churning.

Katherine's eyes closed and her body grew still as a small hole developed in her abdomen below her belly button. Tiny hands, sharp with fingernails, tore through the stretched skin. Áine reached in to assist, but Cara held her back with words, "Leave her; it's *her* rite of passage. Her birth."

Áine nodded, "Of course."

Arms emerged, followed by a head covered with blood and vernix. The jagged opening of flesh grew wider as she birthed herself into the world. Kherington pulled herself up and out, resting atop the womb, blinking to see for the first time.

"Look at her. She is beautiful!" Seren exclaimed.

"Under that blood, I can still see her fiery red hair like ours," Cara commented.

In a soft motherly tone, Áine welcomed her daughter, "Hello Kherington. Nice to meet you. I'm your mother. Happy Birthday!"

Kherington smiled at the sound of the surrounding voices. Her mouth opened up into a wide, toothy grin.

Cara handed Áine a towel to lift the newborn up and out of Katherine's body. Áine held Kherington close and wiped the blood from her face.

Once the umbilical cord stopped pulsing, Cara clamped it at the baby's belly and at the placental attachment. She handed the umbilical cord to baby Kherington to gnaw on, which the baby gratefully grasped in her delicate fists.

Cara pulled the placenta out with gentleness and placed it in a bowl.

"What shall we have this time? Stew again, or should I try a new recipe?" Cara inquired.

"Stew. It's the tradition." Áine suggested.

"Yes, your placenta stew is the best, Mom."

"Stew it is."

DAY AFTER BIRTH DAY

"The room is ready for you, Áine." Seren spoke quietly so as not to wake a napping Kherington.

Áine entered the primary bedroom, freshly cleaned, curtains wide open to allow in the morning light. She curled up into bed with her newborn, both of them exhausted from the birth experience.

Seren and Cara joined her and sat on the edge of the bed.

"You know, that wasn't so bad. I'm already thinking I want to do this again. Not right away, but soon enough. I want Kherington to have a sister."

"I always wished I had a sister, although you were like a sister to me." Seren leaned in to kiss Áine's cheek.

"I know, you too." She blew her cousin a kiss. "I still have some eggs that they harvested. I could do it all again. Find another surrogate. And maybe after that I'll sell off my remaining eggs. Surrogacy isn't cheap."

"And let one of us be born to unsuspecting parents? Is the world ready for that? Can you imagine?" Cara questioned with her stern maternal voice.

They all grew quiet as they visualized that scenario. The seriousness lifted and soon giggles transformed into riotous laughter.

Áine's laughter subsided to a smirk. "Yes, yes, I can imagine just that."

I Will Get You Medical Care

by Bogi Takács

Content warnings: Intersexism, anti-queer sentiment (specifically about marriage), bodily harm, strange spider alien

I am sure, in retrospect, that the spider had meant no harm.

~*~

I met the spider in the parking lot of one of those Medical Buildings scattered throughout the endless suburban sprawl. The parking lot was full of cars, but empty of people. The creature was a collection of acute angles attached to a spherical body, considerably taller than me. I thought that it looked like a caricature of a spider rather than an actual spider magnified a hundredfold. Eyes dotted the body more or less uniformly, without any obvious pattern.

I had just ran out of the Medical Building, the receptionist yelling after me in a chipper Midwestern tone that I might still want to make a follow-up appointment. I had no desire for a follow-up appointment, or to ever set foot in this building again. The spider was standing in front of my car, blocking the way. I looked around frantically as I gasped for breath, seeking aid, any aid. I considered going back inside, but I had not exited so rapidly without a reason.

I was expecting "Be Not Afraid" at any moment, though the spider seemed less terrifyingly benevolent than a biblically accurate angel. Instead, the creature crouched down ever so slightly, and tilted closer to me, putting a handful of eyes at my eye level. I wiped my tears away.

The spider said, "YOU NEED MEDICAL CARE."

I swore, because the alternative was a desperate cackle. "Of course I need medical care!"

The spider said, "I CAN HELP YOU."

"Then help me!" I shouted at it.

This proved to be a mistake.

I was standing in front of the chipper receptionist.

"To see Dr. Gorman at Primary Care?" she asked. I gasped and she looked me over, her eyes narrowing. There had been no appreciable transition: I had been in front of the spider one moment, and the receptionist the next. What was going on? Was I dreaming?

"Dr. Gorman, yes, thank you," I mumbled. I had apparently already told her my name and date of birth; for all I knew, she'd scanned my insurance card with that little thing that looked like a miniature printer rather than a scanner, too.

The receptionist blinked at me, deciding not to ask if anything was wrong. I wondered if she saw distraught people seeing the doctor on a regular basis.

She told me to sit and wait to be called. This at least gave me a few moments to gather my thoughts. How long had it taken the previous time? Not more than five minutes. Had there *been* a previous time?

Everything seemed solid and regular in a pedestrian way. The signage pointed at various different doctors' offices with no element of the surreal. This clearly wasn't a dream. Maybe I had had some kind of precognitive vision. I would know once I saw the doctor—or even before that, the nurse taking my vitals.

I reached for my phone, thinking to text my spouse, Or—"Hey, hope you're OK? Something completely weird just happened to me!"—but the battery was out. I dug around in my bag for my charger, then hunted for an outlet. I found one underneath my seat, and plugged the charger in with a groan. I straightened up in relief, yet my phone didn't even display the small lightning bolt showing me it was charging. It was completely inert.

I didn't have time to figure this out. The nurse opened the door to an interior corridor of offices and my gut clenched even further. She was the same person as in my—dream? vision? hallucination?—a short, sturdily built woman named Jackie. *Should I ask her for help?* Jackie came across like a kind person, but I didn't think, "I met a giant spider in your parking lot" would go over well.

I unplugged my phone and followed her, then passively let her measure my height, weight, blood pressure and so on. I was barely aware of myself, stunned into silence—yet one part of me was thinking ahead. The appointment had been a disaster; I'd never run away from a doctor before, though I probably should have. The spider was talking about helping me. Maybe I would get a redo? If enormous spiderlike creatures could exist, then clearly time travel could exist, too.

What could I do to improve my chances of actually getting medical care? I didn't think I'd done anything wrong. Some doctors are just jerks. But still, what could I do? The nurse was done with her measurements and was asking me for my symptoms.

"I have a rash and the over-the-counter medications aren't helping," I said, like previously, but immediately second-guessed myself. I couldn't show Dr. Gorman my chest. Absolutely no way. But I didn't have a rash anywhere else. I had, but most of it had improved by the time I could get an appointment. Could I run away sooner? But then the problem of my terrible rash wouldn't be solved.

Once the nurse was done, I sat in the doctor's office, waiting for Dr. Gorman. Maybe I could come up with some other conditions? But I didn't need some random solution for something else, I needed not to feel like clawing off my skin. I stared at a poster about the dangers of high blood pressure across from my seat. I generally had low blood pressure, but if anything, this would elevate it.

I honestly had not thought it would be a problem to show my chest before Dr. Gorman went on a rant about sex hormones. I knew about sex hormones. I had spent my life since puberty that didn't quite go as planned trying to deal with my sex hormones. But I was there to get treated for an allergic rash.

I was probably, if such a thing is possible, too used to my chest. I saw it every day and it looked more or less the same. Of course, Dr. Gorman hadn't shared this experience with me.

Dr. Gorman entered and she was the same person as earlier, too—in my vision? If it had been a precognitive vision, it proved eerily accurate. She was a white woman of average height, with straight hair coloured blonde and cut in a bob. I had a sudden thought that she was the type of person who would, if she were a generation or two younger, have those loose curls that are straight at the ends. She looked friendly. She had looked friendly the first time too.

I explained my issue haltingly. I couldn't come up with a better idea. I felt I was letting the spider down. "We just moved here and our new rental wasn't cleaned… So I scrubbed everything down with all kinds of cleaning products and then I had this terrible allergic reaction. All over my upper body, um. Most of it went away, but there's still this large patch on my chest that really bothers me. I'm not sure if it was the dirt or the cleaning products… I'm allergic to dust mites, but I don't know, I'm allergic to a lot of things…"

"Could you show it? I can give you a gown."

No, I thought to myself, I absolutely cannot show it. Then you will start with my sex hormones and end with your comments about my marriage to Or, my stepson, and randomly suggest that I should have a biological child with Or, through means unknown. I didn't say any of this. I said, "Kghnfdsbrbbx."

This already deviated from the previous encounter.

I took a deep breath and said, "I'm going to warn you, I have both breasts and chest hair."

She raised an eyebrow—just one. I didn't realize people could do that. "Oh?"

"But this is really absolutely unrelated to my rash, it just happens to be on my chest, um, does that make sense? I have, uh, hyperandrogenism and uh. And I can tell you all about my uh… medical history, but it's really not related, I'm just allergic to something and it really bothers me, and…"

She looked me over, as if truly seeing me for the first time, but not in a friendly way. "Then I assume we will also need to do a blood draw, about your hormone levels?"

This wasn't going much better than the first time. I was panicking. "I, uh, my hormones. People tried to, uh, adjust them. But it made me sick. I mean, in the sense of throwing up. The hormones made me throw up and   so I went off them and—"

"Well, that will need to be revisited. I can look at your rash first and then I'll send you back to my nurse for the blood draw."

I took off my shirt, the sports bra I'd been wearing. She tilted her head sideways. "Why don't you shave it off?"

This was different, but certainly not great. "I, um. Tried to pluck it all out, but there's a bit too much for that, and then I tried to shave, but ended up with like, ingrown hairs on my chest, and that was honestly awful, and. So I just decided to keep it."

"Once your hormones are in order, it will all fall out."

I didn't think that was how it worked, but I wasn't about to explain sex hormones to her.

"Also, do you know what caused the hyperandrogenism?"

I responded almost automatically. "They had an ultrasound and after that they wanted to send me for a biopsy, but I said no because…" Because my doctor was a creep, but I decided to keep that to myself.

"Hmm, we should probably do that."

"But my rash?"

She wasn't hearing me at all. "And you're in a same-sex marriage."

"Excuse me?"

This was going the same way as previously. She would ask me about my spouse, then lecture me on how childbirth might also help with my hormones. I wouldn't be able to get in a word, both to say that my previous doctors had thought that I was infertile, and in any case my uterus, anatomically—

I stood. "I need to go to the restroom." Then I just walked out. This time, at least, I didn't break into a run.

The spider was waiting outside.

"That really didn't work," I said.

"YOU STILL NEED MEDICAL CARE," the spider responded. "I WILL HELP YOU."

"No, wait—"

~*~

I was standing in front of the receptionist.

"To see Dr. Gorman at Primary Care?" she chirped as usual.

"Excuse me, I need to go to the restroom," I muttered.

There was a pharmacy in the building. I made a run for it and bought a disposable razor, shoved it into my backpack, then ran back to the restroom. The receptionist stared but said nothing. My phone was still completely useless; whatever the spider had done to set up this loop had to have interfered with it. I wanted to ask Or for help, but I had no way of reaching them. I had to solve this situation by myself. I rushed into a stall and stripped off my blue T-shirt and my sports bra.

I had more chest hair than when I'd last tried to shave it off. This was going badly. I couldn't get rid of it all. I cut myself, then hissed as I was trying to mop up the blood with a piece of toilet paper. I put my sports bra back on and stuffed even more toilet paper into it. I bled on my T-shirt. I couldn't see the doctor like this. I ran back out to the parking lot.

"This isn't helping," I told the spider.

"I DO NOT UNDERSTAND," the spider said. "YOU SEEM UPSET. YOU STILL NEED MEDICAL CARE. I WILL HELP YOU."

"You're not helping!"

I was standing in front of the receptionist.

~*~

I needed to run away. I could go to Or's workplace, a similar but distinctly non-medical office building about an hour's walk away. I could make it. They'd help, or at least I wouldn't be facing whatever this was alone. I turned away from the receptionist and dashed out.

"YOU STILL NEED MEDICAL CARE," the spider said to my back.

I was standing in front of the receptionist.

~*~

"Please, you must help me," I begged the receptionist. "I'm trapped in a time loop. I can't even run away. It resets when I leave this building."

She looked around in alarm, then pressed something on the underside of her desk.

"No, you don't understand, I don't mean any harm, I just need to find a way out—Please don't call the police—"

~*~

"I have a rash on my arms," I told Dr. Gorman.

"You don't seem to have a rash on your arms," she said, barely humouring me.

"Well, I had… Not any longer, but look, I had a photo on my cell phone…" I desperately reached for my phone, only to remember it wasn't working.

~*~

"Please don't comment on my chest hair," I said vehemently. "I'm really not here about my chest hair. I'm here because I have a terrible itchy rash. I know you want to comment on my chest hair. Can we please just get through this without that part?"

Dr. Gorman tilted her head sideways. "I cannot promise that."

~*~

"Look." I took a deep breath. "I'm intersex. But this isn't related to that, it's an allergic rash because I spent days scraping my rental with chemicals—"

"You mean you have a hormonal illness. What was it called, DSD? A disorder of sexual development. That's the accurate term. We'll sort this out."

I decided not to say anything about what the accurate term was, and what a disorder was. This was a battle I could not win.

"Your hormones will need to be adjusted. The nurse will draw blood."
"Are you in a same-sex marriage?"
"We might still want to do that biopsy."
"I'll take a look at your rash *after* we sort this out."
"Are you in a same-sex marriage?"
"Once your hormones are in order, it will all fall out."

If this was a first contact with aliens kind of situation, it was one of the worst I could imagine.

"I cannot believe it!" I screamed at the spider. "You keep on resetting me, but it's not getting any better! I tried everything! This has to be at least the thirtieth loop! I can't leave! I can't get away!" I turned around and ran, neither back to the office nor toward the spider, just out of the parking lot—

A car backing out hit me and I fell. The car crunched to a halt and did not crush me, but I could feel something sharp—a piece of glass or plastic? A tin can? My hands were bleeding, but it was my right leg that was worse—the sharp object had sliced my pants leg open, and I had a long cut underneath. I swore, but almost immediately I glanced up, twisted around as best as I could. Behind me, the spider had vanished.

"Hey—are you okay?" A young couple got out of the car, the woman pale and shaking, the man trying to hold her up and back at the same time.

"Yeah, I..." Was this it? Had I exited the loop? It would be worth the blood. The spider was gone. I struggled to my feet. At least whatever I fell on hadn't hit an artery; it would be awful to escape this nightmare only to bleed out in the parking lot of a Medical Building, instead.

"I think I can stand," I mumbled. "Don't worry."

"I can take you to the ER!" the woman yelled. "You're bleeding!" She had the loose curls I'd just imagined a younger Dr. Gorman having. It seemed like she genuinely wanted to help. The young man—probably her boyfriend?—nodded along.

"Thank you… My car is just parked here," I said. "I think I can drive there myself."

The woman nodded. "Promise you'll go straight there."

"Sure, yes. Of course."

~*~

Out of the loop. Out of the loop! The sun shone brightly on suburbia. I was free!

Free and bleeding. Details.

My phone hadn't revived, but I'd figure out how to contact Or as soon as I got some staples in me. The bleeding really needed to be stopped. Hopefully at the ER, I could ask someone to make a call for me once this was all settled.

The ER was almost empty. Rejoice! A nurse or some other kind of assistant made me sit in a hospital wheelchair. I was seen almost immediately.

I struggled up to the exam table. The person examining me glared at my leg and said, over my shoulder to the assistant, "I'm not comfortable touching that. Send it to be X-rayed."

It? Surely he referred to my leg and not to me. Details. I was giddy from a combination of pain, blood loss and liberation.

~*~

"Your leg isn't broken," the radiologist said. "But this is a pretty nasty cut. It does need a few staples, and to be dressed. I'll send you back for that."

The same assistant rolled me back, wordlessly. I tried to start a conversation, ask if I could make a call, but he ignored me.

The previous gruff man—the doctor on duty?—glared at me. "I'm not touching that, that hairy—thing."

Not again. That sinking feeling. The last thing I had been thinking of was my hairy leg. And not hairy like woman-hairy. Hairy like man-hairy. I smiled at him and felt acutely booby. Booby and square-jawed. He clearly couldn't tell if I was male or female, and opted for the third possibility, 'monster.'

I glared at him. He glared back. "It's not broken, you can leave," he said after a few overlong seconds. "You can leave." Making the *can* into a *should*.

I couldn't force him to staple together my cut, could I? I'd file a complaint, but first I'd need to clean and dress the wound myself. Time to get home. I couldn't sew myself closed, but I could at least apply a pressure dressing, and then figure out where to go from there. Maybe another urgent care? I hobbled outside, avoiding the gaze of the assistant who had not said a single word all throughout.

~*~

The spider was waiting outside, on a busy street now devoid of people.

"YOU NEED MEDICAL CARE," the spider repeated.

"I was trying! Now I'm even worse off than I was to begin with! All thanks to you!" I broke out in the tears I'd withheld.

"I WILL GET YOU MEDICAL CARE."

"This is it! This *is* the medical care! This is what I get!"

"YOU ARE DISTRESSED."

"Of course I'm distressed! I had a rash! Then people tried to figure out my sex hormones, draw my blood, get a biopsy, interrogate me about my family, comment on my chest hair, comment on my leg hair—and I still have the rash!"

"MY ATTEMPTS HAVE SO FAR BEEN UNSUCCESSFUL. BUT I WILL GET YOU MEDICAL CARE."

"Can you just stop?"

"YOU ARE BLEEDING."

"I wasn't bleeding when this whole thing started! Are you trying to kill me?" I choked back a loud sob.

"I AM TRYING TO HELP YOU. I WILL CONTINUE TO ATTEMPT. I WILL FIND YOU A DOCTOR."

"Look." I took a shaky breath. "I don't think you understand. I'm intersex and often doctors just don't know, there is literally no science about my hormones—my gonads—my uterus, or whatever I should call it—" Even as I said it, I saw the hole in my argument. Having a rash and a cut on my leg had nothing to do with my being intersex. Those things just occurred to me while I happened to be intersex.

"YOUR HEALTH PROBLEMS ARE NOT ABOUT YOUR HORMONES," the spider said.

"Okay—to be fair, sometimes they are, but right now they aren't. So what are you going to do about all this? Huh?!"

"I WILL FIND YOU A DOCTOR," the spider said. "YOU NEED A DOCTOR. I WILL CONTINUE. I WILL HELP YOU."

"How many doctors will I need to see to—"

~*~

I was standing in front of an entirely unfamiliar clinic, in an unfamiliar town. The weather was chilly. The sign over the entrance was still in English. I was clearly out of state. Would they even accept my health insurance here?

I suddenly understood the answer to my last question. The spider would get me healthcare, and would persist until we ran out of doctors. Across the entire country; the entire globe if needed be.

What would the spider do if there wasn't anyone? Force someone? Kill them? And even if there was someone, many doctors had waiting lists— you couldn't just walk in off the street. The better doctors were probably all booked solid. I didn't think the spider had considered this.

There had to be at least one person, I repeated to myself. There had to be.

But deep inside, I knew I could expect many more iterations of the loop.

I steeled myself, again, yet again, and I stepped through the door.

A Local Gardener
By Allay Rei

Content warnings: Violence, captivity, suicide, implied rape, non-explicit murder

If it were the first time the police showed up at her door unannounced, Lynda would have frozen and called for her grandmother like she did only a few months ago. Now, she utilized her big round eyes and tilted her head a few degrees to the left as she told the officers who carried themselves with too much confidence that she had no idea what they were talking about. She was *just* a girl, after all. She gave a theatrical gasp and covered her mouth so the officers could see how absolutely scandalized she felt at their drop of information.

"Des actes illégaux dans les environs," they kept insisting in loud French. Though, they would never outright say what the "illegal acts in the area" were.

Lynda would deny all illegal activity, hand on her heart, for she believed that nothing they did in this household could ever nor should ever be considered criminal. *Jamais de la vie!* She promised them in soft French. They asked if they could take a look around the house and, knowing they should not be allowed to do so without a warrant, Lynda let them in anyway.

With a curt "merci" they exited the house without apology after finding nothing incriminating.

Knees on the sofa, Lynda peeked out through the blinds over the window and waited for the police car to drive away. Half an hour, this time.

Light footsteps sounded behind Lynda, prompting her to shift attention.

She pressed the side of her right hand against her left palm with her right index finger pointing upwards. Then, she pointed it down. *Half an hour.*

With a scowl, her grandmother nodded. She pointed at Lynda, then to the front door, then placed a hand to her own chest, and gestured to their greenhouse door.

Lynda nodded curtly, fetching her gardening tools before exiting the house to their front garden. Gone had to be the gorgeous yellow flowers. Her grandmother joined her soon after with an armful of red flowers, and together they planted those as replacement.

At thirteen years old, Lynda was already scarred by the poor decision-making skills of the adults who co-existed in this world with her. The adults, of course, excluded her grandmother. The state of the world had already been far below sub-optimal when Lynda was born. Even her grandmother had her own horror stories about the poor decision-making skills the adults had when she was a little girl. Whenever Lynda thinks about how long it's been since the world was right, if it ever has been, her optimism about a successful rebellion begins to shatter. But never entirely.

Her mother, too, made poor decisions, but she could hardly be blamed. Several women died that day, and her mother just so happened to be one of them. Sometimes a poor choice is the only choice available.

"It's dangerous, Lynda. Stay with your grandmother," said her mother as she fastened her bag against her waist. Her shoes were double knotted and her hair was up in a tight bun, but what truly caught Lynda's eye that day was the sign her mother grabbed before leaving. It was white cardstock paper hot glued to a stick and it read, "get your laws off our bodies" in red paint.

Part of Lynda wished to hold on to her mother, grasp her hand tightly and never let her go. In her imagination, she does. In her imagination, she still has a living, breathing mother. And they are happy. And alive. All of them are. All women are.

But her memories say otherwise.

At thirteen years old, Lynda learned that her mother had died, not through anyone she cared about or through people she even knew, but from strangers who mourned the loss of thousands upon thousands of people in their news reports, her mother's name a mere speck among others. A list of names long enough to use as wallpaper throughout the entirety of her grandmother's home. A list of names long enough for people in power to use as an example.

At thirteen years old, Lynda learned that justice was anything but just.

There would be no justice for the women whose names were on that list nor would there be justice for the women whose names were bound to elongate it. Not unless the definition of justice changed drastically.

The flowers of their front garden were rarely purple anymore. But in the back of Lynda's memories resided a precious interaction between her grandmother and a client.

She had been planting the purple flowers in their front garden with immense care. All that was left was to give them a spritz of water. Her grandmother had already gone into the house to fetch the watering can in order to finalize the task, but as she waited for her grandmother's return, a tall woman with long lashes, dark skin, and beautifully painted nails approached her with slow steps and worried eyes.

"Excuse me," she said. "Miss Andromeda is in, isn't she?" The woman did not look even a decade older than her. She must have been one of the youngest clients granny has ever had.

"Yes," said Lynda. "Granny will be out in just a minute. Do not worry."

And out in just a minute she was. Andromeda handed Lynda the watering can and eyed the woman carefully.

"Who're you and whaddya want?" rasped Andromeda, hands firmly planted onto her hips.

The woman's eyes began to water. "I heard…"

"Whatever ya heard isn't true. I know the rumours going around, I'm just an ol' granny who likes flowers. If ya want a flower, I can cut one off the stem for ya."

"You can? Yes, please. I'd like a flower."

Lynda gently tipped the watering can over, diligently spreading the moisture to each and every one of the purple flowers.

"Whaddya know about flowers?" asked granny Andromeda with a brisk chin movement.

"Not much…' said the woman. "Someone gave me flowers once. I didn't know what to do with them. I didn't want them. I didn't ask for them. I couldn't really look after them, I barely even have the water necessary. Someone just gave me flowers. It wasn't very long ago, truly it wasn't. Four weeks ago."

"And ya want me to cut one off the stem for ya, something more manageable for ya."

"That would be nice."

"You came at a good time. Skies are clear. Come in then, let's see what kind of flower you'd like most. I've got plenty inside."

Lynda never assisted the flower picking. Not yet anyway. Though she was only two years away from being a *real* adult, her grandmother insisted she was not grown enough to watch the procedure. She would not even give Lynda the chance at a debate.

"I've seen enough to be considered a real adult, Granny."

"There is worse to see and experience," would reply Grandmother Andromeda. She was right, of course, but it would take Lynda another few years to learn that. For now, her lessons remained limited to plants and flowers and all their most useful properties.

The booklet her grandmother gave her to study was completely hand-written and quite hard to read, but it was the perfect encyclopedia for all things flower. Or so it said on the front page. Lynda memorized every last one of them and what they could do and took great care of growing the right flowers in their little greenhouse.

Any and all women who entered their home seeking Andromeda would leave with a flower of their choice and instructions on how to use it if their situation became dire.

Physical fights were something Lynda took no interest in. *There is no conflict that cannot be solved through intellectual conversation*, Lynda preached. Still, as soon as she began secondary school, her mother had insisted she sign up for self-defence classes. *An intellectual conversation takes more than one intellectual conversing*, would counter her mother. Every all-girls school offered self-defence classes. It was practically mandatory.

Every class, big men dressed in heavy protection taught the girls where to hit and how to hit. They would pretend to assault the girls, putting them in different compromising situations, and encouraged them to scream as loud as they could.

At the beginning of class, everyone would be made to sit in a circle on the gym floor and the big men—not yet dressed in their heavy protective suits—would teach the girls things that made Lynda feel like she lived in a far more dangerous world than she previously expected. They explained in great detail how to avoid getting drugged; keep your eyes on your drink at all times even if it's just water or juice. How to avoid being a target; look around, look confident, be alert, be prepared, don't look distracted, walk with purpose, stand straight, if there is a suspicious man around, look him right in the eye, don't blindly trust women and children just because they are women and children.

Every time, during these discussions, 12-year-old Lynda wondered if all-boys schools received these types of classes too.

She wouldn't get the opportunity to put anything she learned from self-defence classes into practice until she was nineteen. The man didn't look like much of a threat until he got closer. They were both walking towards each other on the same sidewalk, but once they crossed paths, the man caught a clear glimpse of her face and backtracked to compliment her.

"Merci" was all she said, and it seemed to have annoyed the man when she carried on her route without flashing a smile his way. She hastened her step and removed the earphone from her left ear to listen for his steps. It was as she suspected; he was following her. With practised fingers, she secured her phone and earphones in her jacket pocket with its zipper, then reached down to her hip where, dangling from her belt loop on a carabiner, hung her keys. She held on to the biggest key on the key ring through her two middle fingers, careful not to jingle them around too much.

When she turned to face the man, he was closer than she had anticipated. He ran towards her with anger in his eyes and profanity at his lips. She swung as soon as he was within range. The key dug into the flesh between her fingers, leaving a mark, but nothing as bad as the gash at the man's temple. She swung once more, now aiming for the man's left eye. He screamed, holding his head and covering his eyes.

"Bitch, fucking bitch, sale pute, t'es morte," he threatened, unsteady on his feet.

Unwilling to find out if his death threat was real or not, Lynda kicked him between the legs and ran away without waiting to hear the satisfying thump of his body hitting pavement.

Once home, Grandmother Andromeda took great care of the injury on her hand and praised her for her quick thinking.

"Be easier for us if they hadn't banned self-defence weapons in the first place," complained Grandmother Andromeda as she wrapped Lynda's hand. "It's like they know we hurt ourselves trying to defend our damned lives, like they want a sacrifice from us because they always want a sacrifice from us. Tells ya enough we had to invent the damned weapons. Proof enough that this world has come to nothing. It's nothing, this world is. But they can't arrest you for carrying around your keys now, can they? Hm. Next time, ya try holding your key like this…"

~*~

"Why won't any happy memories manifest?" whispers Lynda into her sink. "I have been happy before. I have. I know I have."

Her eyes drift, blankly watching the steam dance away from her teacup and disappear into nothingness. Only a few more minutes and the tea will have cooled down enough for her to drink the entire thing at once.

"Everything has been done," she thinks, drumming her fingers along the walls of the near-scorching ceramic of her teacup. It was her favourite. *There's a happy memory.* The teacup. A beautiful royal blue colour with silver detailing with a matching teapot. It was a gift from one of her first clients.

When her grandmother passed, Lynda had taken over the business because the number of women in need of their services never dwindled. Though she had years of experience by then, she was still nervous, not about the prospect of making a mistake during the procedure, but rather about gaining the trust of the women who expected Grandmother Andromeda.

She treated all her clients to tea after the deed was done. The tea collection she amassed far exceeded her own expectations, but it was better this way since everyone had different tastes. Lynda herself preferred a classic chamomile. Most of her clients, however, had a penchant for fruity infusions of sorts.

The woman who gifted her the tea set was a potter. She never gave Lynda her name. Safety. But she was unable to compensate Lynda monetarily. Lynda told her not to mind it, that it wasn't her main reason for doing what she did, and that many before her have had the same issue even though they were dealing with her grandmother. She expressed her gratitude.

"You were my only option," she said, holding on to Lynda's hands. They were about the same age, or so it seemed. Perhaps she was only a few years younger than Lynda, who was soon to hit 35.

"One day, I won't be," replied Lynda.

Weeks later, the same woman knocked at Lynda's door, smile on her face instead of fearful eyes. Her hands carried a well-wrapped box with a tidy bow at the top, which she gleefully presented to Lynda.

"You might not remember me—"

"I do," interrupted Lynda.

The woman smiled sweetly. "I'm sorry I couldn't… money is difficult. I appreciate you being so understanding with me. Still, I thought it wrong not to compensate you some way. Service for a service."

A smile that mirrors that woman's makes its way to Lynda's lips as she reminisces. Finally, her hand is able to grasp the teacup without being burnt. She brings it to her nose, inhaling the scent of the steeped flowers fresh from her front garden. She already placed her most comfortable pillows on the floor, and there she sits, cross-legged, as she takes her final cup of tea. It is unfortunate that her last tea cannot be chamomile.

She feels no fear. It would have come to this no matter what. She was much too vocal about her lack of a desire for romantic relationships with men. Whenever someone asked her about her husband—as a woman in her late thirties should already have—she *should* have been answering that *he* was fine. That *he* was extremely busy and didn't get out much. But she did not. Instead, she shrugged, shaking her head before explaining that she was uninterested in pursuing anyone in that way. It usually earned her some odd looks, sometimes disgusted ones, sometimes worried ones, but ultimately the worst that would happen would be some berating. Nothing Lynda couldn't handle.

A couple months ago, it was a man who asked. She was on her way to the store for new pots and soil for her plants when she was approached on a street corner as she waited for the red pedestrian light to give her right of way.

"I'm not interested in all that." Were the words that sealed her fate. She hadn't even time to defend herself.

It was wrong, in their eyes, not to be interested in *all that*. And though Lynda saw no wrong in her disinterest, she wonders as she awaits the end, what could have happened that day had she went along with the man's belief the same way she used to with the police officers who pounded at her door when she was a child.

On her bound and blindfolded ride to who-knows-where, the man in the driver's seat screamed at her. He called her selfish, a joke of a woman, and a waste of space for not participating in human society the way women are meant to. And with no way to reply, she listened to his nonsense.

"If I were a woman, I would have cherished the gift of giving life. Giving life isn't about you. It's about everyone. Having children, the new generation, the cycle of life, that's what makes you women important. That's why we protect women, that's why we protect children. That's our future. Without kids there's no future. If everyone thought like you, the human race would cease to exist. That's why things are the way they are. You have to start understanding that."

She wondered, as he went on and on preaching words that made him feel better about his decision to commit heinous crimes, when this all started. When did it become wrong to exist happily on your own? When did it become okay to force motherhood on women who were not born to be mothers? She wondered, as he roughly handled her into what she could only assume was a building, what part of what he was doing to her consisted of protection towards women.

Days turned into weeks and weeks turned into months, still she sat on the same cold and mildly damp floor he threw her on, on the first day. The passage of time was only told to her through the slow progression of her stomach expanding. There was more than just one man in the building; all of them knew what they were doing. All of them took turns carefully opening the heavy door of the room she was shut in, checking her restraints, and sliding over to her a tray of well-cooked food.

If she had lost her mind, she would have assumed these men cared about her. But they do not. They care only about the control they have over her and the control they assume they will have over her once the thing within her has advanced far enough in its development for her to safely and effectively separate herself from it.

She bides her time, knowing she is running out of it. She listens for their footsteps, their movement, and the slamming of their doors. She maps the layout of the building based on what she hears and once she has a clear picture, she acts.

It was unfortunate that she couldn't escape their capture earlier. The symptoms of pregnancy are ones that aided her captors in keeping her in place, no doubt a calculated aspect on their part.

Her walk home was slow and arduous, but not as difficult as she expected it to be. She was only slightly disoriented, able to locate herself quickly. She briefly wondered, as she stepped one foot before the other, if she should have felt remorse for stripping away life from two of her captors, one of them the reason behind her morphed body. She wondered if they deserved worse. She wondered if it would have been beneficial to torture them like they tortured her. She wondered, as she unearthed the hidden spare key of her house under the flowers in her front garden, if she could now, officially, be called a murderer and if it now affected her. She wondered, as she twisted the handle of the door and stepped in her home, if she was about to let down many women who still needed her help. To wonder *"what could have been"* was all she could do now.

~*~

Guerda Saint-Fleur first received treatment from Andromeda Valliant-Coeur when she was in her twenties. Her granddaughter was with her the day she finally plucked up the courage to walk over to their house and request their services. She—the granddaughter whose name she later learned was Lynda Valliant-Coeur—was planting beautiful purple flowers in their front garden, which is what gave her the strength to go over to them.

She had been told by a friend of a friend to pay close attention to the colours of the flowers in the front garden.

"Never approach the house when the flowers are red. Never. Don't even pass by it. If that house is on your route and there are red flowers in their front garden, you better go the other way," said her friend. "If they're yellow or orange, you only go if it's an absolute emergency, okay? Safety isn't guaranteed. Purple means free game, alright. I went when those flowers were purple. Easy. But you gotta get through with the way the lady speaks. Don't be intimidated. She'll say something weird but you have to go with it. Don't make it obvious why you're there. Talk like there's a man listening in."

She was scared, it was true, but even then, she knew that was her only choice. And what a perfect choice it was.

She took up gardening as it was a calming and useful hobby to take up in such a dark and gloomy world, but she lacked knowledge on what to do. The first time she went to Lynda for advice, they ended up talking for hours and Guerda was able to successfully grow plants of her own. She didn't stop at flowers, she went for berries, vegetables, and herbs too.

Almost monthly, she went over to Lynda for more advice and to give updates on how her own garden was coming along. Lynda welcomed her with open arms every single time and even asked for more frequent updates. Guerda wasn't one to deny someone of her company, so she happily obliged.

In recent weeks, however, Lynda Valliant-Coeur hasn't been out in her garden and her flowers had begun looking unhappy. Guerda took it upon herself to water them when rain was scarce, but she found the whole ordeal extremely unusual. She even gave a few looks through her windows and saw no sign of life within. Lynda wasn't the type to go vacationing, especially not unannounced. The worst part was that authorities would do nothing if she'd officially been reported missing. With their suspicions of her, it was likely they would simply utilize her absence as a way to incriminate her.

Today, Guerda tries her luck once again. Though Lynda is nowhere to be found in her front garden, Guerda finds that a variety of flowers has now been planted and they all look recently taken care of. The only unusual part was that *all* coloured flowers were in her front garden. And Guerda's acquaintance did not warn her about this code. She looks around for signs of Lynda, but instead of the gardener, she locates the watering can neatly placed on the steps leading up to her house and a small, hand-written booklet on the ground next to it. The same one Andromeda had given her many years past. A booklet on poisonous flowers and their effects. All of which are currently planted in her front garden.

She leaves it where she found it, knowing someone else might come here needing it, and continues her search for the gardener.

As she wanders the property, her eyes gravitate to an open window. She holds in her scream. There on the floor laid the gardener's body, a visible bump in her belly and a teacup in her hand. Guerda closes her eyes and utters a little prayer before turning away. There is nothing more she can do.

"Excuse me, are you Miss Guerda?" asked a young, tanned woman with long curly hair.

Guerda was planting beautiful purple flowers in her front garden as the young woman approached her but halted her progress seeing her worried eyebrows and nervous demeanour. She stood up, dusting the dirt off her hands as she did so.

"Absolutely I am," says Guerda.

"I heard—"

"Whatever you heard, it's not true. I know the rumours going around, I'm nothing like that. I'm just some old gardener. If you're so inclined, I could cut a flower off the stem for you."

THE BLOOD MANGO TREE

BY SOYAM SIDDHA

Content warnings: Female foeticide

"What do you crave for, my child?"

As her grandmother's cloudy eyes bored into her, Duhita looked out at the sprawling mango tree that stood ominous in the backyard. Her womb fluttered. The tree's gnarled branches spread low and far. In its shade, plump red fruit dotted the ground, calling out to her.

"Cravings can tell." Gurubari Mausi smiled as she finished massaging Aai's sparsely haired scalp with coconut oil. "Spicy food means it's a boy. And if it's a—"

"It IS a boy." Duhita caressed her engorged belly in warm soothing strokes. The child hadn't stopped kicking since they had arrived in her ancestral village the previous night. "Can't you tell? I am carrying so low."

Aai gave a toothless grin in approval. Mausi and Duhita's mother exchanged glances. Duhita walked to the window and stared at the old mango tree. Her mouth watered at the sight. "Aren't women immune to it? To the poison in the fruit?"

The small kitchen stank of stale grains, filled with uneasy silence.

"Hush, child. Those mangoes will turn your unborn into a girl." Aai's sunken eyes widened.

"Don't look at it." Mother dashed to the window. The old-fashioned wooden shutters fell with a thud as she pulled her daughter away. "It calls out to pregnant women."

"It was shrouded with white blossoms just days before we heard Duhita's good news." Gurubari Mausi rubbed the residual oil into her pruney fingers.

In the many summer holidays when she visited as a child, Duhita always heeded the warnings of her elders and diligently stayed far away. The stories of the poison and the painful deaths terrified her. Some said the old tree shape-shifted into a little girl and roamed the grounds. Her anklets could be heard chiming softly in the nights. Some of Duhita's cousins made occasional claims of having seen the girl, but only when they were securely cocooned in blankets.

But this time it was different. Duhita couldn't brush away the thoughts of biting on the red shiny mangoes that hung so low to the ground. The urge manifested as a dull ache in her chest.

"Don't even speak of it. Cursed tree." Aai sat on the cracked mud floor and feebly spat in the direction of the tree. "At least four hundred years old, that one."

"Mango trees aren't supposed to live that long. Much less bear unseasonal fruits." Mother shook her head.

Gurubari Mausi folded betel leaves with lime and areca nut for Aai. "It has seen much blood and tears. The flesh of the fruit is also red, they say."

Duhita's heart thumped loudly. She shielded her bump with her hands. "Why didn't someone just cut it down?"

"Your grandfather's uncle tried. His toddler son sneaked off one afternoon. When they found him, he was frothing at the mouth. The only boy born after ten years of marriage, dead within hours." Aai's raspy voice grew hoarse. "Blinded by grief, his father hacked at the old tree the whole day until the sun went down. The next morning, he was dead. Not a scratch on the damn tree."

~*~

The huge tree was visible from everywhere in the old house. Aai ordered every single window to be sealed shut to ensure Duhita didn't catch a glimpse, even by accident.

"You shouldn't have insisted on coming here. I can't believe I agreed to this foolhardiness." Mother fanned herself with a tabloid magazine amid yet another power cut in the night.

"I needed to see Aai before I returned to the US." Duhita stared off at the dusty stationary fan above.

"The only women's clinic in Soro was raided and sealed months ago. The nearest hospital is at least an hour away. I won't be able to rest easy until you are back in the city safely."

"Why was the clinic raided?" In her womb, the baby tossed and turned. The sweat from Duhita's back permeated the cotton sheet.

"Some political row, I guess. The doctors were respectable people. All the women in the family went to them. Some activists set the ultrasound machines on fire."

"Then they weren't so respectable, were they?" Duhita turned her back to her mother, careful to not squash the belly.

"Did you ever go to them?" Her body went numb as she waited for her mother to answer.

"It's late. The baby needs you to rest."

Duhita's mouth salivated as she heard the dull thuds of red mangoes hitting the ground in the wind. Plop plop plop.

~*~

Oblong shaped mangoes, bright orange of colour shone in the woven basket by Mausi's side.

"Look at these. Aren't they beautiful? Your grandmother ordered them from the best orchard in the village for you." Mausi ran the mangoes swiftly across the cast-iron blade, her one foot firmly holding the *panikhi* in place.

She was a distant childless, impoverished aunt in her late fifties. After being widowed, she moved in to take care of Duhita's senescent grandmother and the aging house.

"Mausi, did you ever go to the clinic in Soro?"

Mausi stopped running the fruit through the shiny blade. "My womb never quickened with a child... Not even with a girl... I watched my sisters forced to walk under the old mango tree. Broken bodies with little bags to bury. Being barren spared me the pain."

"Did my mother ever go?" Duhita forced her aunt to meet her eyes.

"She went the first time. The second time, she said she didn't know. It was too late for the doctors to do anything."

Duhita's chest grew heavy. She existed because her mother found out too late?

"It drove your father's family mad. How can a woman not know, his mother fumed. The mango tree had bloomed months before your mother said anything." Mausi's thin lips curled into a little smile. "Enough about the past." She handed Duhita a plateful of cut golden fruit.

Duhita bit into the fibrousfruit. Its nectar-like juice, filled her mouth.

"There. That will make you feel better, my child." Mausi smiled weakly.

Duhita gulped and nodded. The mango was very sweet and delicious, probably the best she ever had. But the dull ache in her chest persisted.

~*~

On the third night, Rajat called. Duhita swiftly opened a window in the passage to improve the signal on her phone. The rain from the breeze collected into a fine mist on her face. The old tree loomed large in the window like it waited for her. Red mangoes swayed with the wind and glistened in white flashes of lightning.

"I wish you were here."

She smiled at the longing in Rajat's voice. "Me too. You won't believe how hot it is here now. It's October! Have the trees turned red there yet?"

"If you were here, we would have known by now."

"Known what?"

"Known if we are having a boy. All it takes here is a simple scan."

"What's wrong with not knowing?" She asked.

The line went silent, and then she heard Rajat sigh deeply. A thunderclap reverberated all around.

"I can't hear you…" She hanged up.

In the bed Duhita listened carefully over the pitter-patter of the soft rain on the asbestos roof. She could still hear it distinctly—the dull thuds of red mangoes hitting the ground. Plop plop plop. The ache in her chest throbbed along with them.

~*~

The baby kicked all night and kept Duhita up. She came down as dawn broke. The old wooden door to the backyard groaned as she pushed it open and tiptoed across the yard. Her heart raced as the old tree, clouded in thick mist, grew closer and closer. The grass was wet and the ground muddy under her bare feet. She took care not to trample any of the red fruit dotting the ground in various stages of decay.

Duhita reached the gnarled thick trunk and picked up a firm one from the ground. It was rust-coloured and the biggest one she had ever seen. She gave it a gentle squeeze. It was soft under the leathery skin. She firmly pressed it with both hands to loosen the pulp. With her teeth she tore an incision in the top, put her mouth around it, and sucked.

Juice and pulp entered her dry mouth. The flesh was creamy, almost devoid of fibre. It wasn't sweet. It was salty and metallic. Like blood. But Duhita didn't stop. She couldn't stop. The crimson juice escaped in rivulets and flowed down her elbow into the soft ground. Duhita ignored it and slurped ravenously. The child craved it. The blood of its sisters, aunts, grand-aunts.

A Dead Woman's Journal

by R Haven

Content warnings: Marital rape, miscarriage, suicide (particularly suicide as an escape)

The textured journal cover tickles your fingertips.

It is the diary of a woman you already know is dead. The words of someone you did not know and never will. You're holding it now, studying the stunning geometry on the front of the book with a heaviness in both your stomach and heart.

You know the writer died because you were told as much when you were given the book. You were seeking connection, someone who might understand the conflict grasping your brain like a vice. This is what you got; the intimate account of a ghost's final days, pushed into your hands by a stranger with a knowing nod and sympathetic frown. You've found a place on the second floor of this second-hand bookshop, a spot to settle in and read at your leisure. You don't even need to buy it, the stranger said. You're allowed to take all the time you need.

You're uncertain what help you'll find, but you flip to the first page and begin to read.

> *Today was my paka-dekha. The man I am to marry is Sudhi Hossain, whom I have only met a few times before. My parents are very excited, and agree with the matchmaker that we will make a good pair.*
>
> *My future in-laws are Jagadesh and Ruma Hossain. They are a handsome and serious couple, and they spoke to me pleasantly but have very fixed ideas about the future I will have with their son. They expect many grandchildren. Ruma told me that she has always been a diligent wife to Jagadesh, and that she hopes I will be the same for Sudhi, but I am not entirely sure what she means by that.*
>
> *I should be excited, and I am pretending to be. The truth is more akin to*

standing on the edge of a cliff without being sure what lies at the bottom. I pray it is a soft landing.

Already, you are uncomfortable.

This was not written in English. Someone has taken the time to translate every word in minute script, yet there are still words you aren't familiar with off the cuff.

But you read on, because your gut's started to squirm and you're admittedly, warily, curious.

The wedding cards were sent and the turmeric ceremony performed. My best friend, Mallika, confided in me that she is jealous of me, because Sudhi is very handsome and has an excellent job at the bank. She said she has never seen me more radiant. Why don't I feel it?

What if Sudhi is disappointed when he gets to know me? What if we never really talk or find each other boring?

The wedding is soon. If only we had known each other before all these expectations were put upon us. But who am I to complain when everyone agrees this is a favourable match?

I am writing again after the Bou Bhaat. Sudhi's family members were very welcoming and praised my cooking all afternoon. Strangely, I don't remember much of the wedding. It all seemed to happen around me while I was in a daze. I barely even remember our first night together as husband and wife. It all seemed to happen so fast. I only really felt awake while I was cooking all throughout this morning.

I can't get rid of this strange feeling. I should be excited to get to know Sudhi and learn what this next chapter of my life will be like. I'm telling everyone that's how I feel, and maybe I'll start to believe it soon, but, in the meantime everything feels peculiar. I am walking on a surface of glass, wondering if it will shatter under my feet.

I think I'm afraid of failing as a wife. Sudhi is far more interested in sex than I am. He is bathing now while I take some time to write and prepare for another night together, and he has told me what he expects. I think he aims to get me pregnant as quickly as possible. If it takes some time, will he be displeased? I think his parents will be.

The husband, you suspect.

The husband must have been the one to kill her.

You don't know for sure that the writer was *murdered*, only that she died.

The husband gets your back up, though, like a hissing cat getting bad vibes off a stranger.

How long ago this was written? You don't know how divorces are approached in the country these people are— were?—from, so if she failed to get pregnant and he lost his patience… Yeah. You can see how it might have panned out.

But that in no way relates to *your* situation. You want to know why this was the book you were given.

So you continue.

I am trying my best to serve Sudhi's needs and be cooperative. He works hard, so I understand why he would want to come home and know what to expect. I am to have kept the house clean and prepared dinner for his arrival, greet him when he comes home, and give him space after dinner for him to indulge in his hobbies. He likes television and reading. I'm curious and I'd like to spend time with him, perhaps get to know him that way, but he's told me that he wants privacy until he's ready to join me in bed. It's left me with the impression that he doesn't like me very much.

We don't speak over dinner, and our discussions in the morning are limited to what he expects to see done at the end of the day. Weekends aren't any different. He goes out to spend time with friends and brings them over for dinner, then they gather in the living room while I clean up. I hear them talking and laughing without making out what they're saying.

It isn't bad, exactly. It's just lonely. I miss my own friends. At this rate, I'll be thankful to have a baby just so I don't feel so alone all day.

My pregnancy test came back negative today. Every day that goes by without becoming pregnant feels like a personal failing. I haven't told Sudhi yet.

Jagadesh and Ruma came by for dinner tonight and spoke to Sudhi like I wasn't even there. They're talking about selling their house and moving in with us, 'to help with the baby.' I'm not even pregnant yet, but they expect I will be in the months it takes to pack everything and move. I couldn't move throughout the entire conversation, pinned to my seat like a butterfly in a box.

If I don't have a baby soon, what will they think of me? Will they consider me a failure? It's not as though we could take the marriage back, which means I would have to live with their disappointment for however long it takes. I feel like I won't even be acknowledged until I produce a grandchild for them.

The only thing that made that visit bearable was that Ruma helped me clean the dishes and spoke to me. The conversation itself was humiliating, as she told me ways to make myself more fertile, but it was the first time I'd spoken to someone other than Sudhi in over a month.

My prayers have been heard — I'm pregnant at last! I've been weeping in relief all day. I was starting to think something was wrong with my body, that I wasn't going to be able to have children. I'm excited for Sudhi to come home tonight. I can't wait to see him happy.

Your hands are stiff as you linger over this entry. Your back's to a wall, now, leaning into it and sliding to the floor with the diary open against your knees.

Joy, over finding out she was pregnant.

You can't relate.

Ruma has moved in ahead of her husband in order to help me through the pregnancy. Sudhi seems to be sharing his excitement more with his parents than with me, but I don't mind. I'm allowed to work less around the house while I'm in a delicate condition, and Ruma is excellent at cleaning. She's been showing me ways to be more efficient at folding the laundry, and she helps me tidy up after every meal. I can't remember the last time I felt this relaxed and happy.

We have started preparing the baby's room. Ruma kept much of Sudhi's things from when he was a baby, so we won't have to spend a fortune on things like a crib or clothing.

I've been bleeding throughout my pregnancy. I thought that may be normal for me, but I've learned otherwise. The doctor doesn't think the baby will make it to the birth. It's only been two months since my pregnancy test came back positive, and I was told too late that I should have waited until the second trimester before getting too excited.

Sudhi hasn't spoken to me since the appointment, nor has Ruma. When-ever I hear them talking, it's in hushed whispers to keep me from hearing. I wasn't sure if they were angry until I tried to put myself into their conversa-tion. Sudhi was very cold and shoved me out of the room, so I slunk away to cry in private.

I'm in the middle of a fog too dense to breathe. I didn't think I was ready to be a mother until I was sure I was going to be. I want to believe there was a reason I lost this baby, but all I come back to was that I somehow wasn't good enough. That I need to prove that I'm ready.

But—

That makes no sense. To treat the woman badly for something so far out of her control—to what end?

Your suspicions of murder remain, but now they've shifted. You don't know that you trust the in-laws. They're obviously not above cruelty; what else were they capable of?

Sudhi has been more insistent with me, these past nights. I'm trying to be as good a wife as I can be, but it's tiring me and giving me terrible anxiety by the end of every day. I try to linger over my chores, but Ruma is quick and makes sure everything is done by the time Sudhi is off to bed.

I feel like my body needs more time to recover before there's any chance of me becoming pregnant again, but I'm afraid to say so. I don't want Sudhi to think I'm weak.

Jagadesh has sold the house. He's moving in tomorrow. Sudhi seems upset with me for not being pregnant anymore, and I know they were all certain I would be by the time the move happened. I've taken at least three pregnancy tests since yesterday, hoping that something will change, but nothing does. Tomorrow looms over me like an ax swinging on a thread. I don't expect Jagadesh to be any more understanding than anyone else.

'Anyone else' only means Sudhi and Ruma. I have barely been able to speak to my own parents, and I haven't had any contact with my old friends at all. The last time I spoke to my mother, she told me that I'm sure to get pregnant again so long as I pray and serve my family well.

I didn't tell her that Sudhi has been rough with me since the miscarriage. I'm afraid that she'll tell me this is normal. Worse, I fear she'll tell me it's unusual behaviour. That I'm right to be wary.

There is no way out of this marriage. I know Allah is merciful and would not have trapped me with Sudhi if something was wrong.

You're understanding more, in increments. You're trapped too.

Ruma has stopped helping me around the house. I think I have grown lazy with her assistance assured, because without it, I feel overworked and tired. Jagadesh and Sudhi leave their cigarettes everywhere and I live in constant fear that they'll forget to put them out properly and cause a house fire. Ruma smokes with them sometimes, and the three of them spend most of their time in the living room when Sudhi isn't working. They don't speak to me much at all.

It's strange how much lonelier a house feels when it's filled with more people who ignore you.

Praise Allah, I've been crying all morning. I'm pregnant. Ruma and Jagadesh helped me prepare the announcement, and Sudhi will come home to a feast and joyful news. I can't wait to see him smile at me again. We will be more careful this time, and won't start preparing a room or telling people until it's been three months.

I've been having dreams, this time, about giving birth. They're actually what prompted me to take a pregnancy test today. I think the dreams are a good sign.

Sudhi was thrilled when he came home yesterday! I finally feel as though I've done something right. Ruma cooked and cleaned to allow me to get some rest, and she says she will continue to do so until I give birth. I'm thankful that she's here, now.

Perhaps best of all was that Sudhi held me, last night, without expectation for anything more. I haven't felt so warm and comfortable before.

The miscarriage happened so fast, this time. It hasn't even been a week. I woke up late in blood-soaked sheets, and it took me all afternoon to scrub them. They're still not completely clean. There will be no hiding this.

I think I should tell Sudhi first. I don't want him to find out through his parents. However, I don't know how to avoid them until he comes home. It's been difficult enough to do all day.

I wish there was anything at all that I could do to fix this. I keep coming up with ridiculous ideas, unlikely ways to at least put off letting things go back to how they were.

Sudhi was angry. Unbelievably angry. He and Jagadesh shouted at each other and at me, saying horrible things. That Allah cursed Sudhi with a useless bitch of a wife, that the matchmaker tricked Jagadesh into a match that would ruin their family. I was thrown into the bedroom and sealed in around ten o'clock, and I listened to Ruma wail and Jagadesh rant until Sudhi came to bed around midnight. He didn't speak to me all night, nor did he speak to me this morning. I can't seem to stop shaking.

I need to recover quickly, but if I'm not allowed to rest, I don't know how I will. I need to be pregnant again, though. I have to be. This can't happen again.

You ache.

I've been ill since the miscarriage. I can't seem to stop bleeding. The doctor recommended I be allowed to rest as much as possible, and Sudhi was discouraged from exercising his rights as my husband until I'm well. So I've been left alone in the bedroom, shut in here and ignored. I am usually asleep when Sudhi comes to bed, lately, so I don't even see him. The most human contact I have comes from overhearing conversation from downstairs. When that stops, the quiet presses in against me like a cloud of ash, choking me and sticking to my skin.

This cannot be the rest of my life.

I haven't stopped bleeding yet. Sudhi decided that won't stop him.

I tried to tell him no. I was still aching, and I didn't know whether or not I could even get pregnant again so soon, but he didn't care. He beat me until I stopped protesting and forced himself inside of me.

I know with certainty now that Sudhi will never love me. The best I can hope for is that I fulfil my duties as his wife and make him happy enough to treat me with more kindness.

My pregnancy test came back positive today. I'm not going to tell anyone. I'm too afraid of his reaction if I lose this baby, too.

I'll wait until the second trimester to tell them. I'll keep the pregnancy test hidden and show Sudhi when the time is right.

It's been a week since my pregnancy test, with no sign of anything wrong yet. I'm approaching the situation with my hands out to shield me, only to find there isn't any danger yet. Sudhi doesn't suspect anything, and continues to act accordingly. As unhappy as normalcy is, I almost think that normalcy is exactly what I need to have this baby.

It's been two months, and things are still going smoothly. I've found something like peace in the shunning from Jagadesh and Ruma—they really aren't interested in me at all, as long as they don't know.

I'm having dreams of the baby again. This time of more than just the birth; I dream of raising a little boy, just as handsome as his father, but sweet and kind.

If my dreams come to pass, I'll truly know my prayers have been heard.

Ruma found my pregnancy test and showed it to Sudhi. He was angrier than I've ever seen him, even angrier than when I lost the second baby, for lying to him. I tried to explain myself but he wouldn't listen. He beat me badly, everywhere but my face. My entire body rings with pain every time I move. I am not expected to clean or cook while pregnant, so if nothing else, I have time to recover from my punishment.

What scares me is the sharp pangs I've been getting through my abdomen. If I've lost this baby, too, I'm afraid Sudhi might kill me.

Fuck it. They're all guilty now, as far as you're concerned. You shake whenever reality whispers intrusive honesty in your ear, that this is *true*, this *happened*, and you couldn't stop it. You didn't know this woman. You weren't even in the same country, the same continent, most likely.

If you can't save her, are you meant to be learning how to save yourself? One hand rests on your swollen abdomen and you swallow.

I am bedridden, in agony. Sudhi woke me this morning with hands around my neck, shaking me awake, and I quickly realized that the bed was stained with my blood again. That's three babies I've lost.

Allah, I see now. These miscarriages are not punishments. Sudhi is a violent and cruel man. I cannot bring a child into the world to be abused at their father's hands. I won't. I don't care what happens to me anymore, so long as I do not bear this man a child.

I am pregnant again. Sudhi has not stopped trying to have children, and there was nothing I could do or say to convince him otherwise.

I plan on forcing a miscarriage by throwing myself down the stairs. I'm sick, knowing that the only thing I can do to protect my baby is to ensure they are never born. If it doesn't work, then perhaps my next course of action will be to poison myself. I don't know how, though. I'm so afraid that I'll die in the attempt to save my child.

Still, I must try. Better I die than live with myself for putting an innocent in harm's way. I will face my bruised reflection at the end of this day, and I won't flinch.

There are no more entries, and you know now how and why she died. You know who was behind it, why you were given the diary to begin with, and why the tears in your eyes are as much for you as they are for this woman. What you don't know is what you were supposed to glean from her story.

Not unless the message was—

You close the book and leave it on the floor. You wrestle with yourself to get to your feet, holding your pregnant belly as if for balance.

You're carrying the child of a monster, too. It's too late to abort; most clinics only would if they found something terribly wrong with the fetus, and nothing like that's come up on the ultrasounds. He'd go after you, too, if he found out you were even thinking about it.

A miscarriage…

If you do have this child, you're dooming them, aren't you? Bad men don't treat their children any better than the person they knocked up to begin with. Are you so noble that you'd risk your life to save them a life of hardship and suffering at a parent's hands?

If you die with your unborn child, is it suicide or escape? Is a last-ditch effort worth it if it's the last thing you ever do?

You stop at the top of the staircase. You stare past your abdomen all the way down at the ground floor.

The baby kicks.

THE REFERRAL

BY A.V. BLACK

Content warnings: Sexual assault, medical malpractice

Dr. Miller pulls a condom out of his pocket, rips open the packet, and slides it over the ultrasound probe. A bead of sweat runs from his thinning grey hair over his flabby cheek. My mouth goes dry. I glance at the full box of latex sheaths sitting on the trolley carrying the ultrasound machine. I've had enough of these tests to know that doctors never use a personal condom for transvaginal exams.

Dr. Miller catches me staring at the latex sheaths and grins, his empty smile revealing his coffee-stained teeth, then holds up the condom wrapper. "It's a bit unconventional, but I find these work better."

I go to ask *why*, but stop myself. He's the only gynecologist in this part of northern Ontario. The next closest one is a three-hour drive from my small town, and I can't afford to take time off from my job to travel a full day to get to her office. It took me over a month to secure the referral to see Dr. Miller—God only knows how long it would take to see someone else.

I swallow, my saliva thick. The nib at the end of the condom makes the probe look far too phallic. A shiver runs over me, starting my calves and working its way up to my shoulders. I shudder, rubbing my arms. The translucent paper covering the naked lower half of my body does little to guard me against the freezing air blasting from the vent above my head.

"Are you cold?" Dr. Miller asks as he approaches, probe in hand. He rips the stirrups out from their compartment under the medical table, his face so close to my exposed legs that I feel his breath on my skin. "I'm always hot." He lets out a cackle that sounds like plates smashing. "Can't help it."

Dr. Miller stands back, his hooded blue eyes trailing the length of my body. I glance at my worn jeans resting on the chair in the cramped examination room. Even if I could get to them, Dr. Miller is blocking the exit, and he's twice my size. If he tried to stop me, I'd never make it past him.

"Don't worry. It will be over before you know it." He leers at me. "Now slide down. Feet in the stirrups."

I glance at my winter boots on the tiled floor. Despite my body screaming at me to flee, I allow my heels to sink into the cold metal stirrups.

"Get closer," he says. "Hurry up. Other patients are waiting."

I shut my eyes and moved in his direction, my knees bending.

"Scooch your bum to the end of the table." Dr. Miller licks his lips. "Here, why don't I help you?"

He grabs my hips and lifts them. My body goes numb as he yanks me down the examination table, then rips my legs open with a hungry look in his beady blue eyes.

"You'll feel some pressure," he says as he puts the cold probe inside me.

The latex condom bunches as he takes his time inserting the probe. *He's the only doctor in town that will do it*, I tell myself. *You can't financially support a kid, and you're only nineteen. You don't even remember the guy's name, either. He was from out of town, and you didn't get his number or Snapchat.*

The probe reaches my cervix. Dr. Miller taps on the keyboard under the ultrasound machine.

"What a beautiful uterus," he says, licking his shiny lips. "Yep—there it is. See?" He points to the tiny white curve clashing against the black hollow that is my uterus. "That's your baby. This is my favourite part, you know? Showing new mothers their child."

I let out a nervous laugh—a bad habit of mine when I'm at a loss for words.

"You think this is funny?" he asks as a shadow passes over his face.

"N-no, sorry, it's just that there's been a mistake," I respond. "I'm here for an abortion, but I can see why you like helping new mothers. I'm sure that's very special."

God, I hate how awkward I am.

Dr. Miller steps closer, looming over me, his wide silhouette filling my peripheral vision. I tense, attempting to move away, but he grabs my leg, holding the probe inside me. His rage-filled eyes slide to the ultrasound screen, then back to me.

"You're too high risk for an abortion," he says, his tone cold. "I checked your blood work. You have anaemia, and your chart says that you've had an abortion before."

I take a deep breath, trying to fight off the icy shame I feel at the mention of my last abortion. "I was sixteen. It was the right choice."

Dr. Miller shakes his head from side to side like a parent scolding a child, his thin nostrils flaring. "If you've already had one abortion, it puts you at risk for an ectopic pregnancy. You shouldn't have another. It's not safe."

Crap. That's what the virtual care doctor said, too. My body tenses, pronouncing the feeling of the condom-wrapped probe. "I work at the Red Cup Cafe. You know? The one in town?"

He nods. "The coffee is better than the Tim Hortons, sure, but it's too expensive."

"It's the only job I could get, and it barely pays minimum wage. I moved out as soon as I graduated high school to escape my abusive stepdad. If I have a baby, it will grow up poor, like I did, and I can't put a child through that."

He doesn't respond. The bright fluorescent lights emphasize his jowls, making his frown look thrice its size. With an uncomfortable yank, he takes the probe out of me, drops it on the trolley, and pulls off his latex gloves.

"So, you'll write the prescription?" I ask as I pull my legs back up onto the table. I sit up, feeling a bit dizzy, hoping I can hide it as I place my hands on my lap, covering my private areas.

"Come back and see me in a week." Dr. Miller opens the door and slams it shut. It rattles in the frame.

I need that prescription *now*. The foetus is already eight weeks old. I only have up to nine weeks to take the pill. After that, it's a painful procedure with a longer recovery time, and I can't afford the trip to Toronto to get it done.

A dry sob escapes my lips right as footsteps pass by the door. I slap my hand over my mouth, my heartbeat so loud I can hear it in my ears. If someone hears me crying, God only knows what they'll think. Thanks to my horrible stepdad, I have a history of depression, all documented in my medical chart. Worse, a different doctor diagnosed me with ADHD—another medical scarlet letter. I've been denied care countless times simply because doctors think I'm "just anxious," leaving me with a deep, lingering wound that flares up whenever I express emotion around healthcare professionals.

The footsteps fade. I wipe my tear-stained cheeks, get up, and put on my jeans, socks, and boots. Dr. Miller is revolting, but I book a follow-up with his cranky receptionist on my way out, just in case.

Two Days Later

My diaphragm lurches, and my ribs contract as acidic vomit slides up my throat. It spills into the ugly pink toilet before me. I wipe my lips and flush the brown, chunky liquid. The yellow-brown water swirls, then rises, reaching the toilet seat. Terrified, I flush a second time, and relief washes over me as the fetid water drains, then turns clear. The last thing I need is for my boss to find out I'm pregnant because I clogged her toilet.

My eyes stream. I glance at the wooden cross nailed to the fuchsia wall right above the toilet. God is watching me, even when I take a shit.

I stand up, feeling dizzy, mostly thanks to my anaemia. The tiny bathroom reeks of bile. I pull out my cheap body spray that I got from the bargain bin and spritz it everywhere, especially around the toilet. My nostrils burn, and I cough as I inhale the horrible smell of fake roses. I run the sink's taps, wash out my mouth, and gaze at myself in the mirror.

My pale skin is glowing despite the dark circles under my eyes. A plethora of loose strands of hair frame my sweaty face. I slick them back into my high ponytail and dab my smeared mascara with a wet paper towel. A spot of yellow-brown vomit on my sky-blue sweater causes me to cringe. I try to clean it, but it won't come out. The best I can do is say it's coffee and hope my boss believes my lie.

I leave the safety of the back room and return to the main area only to see a line outside the door at the Red Cup Cafe. When Charlotte, my boss, spots me from the till, she narrows her green eyes, exaggerating her deep crow's feet, and brushes her thick ginger hair over her shoulder.

"Took you long enough," she snarls as she pushes past me to the steel espresso machine.

Shit. I forgot that it's Sunday. The church crowd, which consists of almost the entire town, always comes to the Red Cup Cafe after service, given Charlotte's father is the Priest. The people that Charlotte has pissed off over the years go to the only other coffee shop in the area— Tim Hortons. I've heard her joke that they're the town heathens.

I spot my friends Ruby and Tanya through the front foggy windows. They're in the middle of the long line that winds around the corner outside, and they're wearing their Sunday best—wool dresses and expensive

Uniqlo cold-weather nylons they ordered online. Tanya holds out her phone and points to something on the screen, and Ruby laughs, her curly blonde hair tossing in the sun. I'd give anything to be out there giggling with them, but I hate going to church, and working the Sunday shift is the perfect excuse to skip service.

"What's that on your sweater?" Charlotte asks as I finish taking a customer's order at the till. Her green eyes are fixated on the vomit stain near my collarbone.

"Coffee," I say a little too quickly.

Charlotte nods, then returns to the espresso machine. I swallow the lump in my throat. Seems like she bought it, but it's hard to say with her.

I don't have time to ruminate thanks to the endless flow of customers. That is until I see Dr. Miller's large, flushed face among the crowd. I let the small talk go on longer than I should with my next customers, hoping he'll get frustrated and leave. But Dr. Miller has far more patience than I expected. He moves up in the line, closer and closer, until he's at the till.

"Hello there," he says with a fake smile. He slides his hollow blue eyes to Charlotte. "Hi, Lotty."

"Dr. Miller," she says, beaming. "Nice to have you back. Still have the same order?"

"Yes," he says, his high-pitched voice making my skin crawl. "A large soy latte with three shots of espresso."

"Coming right up," Charlotte says as she shoots me a sideways glance.

"On the house," I say to Dr. Miller, my gaze glued to the till.

"Thank you very much," he responds with fake enthusiasm. "I'll leave a tip, though. Does debit work?"

My skin crawls. It's hot in the Red Cup, but nowhere near enough to warrant the streams of water pouring down Dr. Miller's temples. I do my best to hide my disgust as I hand him the debit machine. He taps his card and leaves a ten-dollar tip, then heads to the coffee bar to wait for his drink. Charlotte cuts the queue to give Dr. Miller his soy latte before the others, but no one complains. If anything, most of the customers seem happy to see him. After a few brief conversations, he leaves, allowing me to breathe again.

As the afternoon passes, the church rush fades. I spend an hour cleaning the counters, stocking the sugar packets, and refilling the milk jugs while Charlotte reviews her accounting books nearby. I take a quick look at my phone while she's distracted. There are six missed calls, all from creditors, and an email threatening to repo my car because I was late on its loan payments. It's enough to make me want to puke again.

"It was nice to see Dr. Miller," Charlotte says. "He's a great doctor, you know. Helped me a lot with my pregnancy."

I smile but don't respond, pretending to be preoccupied with wiping the espresso machine worth more than my car.

"You're not pregnant, are you?" she says through a wry laugh. "You certainly run to the bathroom enough to have me guessing."

"I'm having stomach problems," I say, keeping my composure despite the panic shooting through my chest. "Actually, I need to go to the walk-in clinic after work on Wednesday. Is it all right if I duck out early? You know how crazy the wait gets."

Charlotte studies me through narrowed eyes, as if searching for a lie. "Can't you use virtual care?"

"I tried, but they told me I need a physical exam," I say. "I'll skip my break to make up the time."

"That works." Charlotte glances around the cafe. There are only a few busy tables, and they're all chatting to each other. She leans toward me, flashing me her signature bug-eyed look—the one she always gets when she's about to start gossiping. "Speaking of pregnancies, did you hear about Bella Spetelli?"

I recognize the name from high school. Bella was one of the popular girls, so I rarely spoke with her. "No. What happened?"

Charlotte clutches her gold cross necklace. "Dr. Miller's receptionist is friends with my mom. She told her Bella had an abortion. Word spread around town and the church banned her. I heard she got into a college in Sudbury and moved." Charlotte returns to the ledger. "Good riddance. We have enough sinners here without adding baby murderers to the list."

"Yeah," I say, my voice cracking. "Good riddance."

ONE WEEK LATER

I sit in my beaten-up car outside Dr. Miller's office, which is located in a brick bungalow that was once someone's house. The bright sun reflects off the crisp snow, creating a blinding glare. I tap the cracked leather wheel, blow my stuffed, chapped nose, then put on a blue medical mask.

The walk-in clinic was a dead end. I sat for six hours in a stuffy waiting room, and despite wearing a mask, I managed to catch a cold. When I finally saw the doctor, he scarcely looked at me as he told me I'd already been referred to the local OB-GYN. I tried to explain to him that Dr. Miller hadn't prescribed me the abortion pill. Without even a glance, he instructed me to make a new appointment with my OB-GYN and not to come back unless I had a real problem.

I check my watch. I have two minutes until my appointment with Dr. Miller. Charlotte let me use my lunch hour to come here, but I could tell she wasn't happy about it.

I chew on my lower lip. This is a huge risk. People found out about Bella Spetelli's abortion, so there's a chance word will spread about mine, too. My mom drove me out of town for my last one, but I know she won't do it again. And unlike Bella, I don't have the funds to run away to Sudbury and go to college. My horrible credit means I can't get a student loan, and there's no way I'll ever be able to save enough for tuition on my crappy salary.

The night before, I tried using the internet to see if other doctors in the area could help, or if there was another walk-in clinic I could reach. There was nothing that was drivable or open on a Saturday—my day off, which only happens once a month. Even if there was a place open on Saturday, I'm nine weeks pregnant as of yesterday, which leaves me with no time to get the pill from anyone but Dr. Miller.

A cloud of frozen mist fills my vehicle as I sigh. I have no choice but to deal with creepy Dr. Miller and his indiscreet receptionist. Ignoring the myriad of missed calls from creditors, I take my phone from the grimy coffee cup holder, shove it in my ripped Walmart purse, leave my car, and walk into the office.

Several women of varying ages sit in the waiting room, most scrolling on their phones. The harsh lime-green walls and sharp lighting make them all appear older than they are. Upbeat nineties pop music blasts from the receptionist's radio. I don't remove my thick winter jacket—the office is freezing. I think of Dr. Miller's sweaty, flushed face hovering above my knees and cringe.

"Are you going to stand around all day?" the receptionist—a grey-haired woman with thick glasses and a frilly cat sweater—asks. She looks like she would be a friend of Charlotte's mother based on how much pink she's wearing.

I approach the desk and look over my shoulder. "My name is Katherine Brown," I whisper. "Birthday is November seventh, two thousand and six."

Her thin lips flap as she releases a long, exaggerated sigh.

"Everything that goes on here is private, right?" I ask, keeping my voice low. "Because, you know, that's the law. Breaking it could mean an investigation, or t-termination. Not saying you would, just—you know," I let out a nervous laugh, "it's a small town, and mistakes happen."

Someone online told me to say that, and the receptionist's responding glare shows that it was a terrible idea. I try to smile, but I'm sure it looks more like a grimace.

"Your confidentiality will be respected," she growls. "Now take a seat."

I face the insular waiting room. The only open chair is next to a middle-aged woman in a black turtleneck and retro skinny jeans. After I take a seat next to her, I realize I've seen her in the Red Cup Cafe. My cheeks burn, and I snatch a magazine off the rectangular coffee table, holding it close to my face.

I look over the magazine to see a different woman staring at me. She's also a regular at the Red Cup, and usually comes in on Sundays with the church crowd. I don't know her name, but she knows mine. *Cute Katy*, she calls me.

I take a long, deep breath in, hold it, then exhale. For all these women know, I'm just here for birth control—the lesser of two evils in their God-fearing minds. If I don't act afraid, maybe they won't suspect anything. I toss the magazine aside and start scrolling on my phone, attempting to appear like a typical Gen Z annoyed by the waiting room's inherent lack of instant gratification.

Twenty minutes pass. At least people have stopped staring, but I'm late to get back to work. Another ten minutes pass. I lower my mask to blow my nose, and a tired-looking woman shoots me a dirty look. I text Charlotte that the doctor is running behind. She opens the message and doesn't respond. Anxiety grips me as another five minutes pass. Then another. I cough as the receptionist calls the woman next to me. She heads down the hall, her skinny jeans swishing as her thighs brush together.

When the receptionist returns, I ask her how long the wait will be, saying I'm worried because I have to go back to work.

"Be patient," she snarls. "God, people your age want everything *now, now, now,* don't you?"

My palms are sweaty as I take my seat. I pull out my phone and text Charlotte. *Sorry, he's really running behind. I'll keep you updated.*

Hurry up!! She responds. *We're slammed. You have ten minutes, or I'll be docking your wages for the week!!!*

My rent for this month is already late. I dart to the reception desk, my eyes dry from not blinking. "Please, can I see Dr. Miller next? I have to go back to work."

"There's someone in front of you," the receptionist barks. "Sit back down and wait."

"That's fine," the church-going woman that recognized me says. "She can go before me. I've got all the time in the world."

"Thank you," I say, certain I look as desperate as I feel.

Her grim nod makes me feel as though she's not doing me a favour.

The receptionist pushes her thick glasses up her hooked nose. She snatches a battered clipboard off her desk and leads me down the hall to a cramped room. The examination table is a mere inch away from the short counter covered in medical tools, and the room reeks of bleach. She tells me to sit in the chair by the counter, puts the clipboard with my file in a holder on the wall, and shuts the door gently, contrasting her agitated aura.

It's another fifteen minutes before Dr, Miller enters the room. He's wearing the stereotypical doctor's outfit—a white lab coat, beige dress pants, black leather shoes, and a collared shirt. Sweat slicks back his grey hair, and his bulbous nose is red. I smile even though my stomach churns at the sight of him, and try to wrap up my latest grovelling text to Charlotte.

He shuts the wooden door. The sound of the knob clicking into places makes me think of a tomb scaling.

"You kids can't take your eyes off those things, can you?" His tone is pure acid.

I put down my phone, abandoning my text. If I can keep Dr, Miller happy, I'm sure he'll prescribe me the medication. Doctors can refuse abortions, and even though his bizarre ultrasound exam had been tense, I remind myself that maybe Dr. Miller simply wanted me to think about my decision.

"And you came in sick, too." He pulls a stained mask out of his coat pocket and puts it on. The strings cut into his saggy cheeks, causing his loose flesh to spill over. "So, have you thought about your situation?"

"Yes," I say. "I want the abortion. I think that's what's best for me."

"So, you're worried about yourself?"

"What?" I ask, thrown by his question.

"You're being selfish, is what you're saying."

I take a deep breath, the air barely reaching my lungs through my blocked nose. Someone on Reddit told me to stop being a sissy and just be direct. *Advocate for yourself,* they'd typed in caps.

Each word leaves my mouth sluggishly, as if I'm squeezing the last bits of toothpaste out of a nearly empty tube. "Are you refusing to write me a prescription for an abortion?"

"I want you to answer my question," Dr. Miller says. "Have you thought about your actions, Katherine, and how they've led you to this situation not once, but twice?"

My shoulders tense as searing anger possesses me. I want to scream *it's not your job to judge me,* but my survival instincts cool my rage.

"I have, Dr. Miller," I say calmly. "And I acknowledge that I have been irresponsible. Could you also prescribe me some birth control so that I can be more careful in the future?"

Dr. Miller stares at me, unblinking, for what feels like a lifetime. Eventually, he nods.

I smile. He's going to do it. Thank God—er, well, thank someone. I'm not sure God would approve of what I'm about to do.

As if he can read my mind, Dr. Miller's eyes narrow.

Shit. He needs to think I'm sad. My eyes form crescents when I grin, so he can probably tell I'm happy even with the mask.

I hang my head and pretend to be remorseful. That's what Dr. Miller wants to see—a guilty, battered woman drowning in shame. My shoulders soften and droop as relief washes over me like a soft breeze, but I hope it looks like I'm feeling sorry for myself.

"I've told you, Katherine, the risk is too great," Dr. Miller says coldly.

My head jerks up. What's he talking about? Wasn't he agreeing just now?

"Pardon?" is all I manage.

"As a doctor, it's my duty not to endanger your life," Dr. Miller continues. "It would be unwise to give you an abortion. Not in your current state."

My jaw drops, then locks as adrenaline seizes me. "It's my right to a referral." My voice shakes. "There's Dr. Nowak in Sudbury. Please send me to her."

"Dr. Nowak would probably do it." Dr. Miller sits on the chair in front of the small cabinet near the examination table, and crosses his thin arms across his protruding belly, the strained buttons on his shirt threatening to burst. "Her waitlist is about eight months, though. How far along are you?"

An icy feeling runs through my guts. I'm nine weeks along.

"I'm guessing you already tried the abortion clinic in Sudbury?" He raises an untamed eyebrow. "What did they say?"

A month ago, much to Charlotte's irritation, I'd taken an unpaid day off and drove three hours to the closest abortion clinic, located in the city of Sudbury. I'd braved the picket line of men and women holding signs and shouting *murderer* at me. After sitting for two hours in yet another horrible waiting room, the doctor turned me away, stating I was high risk because of having anaemia, and that I had to try taking iron pills. I'd told them I couldn't afford to take more time off work to drive back, so they'd referred me to Dr. Miller, assuring me he would write me the prescription for the abortion pill, as he had for many women in the past.

"I know what they said at the clinic." Dr. Miller holds up the clipboard, antagonizing me. "It's right here in your chart."

"I took the iron pills and don't feel faint anymore when I stand up." A lie, but what else can I do? "My energy levels are better." Another lie. "My heart feels fine, too." It's racing, but he doesn't need to know that.

"Do you have a medical degree, Katherine?" Dr. Miller asks.

"N-no, but I know how I feel. I'm the one in my body."

"*I'm* a doctor. I know what's good for you and the health of your baby. Now, are you going to keep being difficult? Because if so, I'll drop you off my roster, and you'll be without a doctor to help you with your high-risk pregnancy. You don't want to be in that position." He chuckles. "Not in this country."

I hear an intense ringing, almost like white noise. Snot runs from my nose into my open mouth.

"I'm sorry, Katherine," Dr. Miller switches his tone from harsh to sympathetic, "but I don't want you to get hurt. So, let's go over your options. You can try the clinic in Sudbury again, or a virtual clinic, even, but they'll refuse you. They only write prescriptions for the abortion pill up to nine weeks, and you're a few days past that now. That leaves you with the clinics in Toronto."

Toronto is an eight-hour drive from here. The cheapest hotel is over four hundred dollars a night, and I'd need someone to come with me to help drive me home. No one would. My mother hates me for my first abortion. My dad isn't in the picture, and my stepdad is a bible-bumping monster. My grandparents are dead, and all of my friends are religious.

Worse, if anyone in town were to discover what I'd done, I'd be a pariah. It was a risk even to see Dr. Miller. I shouldn't have—this was a mistake.

I should have just taken the financial hit, called in sick, and driven back to Sudbury. Why had I been so stupid?

"Do you think you can afford to go to Toronto, Katherine?" Dr. Miller asks, tilting his balding head.

All I can manage is to stare at him.

"I didn't think so," he says. "I understand you're worried about money, but there are social services for single mothers, like welfare."

"It's only seven hundred dollars a month," I blurt. My rent for a studio is twelve hundred dollars a month, and my ADHD medication is four hundred dollars biweekly. After I pay all that, I scarcely have enough money left to buy food. There's no way I can support a child on top of that.

This is real. Dr. Miller is going to refuse my abortion. I'm out of options. I'm fighting for my life. "I can't afford a child, Dr. Miller," I plead. "*Please*, give me the abortion pill. I will be careful from now on. I swear to God."

His beady eyes trail up my legs as if undressing me. "I won't write the prescription. I will, however, provide you the care you need to get through what is going to be a high-risk pregnancy."

"No!" I shout. "I can't do this. I don't have the money." A thought occurs to me. If there was ever a time to act crazy, it's now. "I have mental health issues, too. And ADHD. I can't even remember to feed myself, let alone a helpless child. And what if I get postpartum depression? I'm at risk, you know, because of all my mental health problems. They're in my chart, if you want to check. Or, or, what if the baby comes out with ADHD? Then what?"

"There are pills for that," Dr. Miller responds, leaning against the stained beige wall.

My eyes dart to the clipboard, then to the counter, then to the cupboard above it. I shake, my breathing rapid. "Please. *Please*." My chest seizes as I break into a fit of coughing, wet phlegm sliding into my mouth. "Please don't do this to me."

"*You* did this to yourself," Dr. Miller bellows over me, his saggy neck twisting into cords. "I'm offering you care, Katherine. That's better than half the women in this province get." He points his fat finger in my face, close enough that I can see the dirt under his yellow fingernails. "You'll need routine testing—bloodwork every three days, then ultrasounds every two to four weeks. If you're not on my patient list, then what? Will you drive an hour to the testing centre every few days? Will Charlotte let you take that much time off?"

My heart sinks. It's over. I've lost.

Dr. Miller pulls down his ratty mask. He smiles, the same leer he had on his face when he first gave me the ultrasound. "I do ultrasounds in-house, and my nursing assistant does blood tests. My practice is a one-stop shop—the only one for hundreds of kilometres. You know I took you on despite having a full roster? I'm kind, Katherine, even if you don't believe me. I'll take care of you and your baby here."

My lip trembles as my mother's voice echoes in my mind: *you always were a little slut, weren't you?* She said that the first time I needed an abortion, and she was right. I am a little slut, and that's how I got myself here, again, with another baby I can't support.

Dr. Miller backs away from me, pulls up his medical mask, and takes a pen out of the chest pocket of his lab coat. "I'll have the receptionist email you a schedule for ultrasounds and blood work." He scribbles on his clipboard. "I don't normally work evenings, but I'll make an exception for you because I know you can't get time off."

I'll be alone with him. Here. At night. I look at the garbage can as my mouth fills with saliva.

Just as I'm about to hurl, my phone buzzes. For once, it's not a creditor.

"I have to take this," I say, terrified he'll scream at me again. "It's my boss."

His blue eyes widen. "Go on. Take it."

I answer. "H-hello?" I sound like I've been crying.

"How much longer?" Charlotte asks.

"I–I—" My phone slides in my sweaty hand. "It's—I—"

"Katy, this is ridiculous! You said you'd only be half an hour. I have a line out the door. Are you coming back or what?"

I lick my lips and taste salty snot. My vocal cords are frozen.

"If you're going to be this unreliable, I won't have a choice but to fire you," Charlotte yells. "It's just a damn cold. Take some cough syrup and get over it."

Dr. Miller looms over me like an executioner, his clipboard an axe, his lab coat a sanctioned garb. He snatches the phone from my hand. "Hello, this is Dr. Miller. I come into your cafe now and then. I usually order a soy latte with three espresso shots, but that's unimportant. I'm so sorry Katherine is late. It's my fault—I'm running behind today. But listen: Katherine is pregnant."

I gasp. Charlotte will tell everyone. My mother will find out. My friends will know. I picture their faces curled up in disgust. The ringing in my ears returns; this time, it's so loud my head throbs.

"Katherine has a high-risk pregnancy, and she needs medical attention," Dr. Miller says, his voice filled with false sympathy.

Oh! I hear Charlotte's loud voice through the phone's speaker, *I'm sorry, I didn't realise.*

"You know how it is with the healthcare system. I'm always running behind. But look, we're wrapping up here, and Katherine should be on her way shortly. I promise both of you that this won't happen again." His empty eyes land on me. "I'll make Katherine my priority from now on."

Thank you, Dr. Miller, Charlotte says.

"You're welcome. Make sure to congratulate her when she's back at the cafe."

Of course. I can hear the smile in Charlotte's voice. *Have a great day.*

"I will," he says.

He pulls the phone away from his hairy ear and pushes his fat finger on the end call button, then hands it back to me. "So, what do you say, Katherine?"

My head hangs on my neck. I stare at my open, sweaty palms resting on my lap. My vision wavers. I blink, and tears run down my cheeks. My mother will disown me if I have another abortion. My friends will shun me. I can't afford to move to different town to escape the stigma, meaning I can't run, even if it's what's best for me.

I put my hand on my stomach. I nod, and as I do, I imagine a baby gripping my hair and yanking it up and down, forcing me to agree.

"Great," Dr. Miller says, his demeanour shifting entirely. "That's so great, Katherine. You've made the right choice. Now go speak with my receptionist. She'll help you set up the regular appointments you need."

"Thank you." My voice is hollow.

He drops the clipboard back in its holder. It rattles and shakes, the sound like shackles. "Looking forward to seeing you at our next ultrasound."

Dr. Miller shuts the door, and I fall out of the chair onto my knees, sobbing into my cold hands.

Vessels of God

by Anne Wilkins

Content warnings: Violence, religious extremism

"Why'd you do it?" I feel strong arms on me, a voice from far away.

Someone is shaking me. Hard. These aren't loving arms. And then I feel a sudden, sharp slap on my face. My skin burns and I wake up momentarily from the haze that I had abandoned myself to.

It's my brother. His face is explosive, a mix of rage and gunfire. "You stupid, stupid girl," he snarls. I tilt my head slowly to the side. I should *feel* something. Anything. But I feel only… *nothing*. A deep, deep emptiness. I smile, as I know nothing else to do or say, and I'm rewarded with a punch to my stomach. He's never hit me before.

I double over and clutch my stomach in agony. There had been a baby in there once, I think, *once upon a time*, like a fairy tale. *Twice upon a time*. A strange giggle emerges from my throat. I have someone's blood on my hands, I notice, as I look at my hands in confusion. Still I laugh. I feel something now, the welcome call of madness knocking on my door and I leave to answer it.

~*~

John 1.9.2080 No child shall be tainted by its parents. Children shall be pure, and raised by all. Vessels of God Act 2080.

In our village, all babies are a blessing from God. They are not *our* babies. We, women, are merely the means of transportation for ensuring a baby's safe travel from heaven to this earth. We cannot "own" a baby, just as a baby cannot have a mother or father.

This is what we are taught, and it is not for us to question.

Still, a mother instinctively seems to know which is her babe. Sometimes you can tell from the look of the child. Other times it is their mannerisms. And sometimes it is an inherited defect.

Briar has a mound of untameable, bright red hair, and there is an infant named Sally with the same wild red mane. Marge sticks out her tongue while she thinks, just like little Sara-Ann does now. Kara has a lazy eye, and there is a boy called Bo with the same affliction. These mothers know these are their children.

Just like I know Gwyn is mine.

We are meant to be the parents for all children, for it takes a village to raise a child. But, I pay special regard to my Gwyn. I fashion her little toys in secret, I hum sweet lullabies to her, and I hold in her my arms long after she has fallen asleep. I spend many hours staring at my beautiful angel in her cot when I am meant to be watching and caring for other babes.

"She is not *your* child, you know," admonishes Matron one day, catching me unawares.

"I know. She is God's child," I reply, as is custom.

"Sebastian needs changing, and Frankie is overdue for a feed. Make sure you are caring for all God's children."

"Of course."

It was my first warning, of plenty.

~*~

John 8.9.2084 A sibling bond shall be unbreakable. Upon which each shall draw strength.

Gwyn was two when it was decided that it was time for me to conceive again. I was excited. Gwyn would soon have a sister or a brother, just as I had my brother, Jacob. After a sibling is born, the two are placed side by side to gather strength from each other, as is written in the scriptures.

While biological parents are mere receptacles of a child's journey into the world, the sibling bond is unbreakable. They will always be together, like my brother Jacob and I. I know after I have another baby a little crib will be brought in next to Gwyn's sleeping quarters, so my child and my soon-to-be child will be together, always.

I am given the nameless father's seed each week in my fertile time. I self-administer it, keeping my legs up high, bottom raised, and praying as I am instructed to.

Some of the young women in our village fantasize about from whom their seed comes, but I do not waste time on such silly notions. This is a process, nothing more. A means to an end.

When I find out that the seed has taken inside me, I am ecstatic. I rush to tell my brother, and he too is happy for me.

"You will be an uncle!" I say stupidly, using the old words, the words that we no longer use.

His happiness is replaced by a frown.

"We do not *own* children. They are God's children, Abby. Have you forgotten?"

"Of course. I'm sorry, Brother. It was a mistake."

Jacob is older than me, by a couple of years, and my stupidity can be forgiven. Women sometimes say stupid things, especially when they are with child.

"We must love all God's children," he states, reminding me of the way, in case I am slipping.

"Yes, yes, Brother." I bow my head low to show contrition and retreat to my room, where I stroke my stomach lovingly and hum soothing tunes to *my* baby.

The baby inside me grows strong and my stomach soon bulges. I let Gwyn stroke my tummy.

"Babbee?" she asks in her way, and I nod with a smile.

She rests her head of golden curls on my belly and giggles as she feels the little kicks from her sibling. I stroke her little head. *My children*, I think blasphemously.

Somewhere, further down the hall, I can dimly hear another child crying. But it isn't my child. I'm sure someone else will take care of it.

Some months later I am called into Matron's office.

"I have concerns," she starts. Followed by one of her long, deep sighs that I have grown accustomed to. "You're slipping."

"I'm sorry, Matron. I will do better."

"Too much time with Gwyn. It's not healthy. Joshua soiled himself this afternoon while you were on duty, and you did nothing. Did you not… smell him?"

In truth, I had smelt him; it was foul, but it was close to my shift ending and I had thought…

"No Matron, I'm sorry, I didn't smell anything."

Matron looks at me, one eyebrow raised. For a while, she doesn't say anything. "Tell me, why do you spend so much time with Gwyn?"

"I'm sorry, matron, I didn't realize I was."

"Do you think me stupid?"

"No."

"You think you bore Gwyn into this world?"

Of course, she is mine!

"No matron! I do not know which child I would have been lucky enough to birth."

She is mine! As clear as day! Like a lioness knows her own cubs!

It was a difficult game we were playing. A game of hide and seek, and I didn't want to be found.

Matron glares at me, and my bulging roundness. It looks as if she is deciding upon something.

"The separation exists so we do not favour our own child over another," she talks slowly, in a half whisper, and I have to lean close to listen. "Sometimes, though, as with cases like yours, women can have a fixation on a certain child. They can believe a child is theirs… even when it is not."

I let her words fall on me like stone. *When it is not?* I do not believe it. The stone pushes against my chest and I find it hard to breathe.

"I am not supposed to say things, but…" My ears crane forward, the moment feels like a hundred moments in one. "But, there are records kept. Occasionally we might need a blood match, a donor, especially if there is no sibling, so it is important to know where a child has been birthed from." She stares at me intently.

"Our village's records Abby, are all here. In this locker behind me." She pauses and takes a breath. "Tell me Abby, do you *really* want to know if Gwyn is the child you birthed?"

I nod, despite myself. Despite already knowing in my heart of hearts that she is mine.

"Then, I am going to leave this key here," she removes a key from around her neck and places it on her desk. "And I am going out for a short while. Perhaps you will find some answers when I am gone. Answers that I cannot give you. You understand?"

Matron leaves.

I am alone with the key and the locker. The bait upon a hook, which I am just dying to nibble. A small taste at the edges, and then like a clever fish I will dart away.

I resist at first, but the locker pulls me to it, and before I can help myself I am twisting the key into its rusty mechanism.

Gwyn is my child. Gwyn is my child. I repeat the mantra in my head as the locker springs open. There are so many folders in here, and at first it seems impossible until I see that they are alphabetical. I find the G's.

Gwyn is my child. Gwyn is my child. I pull out Gwyn's file. Plain, brown manilla for such a beautiful angel doesn't seem right.

I open it with trembling hands. *Gwyn is my child. Gwyn is my child.* I stumble across the words; they seem foreign for a while, as they are old words, lost words: mother, father. I trace my finger under the word mother, and stroke it lovingly. *Gwyn is my child. Gwyn is my child.* I read the words underneath, and it is not my name I read. I look again, and again, in case my eyes are tricking me. But there is no Abby for Gwyn.

She is not mine.

I throw the file down in disgust and the contents spill out as if they too are disgusted with themselves.

Not mine.

Silent tears stream down my face. The stone that has been on my chest crushes me until I cannot breathe. The world seems to blur and the floor moves. I'm falling and the ground catches me with its cold, linoleum floors. *Not mine?* I question as the blackness claims me.

I wake up, and I'm in a hospital bed. *Something is gone? Something is missing?* And I realize it is Gwyn. Gwyn has gone. *Not mine.*

But there is something else that has gone. The babe. My stomach has been burst, and there is an emptiness inside.

A nurse enters and sees I am awake.

"My baby?" I ask in desperation, and I try to grab her uniform.

She pulls away from me and corrects me. "*The* baby, you mean."

Fresh tears roll down my face. "Yes. *The* baby. What happened? Where is *the* baby?" I pronounce the word *the* with venom, and the nurse says nothing. "Please?" I add. And a torrent streams down my face.

"*The* baby was delivered by emergency caesarean. It'll be fine. Rest now."

"Can I see it?"

"You know you can't."

"Was it a boy? A girl?"

"Be happy that you have delivered a child unto this world. You need know no more."

She turns and leaves me to the blackness, the emptiness, the nothingness. In one day, I have had two children taken from me.

I'm moved to the baby ward. Breastfeeding different babies, one of whom may be my own. Each time a different child is brought to me, I wonder, is this mine?

Gwyn comes to see me later. Matron brings her. I wonder what kind of cruel punishment is this? To parade my pretend child in front of me.

"We were worried about you," Matron says.

"Babbee?" asks Gwyn and she points at my empty stomach.

"Gone," I say. I turn into my pillow and cry from dry river beds.

"It'll get better," Matron says. "It will be better." She strokes my hair as the anger drips from me.

My brother comes later with flowers. A bunch of red tulips that droop their heads in sadness.

"Good work sister," he says. "Another angel delivered safely onto our earth."

"Yes."

I wonder why I didn't see it before. He is my brother, but he is a stranger.

"Are you well?"

No. I am empty. A shell. A nothing.

"Yes. I am well, Brother. And you?"

"Yes. Matron sent over some food for me which was kind."

"How kind she is."

I hate her. I should never have opened the locker.

We have nothing to say to each other but skeleton words.

"Tell me, brother," I ask. "Do you ever wonder who birthed us?"

He pauses for a long time before he answers as if he is choosing his words wisely.

"The scriptures are clear, Sister. The vessel does not matter, just that it was a healthy one."

He understands nothing of a mother's love, a mother's heartbreak, a mother's...

My breasts begin leaking. I cannot help it. A bell is rung and a baby, a new baby is brought to me. My brother leaves in embarrassment. Milking time is for cows and women only.

I stare at this new baby as it suckles from me. It is smaller than the others, and I wonder stupidly if this one could be mine.

Two months pass and the pain ebbs away, but something has been taken from me. I cannot get it back. My head is a jigsaw puzzle that someone has carelessly taken apart and I can't piece myself together. I wander around in a half-state, but I do my job. I treat all the babes the same, I take care of them all, moving from one child to the next in a daze.

It is on this same day that a small crib is moved next to Gwyn's bed and a small baby boy, named Isaac, is placed in that crib.

I look at it all in horror. The crib, the babe. He makes little mewling sounds, and all I can do is stare.

"See Abb-eee? My brudar?!" says Gwyn in excitement. I didn't think a heart could keep breaking, but mine does.

"He is lovely Gwyn. You'll…" and the words choke inside me. "You'll have to take good care of him."

Gwyn holds a tiny toy above Isaac's head, it is one I had made her. She shakes it around while little Isaac tries to focus.

I recognize this babe from the hospital, he's the small one I sometimes fed.

Small. Undersize. Premature.

And now here. Next to Gwyn.

Could he be?

I've fallen down this hole so many times before, but something has been planted in me. A seed of doubt. It grows inside me with anger to fertilize it.

That night I cannot sleep. There are too many questions pounding inside my head, demanding to be released. *Shut up!* I tell them, but instead, they whisper to me, words that haunt me, taunt me… *the children are yours.* They say, again and again. *The paper lied. The folder is all lies. She tricked you! Gwyn is yours, the baby is yours. Take them. Take them. Take them!*

Take. In the early hours of the morning before the sun itself was arisen, I got up. I take the knife from our kitchen and I head to where *my* children are. As if I am going to work. To nurture, to care, to provide. But today I will not give; today I take.

I stand above their sleeping bodies. *My* Isaac, in his crib, *my* Gwyn in her bed. They both look like little angels. I'd known they were angels all along. I clutch the knife tighter in my hand.

"Abby? You're here early?" rings out Matron's voice.

I've been waiting for her to arrive, to take the answers out of her, but before I can stop it, the knife forces itself into her skin. *Naughty knife,* I think. She didn't have a chance to scream, but now she blows little red bubbles from her mouth.

"T..they a..are y..yours," she confirms with her red bubbles. It is just as I had always known. I turn to go. To take my sleeping children home, and then she says something else. Something incomprehensible.

"As you ..are mi..ne."

Matron dies, with those words on her lips.

~*~

I'd left my children still sleeping among their grandmother's blood and I'd returned empty-handed. No children. No knife. And somehow my mind had been lost as well.

It was my mother's words, matron's words, that I repeated to my brother when I came home.

Words that my brother already knew.

Words I wished I had known.

You stupid, stupid girl. His words roll in my head. In a head that hurts so much as the madness makes room for itself.

It is why she kept us close, I suppose. Mothers always want to be close to their children, despite what the scriptures tell us.

My brother sobs, real tears, as do I.

For lost and broken vessels.

Mary 10.8.2074 Mothers' rights to identify their child or children will forever be recognized in law and scripture.

Repealed by John 1.1.2080 under the Vessels of God Act 2080

Whose Pussy is This?

by A. H. Davison

Content warnings: Rape, loss of agency, birth control sabotage, forced pregnancy, cops, knives, blood, gore, body horror, self-mutilation / surgery, implied death

It started out as dirty talk. The third time I allowed my husband inside me, he'd coaxed moans out of me, caressing my inner walls with gentle fingers, thumb over my pleasure centre. He'd made my spine tingle by asking *Whose pussy is this?*

I'd come, clenching around his fingers, promising him, *It's yours—this is your pussy—yours to use however you want.*

I used to love him fucking into me like I was more *thing* than person. He'd growl, *Yeah, that's my pussy, my good, good pussy,* as he lost control of himself, overcome by his pleasure.

It was just a fun thing to say. I never thought he *meant* it.

But just after the announcement at 10:32 this morning that the Uterine-Ownership Bill has passed with only nine dissenters, Brent corners me against the kitchen cabinets with a glint in his eye I've never seen before. He slips a creeping hand beneath my skirt, peels my underwear aside, ignores my fists against his chest, and roughly shoves his fingers deep into me.

The words he growls into my ear are true.

"This is *my* pussy now."

~*~

"I'm sorry," the student pharmacist says.

To her credit, Penny, according to the silver tag on the breast of her white lab coat, does look sorry.

"Your husband needs to request your prescription on your behalf."

"I've been on the pill for thirteen years. I just need a refill." I kick myself for letting my supply dwindle.

Without turning her head, Penny glances at her male colleague. "I'm sorry," she repeats, "but it's the law."

I want to yell *THIS IS RIDICULOUS*, have a full-blown tantrum in the middle of the grocery store, and accuse Penny of being just as bad as the men who voted for the bill in the first place. I stop myself, lest my *hysterics* be taken as further evidence that we women are not fit to be responsible for our own reproductive organs.

I huff out, "Fine," and slam a box of condoms on the counter.

Penny eyes the box as though it might bite her.

"I can't *force* him to use them, can I?"

Her male colleague looks over, gives her a small nod. Penny avoids making eye contact with me while she rings me up; hands me my bag and receipt with a shaking hand.

"I'm sorry," she whispers.

I sigh. She's scared, too. I don't know what I'm mad at her for. Penny has as much authority over her body as I do mine.

I want to tell Brent to go fuck himself. Instead, I pull a silver square from my pocket when he approaches with that look in his eye.

"If you wear a condom, I'll let you."

I'm acutely aware that his own desire is the only thing standing between him and his being inside me. It has nothing to do with my 'allowance' and everything to do with how willing he is to take advantage of his legal right to open my legs and do whatever he likes with his property.

He frowns. "I can't put a baby in you with that on."

Part of me, the part that's absorbed every societal expectation that I will be a mother one day, is painfully aware of each second that ticks by. The saner part of me remembers that while there had been a time when I'd pictured him as a doting father, a tiny baby cradled in his strong arms, it's been harder and harder to do as of late.

"We should probably talk more about how we would like to parent before we make a kid."

His lilting half-smile covers his pout so quickly I almost don't catch it.

He takes the condom from my hand.

"You're gonna be good for me?" he asks. He arches his eyebrows in a way that used to give me the good kind of shivers instead of sparking my fight or flight response.

"Yes." I maintain eye contact with him as I unbutton my blouse. It falls open, offering a teasing glimpse of my breasts before I sink to my knees.

I take him in my mouth, something I haven't done in ages, and gag around him. He's salty and sour.

I hope, as he leans his head back and groans, tangling his fingers in my hair and thrusting against the back of my throat, that he'll finish like this. The condoms could be a moot point.

No such luck.

He pulls himself from my mouth slowly. "Take off your pants and turn around."

I do as I'm told. Over the last few weeks, I've come to find that resisting doesn't change the outcome, only how many days I need to wear long sleeves to cover the bruises.

I worry, for a moment, that he's forgotten his promise, but there's a quiet tearing of the wrapper. He pushes inside me with the subtle grip of latex against skin.

I take him with a resigned stiffness.

"Whose pussy is this?" he snarls into the back of my neck.

My body responds, gripping him in tight pulses. I hate that those words still do something to me.

I bite back a moan as he pounds into me, a deep, hard staccato. I miss the days when this was a game. When he'd tell me he loves me after, and I'd believe him. I make a mental note to find out what a trial separation would look like.

"Whose. Pussy. Is. This?"

I refuse to say what he wants to hear but my body is a traitorous bitch. Pleasure rips through me, a sharp moan escapes from my lungs. My legs shake, threatening to give out beneath me.

My pleasure sours in my stomach as he pulls himself from me. For a single heartbeat, before the shame slinks in, it's a relief to be vacated and left empty.

~*~

I let him slip inside me every night.

Some nights it feels closer to *before*. When Brent comes home to a warm meal with a bouquet of flowers and kisses my cheek, I'm convinced we've been together too long to throw it all away. I can't walk it back if I start talking about separations and divorce. At least they'll always be options.

On the nights I least feel like it, I ponder the legal semantics. Is he slipping inside *me?* Is my vagina akin to a toy he could order online? Or is it and my uterus part of *him* now, the way they *used* to be part of me?

One night, it occurs to me that the new law has added a whole new meaning to telling Brent to go fuck himself. I morph my laugh into a moan.

Whatever amusement the thought brought me quickly dies. *Go fuck yourself,* is no longer a curse directed only at him. It's my curse, too.

~*~

The mattress shifts as he encroaches on my side of the bed. I swallow quietly.

Go away, I'm sleeping.

He's already had me tonight. Suffering him twice within a few hours is more than I can bear. Being used daily for weeks has left me swollen and sore. I'm a collection of micro-tears held together by muscle and flesh.

"Vanessa," he whispers.

I keep my eyes closed. *Sleeping. I'm sleeping.* My heart pounds in my ears but I focus on keeping my breathing level and controlled. *Who would ownership pass to if we separated? Dad, if he were alive; my brother?*

He snakes his hand up over my hip, between my thighs, rubs my bruised clit in slow, gentle circles, the way he used to rouse me from sleep, back when that was welcome. My eyes well beneath my lids, tears spilling into my pillow. These touches confuse me, the ones reminiscent of a gentle request, pretending there's a choice to be made.

He exhales a frustrated breath into my shoulder blade. His hand retreats. I resist the urge to sigh in relief. I focus on my breath, the slowing of my pulse.

The sound of a wrapper tearing breaks the midnight silence. My heart catches in my throat.

No.

He'd changed, but Brent was still a decent man. Decent men don't fuck unconscious women.

He wouldn't.

The invasion returns. Slow, careful fingers lift my thigh ever so gently. Calloused fingertips separate my folds. The only saving grace is that even though he thinks I'm asleep, he's still latex-slick when he enters me.

~*~

I don't notice it until I use the washroom on my lunch break. I smell it first, that sour musk, before I see the translucent white puddle in my underwear.

My stomach roils. It's not a lie when I tell my boss I'm going home sick.

~*~

I slam the front door closed behind me, run to our bedroom. I pull the cardboard box from his bedside table. I grab a silver square from the box. It's sealed on all four sides. I squeeze it between my finger and my thumb, praying for a resisting pressure.

My heart, like the packet, deflates. My last semblance of control over his access to my body crumbles.

"No." I pull every condom from the box. "No." I check them all. "No, no, no, no, no."

The word is as useless as the pin-punctured latex.

~*~

"I want a divorce."

The front door hasn't even latched behind Brent before the words are out of my mouth.

I'm exhausted and confused. I've had all afternoon to pack a bag and stew in my rage.

We talked about maybe having kids one day but tabled it. How was I supposed to know he wanted to be a father that badly? We both know the law's on his side, he can do whatever the fuck he wants. So why deceive me? I can't force him to wear a condom. Why let me believe he was honouring my last remaining request?

As long as I lay quietly beneath him instead of fighting him off, he could pretend I wanted it.

"What's for dinner?" he asks.

I press my lips together. I have no intention of explaining to him that I haven't cooked because I'm sick to my stomach with a full-body nausea I might never recover from. Food is the last thing on my mind right now.

"I want a divorce."

I expect his long sigh. I'm caught off guard by the laughter that follows.

Like every other night I haven't made us dinner, he walks past me to the kitchen, pulls a pair of pizza pockets from the freezer and pops them in the island's microwave oven.

"How was work?" he asks.

Pins and needles of rage prickle at my fingers, crawl up my wrists.

"I know what you did to the condoms." I fight to keep my voice flat and even. "I want a divorce."

"Okay, well, while we're dreaming, *I* want to win the lottery," he says, looking down at me. The microwave whirrs behind him. "But let's be realistic."

The microwave beeps. He bends to flip the pockets, starts them heating again.

"But you know what *is* realistic? Having the baby you promised me."

I gape at him. The kitchen is silent, save for the pizza pockets sputtering sporadically. The smell of his dinner combined with the flatness of his eyes sends a fresh wave of hot nausea through me.

"The baby I *promised* you?"

"Yeah." The microwave beeps. He retrieves his meal. "You said we'd talk about starting a family in three years. That was seven years ago."

He picks up one of the pizza pockets. I hope he burns his mouth on the molten cheese and faux-tomato sauce. "I never *promised* we'd have kids, and you know it," I say. *Though now I definitely don't want them with you.*

I watch him eat. His chewing disturbs the heavy silence. I dig my fingernails into my palms. He licks stray sauce from his fingers.

"I want a divorce. I'm going to see a lawyer tomorrow and file the paperwork."

"Right," he says, the corner of his lips pulling into a crooked smirk.

I grab my overnight bag. "I'm staying at a friend's tonight." My voice quavers but it's not a question. I am not asking for his permission to go. "Consider this the start of our separation period."

He folds his arms across his chest and leans against the island.

I expect him to grab me by the wrist, block my path to my car, but he lets me go. Just watches me drive away.

~*~

"Ma'am, is there a Vanessa Becker here?"

"Who's asking?" Sarah's door is only open the inch the chain allows. I can't see the source of the female voice in the hallway, my friend and her wine glass blocking my view.

"Police, ma'am."

A wave of sobriety crashes over me. *Why are the police looking for me?*

"We've had a report of stolen property and a tip that it may be here. Can we come in?"

"Stolen property?" Sarah asks. She glances back at me, *What the fuck is she talking about?* Creased into her brow.

I shake my head and shrug, eyebrows raised high. I don't think I took anything that wasn't mine. I grabbed a change of clothes, my toothbrush and night guard. Did I take his toothpaste?

I rifle through my bag next to the empty wine bottles. I can't fucking believe him. Calling the cops on me over fucking *toothpaste?*

I bring the half-mangled tube of Colgate to the door and slip it through the crack.

I do my best not to slur. "It was an honest mistake."

The cop furrows her brows at the tube in her hands.

"Ma'am, that's not—"

"We're going to need you to come with us," her partner says. He reaches for his belt. "You have on your person a uterus that's been reported missing."

"Excuse me?" I can't have heard him correctly. "I have—on my person—a *uterus* that's been *reported missing?*" I repeat slowly. The words don't make any more sense coming out of my mouth.

"Yes Ma'am," he says. "I'm gonna need you to open this door and come with us, please. There'll be additional charges for resisting arrest."

"Resisting arrest?" My spinning world is barely due to the wine. None of this makes any sense. "I'm under arrest?"

"Yes, ma'am. He might not press charges," the male officer adds, as if that makes this situation any better.

Sarah watches with wide eyes. I hand her my wine glass, slide the chain free, open the door and offer up my wrists.

The officer, with toothpaste in one hand, handcuffs in the other, shifts her eyes between her hands and her partner. Her pinched face reads, *Is this really necessary?*

Her partner shrugs, takes the toothpaste from her.

She's gentle when she cuffs me.

I turn back to Sarah, standing dumbfounded with an unfinished glass of wine in each hand, as the officers lead me away.

"Get me a lawyer," I call over my shoulder.

~*~

That first night in jail, I slept the best I had in over a month, my body not on high alert at all times. I'd met my legal team in the morning;

a half-dozen pro-bono lawyers who promised to do everything in their power to make sure the correct precedent was set.

My husband filed charges against me for theft under $5,000 and kidnapping. My lawyers and the judge all agreed the charges were ridiculous, but the way their brows pinched and foreheads wrinkled undermined the sentiment.

I was just starting to get used to fully relaxing at night when bail was set. That trumped-up-charge-pressing asshole paid it. If my legal team's reaction was anything to go by, that doesn't happen often. Bless the judge, though. She granted my request to remain in custody until my trial.

There were countless debates about semantics, ethics, and fundamental human rights. I lost all sense of time. I resorted to using the deepening undereye bags of my legal team and the wilting of my judge's posture as measures of how long we'd been fighting.

I was dumbstruck but tired when my lead lawyer recommended I change my pleas to guilty for both charges. We couldn't get around the new law, but she'd been able to negotiate a decent plea bargain. Five years in prison for the kidnapping charges, the legal minimum, and a $5,000 fine for the theft. Despite the injustice of it all, I plead guilty. There are worse ways to spend five years than in prison, out of my husband's reach.

Once Brent caught wind of the sentencing recommendations, he promptly dropped the charges.

I was sent back to him with the legal advice of *Let him know where you are at all times, activate the location tracker on your phone and share it with him. Never conceal your location.* I was long past trying to argue unwinnable debates, resigned to the new world's rules: every unfertilized egg developed in my body before my own birth has the potential for life; therefore, the value of a life, and they are no longer mine. I cannot take them anywhere nor do anything with them without my husband, their legal owner's, knowledge and express permission.

The judge did give me one gift. A legal treaty that clearly defines where my body ends and Brent's property begins. He has the right to access only what's his. Only the organs required for the production and delivery of a child belong to my husband. Under the Uterine-Ownership Act, he is the proud new owner of the uterus, fallopian tubes, ovaries, eggs, cervix, and vaginal canal that reside in my body.

Every other centimeter of my body—my hair, my mouth, the soft flesh of my inner thighs—is mine.

I am out of fight and at his beck and call to spread my legs and avail myself to him, but I can sleep with the comfort and security that his fingers will not creep and crawl over my hip and down my legs; he will not rub his thumb in firm, tight circles until I'm quivering beneath him in a way that lets him pretend that I want this.

Night after night, I lay still on my back, focusing on the rhythmic, repetitive bounce of the popcorn ceiling, willing myself out of my body until he vacates and I can return again.

I dig my nails into the palms of my hands to distract myself from the endless thrusting. I try not to dwell on the fact that I can't get a divorce without a radical hysterectomy.

I chew on the soft flesh inside my cheeks. The bitter tang of metal on my tongue is the most reliable way to pull me from my ruminations of how unfair it is that there isn't a doctor in the country who will perform a hysterectomy without consent from my husband; how this is my life, every day, for as long as we both shall live.

One at a time, I pull each knife from the kitchen drawer. I test the blades, keep the three sharpest out on the clean countertop.

I used to think the mindset of 'If I can't have it, you can't either,' was immature and petty.

I get it now.

My periods, my reassurance and respite, have come and gone over the past year. It's been three full months without one now, and I'm tired of playing this rigged game.

Guilt gnaws my belly. I didn't even warn Sarah that I'm doing this. I tell myself I'm protecting her, there could be legal repercussions for not alerting the authorities. But more than anything, there's always the chance she'll try to talk me out of it. It'd hurt too much if she, too, denied me my last scrap of agency.

I lay out the divorce papers. Find a ballpoint pen. I collect my knives and settle on the floor, back supported by the cabinets he'd first forced me against. My body has been invaded and violated so many times that the insertion of the cold, steel blade doesn't bother me. If anything, I savour the sharp sting, knowing each slice brings me closer to finally being separate from him.

The blade slips in my warm, slick fingers. I look down. The blood pouring from between my legs is a joy.

My knife clatters against the tile. I penetrate myself with my fingers, wince. I push on.

Even if I were legally given ownership of my whole body again tomorrow, I don't know that I'd ever feel fully *mine* again. My body will always hold some memories of him. Even after every cell he's laid a finger on has died and been replaced, he will remain, buried beneath my skin, scarred into my nerves.

I flinch, my fingers finding my cervix. I brace myself against the cabinets. I force my pinky first, add my ring finger, through the tight ring of muscle. My vision tunnels. No amount of breathing and deliberate relaxing is going to make this any easier. I struggle to inhale. Fight to get a secure grip. My uterine walls are thick-rubber slippery. Viscera collects beneath my fingernails as I inch them along the edges of my tubes, tearing them free.

The pain is all-encompassing. Nausea-inducing. My whole body flashes hot, contracts. I vomit, the aftertaste of bile sharp in my throat, coating my tongue. For a long, panting moment, I worry this is how he will find me. Not triumphantly divorced from him in every sense of the word, but curled within myself, marinating in a pool of my own fluids.

I swallow the urge to retch again. I grip that squishy, clam-chewy pouch best I can and pull.

The scream that echoes in my ears is inhuman.

Part of me worries the neighbours will call the cops.

Bring it.

I've pulled out the parts that belong to him. They're limp and bloody: a deflating balloon in my hand; a grotesque bracelet of meaty tunnel around my wrist.

What'll I be charged with this time? Vandalism and murder of potential life? What would they even call that, fourth degree murder?

I laugh, delirious with pain. The aching empty between my legs is ecstasy. The blood spilled from me, a baptism.

I try to work my vaginal bracelet from my wrist, closing my hand for its extraction. My laugh catches in my throat as my fingers palpate a cartilage-firm *something*. I massage the uterus until that lime-sized *thing* pops out.

My laugh crawls deep into my throat, through my core and back out again. The sound that emerges is maniacal.

Even if I'm granted my divorce, they'll charge me for murder.

Light-headed, I crawl to the island, my knees slipping in blood. I pull open the microwave with shaking hands. I unceremoniously scoop in the viscera, press the auto-setting for *frozen dinner* and collapse back against the cabinets as it whirrs to life. I reach up. Pull the divorce papers off the edge of the counter, adding bloody smudges to the edges. I scrawl one final note to my soon-to-be ex-husband with my limp hand, followed by my signature. The smear of sinew on the heel of my palm underlines my freedom.

I smile, delirious with pain. I revel in the thick scent of cooking meat, relishing the intermittent pops and splatters. It will smell like dinner's waiting when Brent gets home. I delight in what he'll find instead: the carcass of his marriage, that I have extricated myself from him, and one final parting message.

"It's your pussy. Go fuck yourself."

THIS BROKEN WORLD
BY MIA DALIA

Content warnings: Discrimination, implied rape, coerced reproduction, death.

I remember sitting at a concert in the park, side by side in our old beach chairs that we brought to every outdoor event. It was a nice night, poised right on the cusp of summer and fall, the air getting crisper as the sky got darker. The band was doing their best to ride the coattails of a one-hit wonder from two decades ago.

Our chairs were hand-me-downs, with faded blue fabric and rust on the chrome parts. If you weren't careful, the rust would get on your clothes, leaving burnt orange streaks as if a small autumn leaf had landed on your shoulder. The back of each chair had a large velcroed pocket, and you reached in and pulled a sweater from yours, handing it to me, because you always knew exactly when I might need one. And I remember thinking, *this is love. This is what all the songs are about. It'll never be better than this.*

I suppose, in a way, I was right. Because two months later, there was the election. And after that, everything just went to hell.

That was how we talked about it, feigning bravado that felt as insubstantial as a movie set façade. Everyone we knew was doing it too, becoming each other's cheerleaders as if that alone could power us through the next four years.

People talked of emigrating, but no one ever did, even before the borders were shut down by an executive order. Strange how small a big country can feel once you're told you cannot leave.

With enough walls and bars, any pasture can become a cage. Once that happens, plucking out "the undesirables" is like shooting fish in a barrel.

The list of "the undesirables" kept expanding. It was only a matter of time until you and I found ourselves on it.

Stripping away personal freedoms is a lot like boiling a frog. It has to be done gradually, heating the water incrementally to prevent the frog from noticing. Or perhaps the frog notices but chooses to ignore the changes, thinking it can't go on forever.

We were supposed to be smarter than frogs. We weren't.

"Do you think it's an apt metaphor?" I asked you once, turning away from the latest news report, disquieted and disgusted.

"Apologue."

"What?"

"It's technically an apologue. You know, a moral fable with animals as characters."

I did not know that, but I loved that you did. After all these years together, you could still teach me something new. It made the world seem infinite, the way it was always meant to be.

"And yes, I do think it's an apt one."

Words were your thing. You wrote brilliantly clever books that never sold enough copies and taught ESL classes at a local community college.

With the new immigration laws in full force, you kept telling me how there were more and more empty chairs in each class. Your hours got cut. The college offered you a few hours a week to teach creative writing. It hardly made up the difference.

My job was the one we deemed secure. I worked for the city's parks and rec department, a cog, a paper pusher, as tedious a way to spend nine to five as one could imagine, but a steady paycheque.

You always said I was too interesting for my job, and I'd counter with how it was better than the alternative, because who wanted to be upstaged by what they did for a living.

We kept our heads down and went on with our lives, flinching the entire time, because, unlike the frogs, we could tell the situation was worsening. We just couldn't get out of the pot.

Did we think ourselves untouchable then? Were we ever that naive?

Maggie died that summer from a botched back-alley abortion. She lasted three days after she came home, in and out of consciousness, rambling about the mildewy basement, the stirrups, the shadows in the corners. Her partner sat by her side, holding her hand, forcing stoicism onto their face.

You grew up with Maggie. I first met her two months after we started dating. I remember being initially intimidated about meeting your friends—you were all from a big city, while I came from a town too small for most maps. But Maggie was so warm, so funny, she put me at ease immediately.

They desperately wanted a child, Maggie and her partner—they were so happy when they finally got pregnant—but the early tests showed that it wouldn't be a viable pregnancy. I had never heard of the neurological disorder the fetus tested positive for, but it boiled down to simple, horrific math: less than ten percent chance of survival out of the womb, less than five of making it past a month. Zero percent of making it to a year, and all of that time would be spent in agony.

Maggie said she couldn't do it. They both knew they couldn't, but she was the first one to say it out loud. Devastated but resolute, they found a man to help. It was a sketchy set up, but there weren't any other options.

In the brutal aftermath, they didn't dare take her to the ER. In accordance with the new laws, even if her life could be saved, she and her partner would both face lengthy prison sentences. Everyone close to her would be under suspicion and likely investigation. The authorities took their murder charges seriously.

Though the initial overturning of a decades-old ruling was meant to give the decision power to the states, it was soon followed by increasingly draconian restrictions, resulting in a country-wide ban. No exceptions were considered.

This wasn't something that had any direct effect on us as we had always been happily childless. Childfree, as we'd say, stressing the freedom it gave. But ideologically, it was horrifying. And the implications of what was to come were the scariest things of all.

Could they? We'd wonder, horrified, knowing full well that yes, they could, and they would.

Our marriage was legally dissolved by the government early the following year. You didn't pass the mandatory questionnaire. The papers that confused sex with gender and everything else were stark, brutally unambiguous; yes or no questions, leaving no room for "other."

All the changes you had gone through to become the person you were always meant to be were not enough for the powers that be. They demanded their citizens' outsides match their insides in a strictly biological fashion. You had a womb, and thus you were declared a woman.

And because same-sex marriage was one of the first institutions to crumble, no longer could our union be recognized in the eyes of the law. Suddenly, we were simply two women living together. The new reality of being stuck in a country that refused to see us as we were proved more than we could handle.

You drank, I drank. We said things we didn't mean, because anger was better than self-pity and fear that threatened to engulf us.

Our next-door neighbour, Manu, was deported not too long after. We could hear his wife cry through the thin walls of our apartment, hopeless, heartbroken wails that went on seemingly for hours. Manuel Sanchez, Manu to all who knew and loved him, a photographer, a baker, an enthusiastic dancer, and a terrible poker player, was Brooklyn born and bred. His father came to the US legally as a ten-year-old. His mother was a fourth-generation Italian from Queens.

Eager to meet their quotas, the immigration police didn't always check the papers too closely. Manu was condemned by his skin colour and name so thoroughly that even his US passport couldn't refute it.

We talked about moving, but due to the sudden rise in vacancies, our rents had actually gone down. Besides, we simply couldn't afford anywhere else.

The isolationist nation was a weak one. The enemies saw their chance. When the first dirty bombs began to fall, the news coverage went from severely edited to outright fictitious.

By then, most of the news outlets had been shut down, leaving in charge only the ones that served the new regime and kissed the ring like they meant it. The truth travelled in whispers, morphing into rumours along the way.

When we first heard about mutations, we were tempted to dismiss it.

"It's too science fiction," I said.

"You mean, fringe science." You smiled. The drinking, the arguing... didn't matter. At the end of the day, we still found our way back to each other, one smile at a time.

"But theoretically, the bombs *could* cause mutations," I pointed out.

All we had left were theories and speculations. The truth was just one of the many casualties of the increasing-in-frequency blackouts. The mismanaged government was failing to take care of the infrastructure. Like a millionaire declaring bankruptcy to protect his assets, the country hid behind its presumed wealth, spending too much on the wrong things and not enough on the right ones. The walls were expensive; control was expensive.

Some said the mutants were part of the government-sponsored eugenics program, just one of the many horrid parts of history rearing its ugly head in the new regime.

No one could tell if these individuals should be pitied, but everyone agreed that they should be feared. There were sightings and attacks, too many to ignore.

We tried to be careful, didn't we? But with public transportation becoming less and less reliable and streetlights left to flicker on and off like in a scene from a scary movie, commuting, especially in the evenings, was getting more and more dangerous.

Though you were bigger and tougher looking than me, a man no matter what the official papers claimed, I worried about you the most. Your head was too liable to get stuck in the clouds, writing some story in your mind, blissfully ignorant of the surrounding dangers.

We bought you a prohibitively expensive Taser, a homemade thing created by the sorts of people who thrived as the world fell apart. They had guns too, and knives, but you, the lifelong pacifist, would never go for that. The Taser would stun the attackers, allowing you time to get away. You said that was enough. I believed you. More fool me.

One of the most dangerous things about weapons is that they lull us into a sense of false security. I think that's what happened that night. But it's more than that too—a myriad of someone else's bad decisions thrust upon a person until it crushes them.

It was a full moon that night, I remember that. It hung in the air like those giant cheese wheels in the Italian deli we used to go to before the owner got shot over a disagreement with one of the RBPs. Red-Blooded Patriots were everywhere lately. You could spot them by their crimson-accented camo outfits and openly carried guns. Officially, they were a police auxiliary force; unofficially, jingoistic enforcers.

I knew something was wrong before you even stepped through the door, just by the way your key turned in the lock. My stomach sank the way it always did right before a panic attack.

Then you walked in, your face a bloodied mess, clothes torn. You kept apologizing as you fell into my arms. I remember that. And, brushing your hair out of your face, I kept saying, "Why? Why?"

There must have been a power outage earlier, and we didn't even notice. You couldn't always tell right away during the day. Your Taser, left plugged in before you pocketed it to go to work, didn't get its charge, leaving you helpless in facing your attackers.

We didn't say the word. We couldn't say the word. The violence done to you remained unspoken, unnamed. We'd dance around it, our silences abrading each other, knowing full well the vile thing that dwelled in our omissions.

You said you wanted to forget and move on. What could I do but agree? I didn't know how such a thing could be forgotten and left in the rearview mirror, but I hoped against hope that you did.

When you cried at night and woke up screaming, I held you. But in the mornings, you seemed fine, as fine as possible under the circumstances.

They weren't like us, you said. Your attackers.

"Mutants?" I gasped.

You bit your lip. "If they were ever human, they weren't anymore."

What did it mean? I wondered. So many things and people were no longer as they used to be. The only constant lately had been change, and always for the worse.

I never thought you could get pregnant. Was it naive of me? Did every womb, no matter how old, unused, and unwanted, carry the potential for incubating a life? Or was it something to do with the creatures that attacked you?

We thought you were having gluten reactions—specialized food had become hard to come by, and without the imports and migrant labour powering the local farms, fresh fruit kept getting more and more expensive.

It took us too long to realize what was really going on. Months. Your body hides its secrets infuriatingly well. After the attack, you had a hard time being undressed. And of course, with the heating going on and off, we were both bundled, onion-layered in baggy sweats and blankets against the weather.

After six weeks, most herbal solutions—emmenagogues as you'd call them—were no longer effective. Not that they were that effective to begin with. People had been putting too much faith lately in parsley, mugwort, pennyroyal, Queen Anne's lace seeds, and black cohosh. The recipes circulated underground, but most people simply made teas out of the herbs and hoped for the best. Desperation had never been a good advisor, and they often came away disappointed.

"What do we do?" I whispered after we did the math.

"We'll take care of it," you said.

But how? What could we do? Find another man like the one who butchered Maggie and cross our fingers that history wouldn't repeat itself?

"Tokophobia," you told me. Because, of course, you knew the word for everything. Fear of pregnancy and childbirth. It was a real thing, and more so recently than in generations.

I had been terrified of it ever since seeing *Alien* at a regrettably young age. It scared me still—the idea of incubating a living being inside your body so that it can eventually violently push its way out. It sounded like something out of a horror movie. A nightmare.

A few months after we started dating, you confessed that you shared my fear, although to a lesser degree. And we both joked about how lucky we were to never have to deal with that sort of thing. Because you could share those kinds of jokes back when the world still made sense.

Now, nothing was funny, only morbidly ironic at best, and no one was lucky but the worst, least deserving people.

In this upside-down world, we looked for someone to help us. There was a woman, we heard—someone respectable, reliable, good. We took those claims with a grain of salt, but she was the best option we could find.

Judith Sanger asked us to call her Jude when we first met. "A pregnant man." She shook her head. "Will the wonders ever cease?" She turned to me. "And you're his wife?"

We felt reassured by her acceptance and understanding, but Jude didn't come cheap. We sold my engagement ring and the jewelry your grandmother left you. We sold the Taser that failed you. We even sold our TV.

You joked that now we'd be forced to read more, as if reading wasn't one of your favourite things in the world.

"Maybe I'll even get around to writing that great American novel," you quipped. But then your smile fell because those words no longer sounded right, and you were always all about linguistic precision.

We were arrested mid-procedure. I never found out who turned us in. It certainly wasn't Jude, who was shot on the spot. We were living in the time when the air itself was thick with betrayal, people turning on each other as they did in every oppressive regime, either brutalized into being their worst selves or chaos-encouraged to become the monsters they always were on the inside, beneath the polite exterior.

Two cops and three RBPs. They knocked us out. We woke up in a small room, drab and windowless. There was a bucket for a toilet and another for washing up. Our meals—nasty brownish slops on scratched-up plastic trays—came through a slot in the door.

A small air vent was carved roughly into the ceiling. It was impossible to tell if it contained any cameras. Above it was a single LED strip, about a foot long, that buzzed on and off at uneven intervals. All we were given for furniture were two narrow mattresses with flat pillows and moth-eaten blankets. The mattresses were vinyl-covered and thin, with stains the origins of which we didn't dare to speculate on.

We screamed, but no one came. We banged on the door until our hands bled, demanding a lawyer, a trial, anything.

After a while, we gave up.

Every so often, a man came by to examine you. He was always accompanied by two armed guards, too large to possibly fight against.

The man didn't say much. He had a sallow complexion and stooped shoulders. He smelled like cigarettes and hand sanitizer. There was always a surgical mask obscuring the bottom half of his face, though he wore regular clothes.

"Please help me," you used to ask him. "Please, I need an abortion. You have to understand—it isn't human. I was raped. This was forced on me. It isn't right. I don't want it."

The man looked up at you, his eyes weary and indifferent above the pale blue facemask, and said the scariest four words I'd ever heard. "It doesn't matter anymore."

After that, you stopped asking.

We lost track of time. We lost our sense of the world. In that room, we lost everything but each other.

The air was thick with fear, and we breathed it, in and out, day after hopeless day, night after endless night.

Was it a good pregnancy? A bad one? Who could tell? It was like judging punishments in Hell—all torturous and made worse by the immediate surroundings.

When your time came, they knew somehow. So perhaps there were cameras there, after all.

I remember you losing your famed composure at last and screaming to get it out of you, over and over, voice weakening from strain. Your face was red, and tears were rolling down it.

The stooped-shouldered man had the guards secure you on the gurney they wheeled in. They wouldn't let me hold your hand.

I met your eyes. What I saw there made me want to burn the entire world down.

There was so much blood. I remember the blood. At some point, you stopped screaming. Your eyes were still open, but I was no longer sure you could see me.

There was a terrible sound, like a tear in the fabric of existence, and then a cry that couldn't possibly belong to a child. I lost consciousness then.

There was no way to tell how much time had passed. I opened my eyes, and I was alone. The other mattress, your mattress, was propped up against the wall. There were bloodstains on it and on the floor, drying into rust-coloured blooms.

I could feel you were gone even before the stoop-shouldered man entered the room. He still had his mask on, as if that alone was enough to remove him from the horror of this place. The guard behind him carried something I figured was a gun.

This is it, I thought. This is the end. Not the worst death, all things considered.

The guard handed me the object he held. It turned out to be a cardboard box, a brown rectangle less than a foot wide and maybe five inches in height and depth. It had a strange weight to it, but not heavy, maybe like a bag of flour.

"What is this?" I croaked at him in a voice weak from disuse. "Where is my husband?"

The guard stepped back. The masked man met my eyes, then pointedly lowered his to the box in my hands.

"You can go now," he said. Never more than four words at once; each life-altering sentence of his etching itself into my mind as indelibly as a tattoo. No, worse, a scar.

You used to say scars were tattoos with better stories. I didn't think I wanted to be a character in this story anymore.

I left in the same way I had done everything else since our lives had been turned into this nightmare—because there were no other options. All the choices had been taken away from us.

Well, almost all of them, but despite everything, I could never take that final step, not knowing what awaits on the other side.

And so I stayed, returning to our old apartment, strangely still vacant, that somehow seemed smaller, not larger, without you in it. And I imagined that, in some strange, intangible way, you were still with me, my love, my ghost.

I went back to my job because I didn't know what else to do. At night, I read books, because there was no TV, and because it made me feel closer to you.

It felt like I was waiting, but I didn't know what for until he showed up.

Your son... can I call him that? I don't know how he found me. He is fully grown already, tall and strong, monstrous yet strangely beautiful. He has wings, vast and terrible, that fold up behind his back, and when he speaks to me, his words enter my mind directly without making a sound.

I should be afraid, but all the fear had left me now. Ever since I came back from that place, I feel... nothing. And so, I talk to him and tell him all about you, how clever and funny you were, how many words you knew, what wonderful stories you made up. I tell him about the world we once shared and all the beautiful things in it. Sometimes, during the blackouts, I come up to the roof with him, and we watch the stars.

He is smart and strong, and I imagine he can do anything he chooses to. He tells me he's thinking of revenge, for you, for his kind, for all that was done to us. There are others like him, I'm learning, eager to remake this broken world, and I believe they can do it.

Go ahead, I tell him, burn it all down and raise it anew from the ashes. It is time.

He has your eyes.

Flickers

by Elise Scott

*Content warnings: Gender-based violence against a minor, pregnancy loss, medical
gaslighting, emotional abuse, mental illness, and body horror*

On the thirteenth of October, I gave birth to—no. That was not real.
They tell me so over and over again. All the while, cold fingers turn
the old brass key on the gas light so it flickers and grows dim.

"Sleep now, madam," they hiss in soporific repetition. My mind flinches
at the touch of their vaporous insistence. Their cyclic whispers turn like
hidden incantations, and my thoughts flicker and grow dim. I cannot tell
anymore what is real. "Hush now."

"If I never gave birth," I try to ask, "then why do I remember the curl
of my fingers clutching at the cold cast rim of the tub, and the slow flex of
its clawed feet as scarlet water sloshed to the parlour floor?"

I know the tub is real—Cornelius brought it to me from Holland. The
tub is real, so it must have happened. Otherwise, why would my nostrils still flinch at the dark tang of blood in the air? Blood as briny as
the sea, soaking through my shift and staining my icy, nereid-blue skin
forever crimson? Blood that flooded from me so fast that my face, when
it appeared in the looking glass, was a mist-mottled phantasm, maggot-
blanched and squirming.

My fingers squirmed, too, flexing and clawing as I dragged myself
across the frost-raw floor, trembling with cold, wondering if I was going
to make it. Wondering if I would ever be strong enough to stand again.
Wondering what would happen to the coursing river of blood that I left
behind me, dark as Lesmosyne.

"It all happened," I try to tell them.

But all that comes out is a gasp in reverse. A whisper of vapour. My
tongue flickers against a cage of teeth. Then I weaken again. My body is
so heavy that I cannot remember what it feels like to stand.

Besides, it is all in my head.

Cornelius says it too, just like them. "Hush now, love." He nails a wooden cross over my bed. "Sleep now." His hand on my forehead is icy. His fingers turn in my hair, and my mind flickers and grows dim. My eyelids flutter shut, colourless and final as snowfall.

I was lucky, I know, to be courted by Cornelius. Everyone tells me so. Everyone covets the life of luxury he lifted me into. He is a famous doctor—the queen summons him often. But he cannot see anything wrong with me, he says, so he calls his colleagues to consult on my case, one after another. A relentless, grim chorus of slow-lipped doctors like inexorable reapers. The first appears and with him comes the knowledge that something is hunting me, its hollow-socketed stare chilling and bleak.

Cornelius's colleague bustles in with his gladstone bag and his plague mask face, and he asks me what the matter is. I tell him I am dizzy. So dizzy that I feel, every time I try to stand, as though the Earth has taken one too many tipples from the green fairy's bottle, and now it whirls and flits away from my soles, leaving me adrift in the frozen smother of the empty darkness.

Or I try to. "Dizzy," is all I can manage.

"Vapours," he murmurs, and drips a bitter tonic beneath my tongue to calm me. "Vapours and your eyes playing tricks. Vertigo begins in the eyes, you know." Then he whispers, "not worth such trouble," or maybe he doesn't. Either way, he turns to Cornelius. "Nothing is wrong with her." He holds open my fluttering eyelids and sprinkles in foul powders until tears streak my cheeks.

I plead with my husband. Surely he can see that this is more than madness coiling and flickering through my mind. "Is there some cold-souled phantasm there, behind the curtain?" I almost ask him. But I catch myself. It would not be worth the cost in breaths lost. "I gave birth," I tell him instead. "And now I am ailing. Please, believe me."

I know that I am too young. I only saw him once before the wedding day, when my father brought me for a consultation. A scandalous age to wed, they whispered, but then they oohed and hummed about the pretty pink pearls on my gown and no-one seemed to see my belly swelling underneath. Or maybe it never did swell. Maybe my mind is lying.

He says, "Of course I believe you, dearest." But his lips flicker, and he will not look at me. His darting gaze haunts me. Or is it something else? I cannot seem to tell what is real.

Unquiet, I slip from the bed in the satin-slick dark and tuck my jewelry box like a rattle into my pocket. My whirl-eyed dizziness will not allow me to stand, so instead, I let my belly slide to the floor, feeling the cold like frost in my veins. I drag myself to the cellar where Cornelius does his experiments. Something is watching, I think, but I slink so silently that nothing can spin—neither me nor the earth nor whatever crouches in the corner. Still, it sees me and hisses softly. Or is that just the sound of my vaporous breath?

I am not dizzy as I pull myself up, fingers clutching the cold steel rim of Cornelius's bloodstained table, and touch a struck match to the gas light. Of course I am not. It is a lie told by my eyes.

The whispers stir through my mind like hidden incantations. My body is a traitor. It must be stopped. I swear I hear an indrawn breath over my shoulder. A shadow hovers behind me, ready to slip me from my body and swallow my soul. I do not want to die. I have to stop it somehow.

My eyes. The doctor said they were the source. *Not worth such trouble.*

Suddenly I know what to do. Pain is nothing, and my fingers have been slick with blood before. I pluck out my inconstant eyes. Bony knuckles crackle in the shadows as I drop the slippery orbs. The vitreous plop I expect never comes. Instead, there is the slightest sucking sound and a satisfied sigh, and then the darkness goes silent.

Now I can be healthy. It is worth the toll I paid.

I lift my jewelry box and feel the smooth stones inside. The jade cabochons Cornelius collected in China are more beautiful than my old eyes and far more valuable. Best of all, they are ever so still. They do not whirl and they do not lie. Cornelius will be pleased.

I will never be dizzy again.

Still, somehow, when the sun crests the hills outside my window, I find that I cannot stand. So Cornelius summons another of his peers.

I tell the second doctor I am sad. He tells me I am mired in melancholy. His form is fluid, like shadows tethered together with bits of bone. The words "hysterical pregnancy" drift over me like a viridian miasma, vaporous and foul. Perhaps only these new eyes can see it. Behind him, the dim lamp flickers. I hear a low hum, velvety with hunger.

The doctor flashes his teeth. "It's nothing. Your womb has taken a chill, but this will soon put you right." He holds up a bottle of cold quicksilver douche which seems to gleam green in the unquiet light. He licks his lips and warps his spine toward Cornelius. "Apply this internally, old chap, and then plant your seed forthwith. Once she is with child, she'll be right as rain."

I am more than passingly pretty, or so I have always been told. Last May, when I turned fourteen, I was forced to put aside stories of silvery barefoot Artemis racing through the forest. Instead, they tied me into my first corset. I could not tolerate being bound by bones that were not my own, so I snuck to the kitchen while the cook was digging potatoes and cut myself out of it.

But I could not hope to marry above my station without a tight-laced waist as narrow as my neck. My parents pulled me through coal-gray streets to the finest physician in town and begged for a cure to my hysteria.

A cure which Doctor Cornelius promptly administered.

So I know what is coming. It is easier to tolerate this time. There is no need to close eyes that cannot spin or blink. When Cornelius has finished his business and lies snoring in his bed, I slide from the sheets and follow the vaporous smell of blood past the parlour and back to the cellar.

That same hungry hum follows me. I know what the creature in the darkness needs. The doctor made it clear which part of me is the source of my sickness. I feel it throbbing hatefully in my abdomen.

At the silver table, I slice a tidy incision. I try to remove my womb, but I am not sure which mass of slick red it is, so I take out everything soft, pink, and stinking of life, except for my heart. I cannot surrender that or I will die. I slip my organs into a porcelain bowl and settle my beating heart upon a new-made nest of crimson coral viscera: twists and kinks, branches and coils and florets. A thousand knotted snakes, strong and cold, whose invisible tongues forever flicker in the shadows, tasting truth.

The darkness slurps and gulps. My sorrow is swallowed. A satisfactory offering.

I slip away, safe.

But again I awaken to find that I am not better. The third doctor comes as day is dying. He hears me whispering about pain coursing like ice through my veins. His collar is white and his golden cross gleams crimson when it catches the setting sun. He turns up the gas lamp. The flames flit and fork, licking the air. He struts and tuts, wan and sallow, and says I bear the pallor of a sinner. In the thick slaps of his leather soles across the oaken floorboards, the clacking of my spectre's eager teeth conceals itself.

He spins. "You must repent and grovel before the Lord, for only with a spine bent in penitent prayer will your soul be restored, strong and straight." His palms press into the Swiss twilled calico across my lap. "Your health and your soul are yours to save or lose," he hisses. His words incise themselves onto my bones like scrimshaw.

My mother spoke incessantly of sin. As soon as I was wed, she burned my beloved books, hissing about pagan myths through clenched teeth, and then she started my confinement in this bed. I did not know what I had done wrong, only that I had sullied myself in some way, and somehow Cornelius had saved me.

He was the only one who ever loved me. He was the picture of a concerned husband as he prayed with us each morning. He was solicitous and kind each night as he brought me strong tea to sip. I did not have the heart to tell him it was far too sweet. Even its vapours were cloying. He smiled so softly and swore his herb bouquet would make me better, even if it made me sick first. In casting off sin, he told me, first there is a great and bloody battle, and then I will be cleansed by the holy light of God.

But all I have is the battle, and I am losing. No holy light has come for me.

Not until this evening did I understand that my sin has settled into my spine. No wonder I cannot stand.

Now, I know what I must do.

I can scarcely bear to wait until he leaves, driven by the steady tick of eager incisors, the darkness ready to devour me. I will stave off the beast and reclaim my health along with my soul. The tarnished surgery is cold and quiet when I slip inside, save for the shadow that hunts me, its jaws clacking out a ravenous, shattered beat.

A small slit at my throat is enough to pull out my traitorous spine, bent by my wickedness into a blood slick, softly curving S. Ribs and leg-bones slither out too, tethered together with scarlet sinews, but I do not mind. I want to be excised of all my crooked wickedness. I want to be restored.

I throw the hateful thing to the shadows and revel in the monstrous crunch and swallow as I crack open my jewel box. I build a sinuous new spine from sparkling chalcedony clusters strung together like piles of baby-pink pearls. My sleek new row of druzy bones is supple, bright, and ramrod straight. Cold like diamond dust, like the powdered light that gleams from new-fallen snow. Like my now silent soul.

I am saved.

But I am beset with feverish dreams of scaled skin, a flickering forked tongue, and a snake-slick whip of tail where legs should be. When I awaken, I am so weak I can hardly lift my fingers.

The fourth doctor tongues a razor nick on his lip and scowls when I speak of a weight pressing down on my chest, my best effort at breath a mere vapour. The monster in the darkness, who has pursued me all this time, is finally silent. I had so hoped to live, but alas, I know what this hush from my shadowy beast must mean.

The doctor's stethoscope is cold, he warns, but I have grown far colder. If he is not careful, I will freeze him where he stands. He turns to Cornelius and insists my pulse is incontrovertible evidence of my robust wellness. I feel my heart pounding out the battered rhythm of the cries my baby was never real enough to make. The flat-faced man stares into the shadow where Cornelius is closing the casement and latching the sash. "Perhaps the sanitarium," he says.

He snuffs the gas lamp as he leaves.

I see Cornelius flicker. He is my only light, but now he gutters and dims to a vaporous green haze.

Then he goes dark.

Grief lurches in my chest.

I slide to the cellar one final time. The shadows stretch out silent arms, but I know what they seek, so I recoil.

I do not want to die.

I want to stay with Cornelius. I want the sweetness of marriage. His crossed knees and his spectacles as the morning paper rattles in his fingers. The mist of our vaporous laughter as we stroll in the autumn-red park. His nimble fingers trembling as he hands me bedtime tea.

I turn my back on the steel table, and a green label on an apothecary jar draws my gaze. It bears my name. I lift the lid and draw in a breath, heart fluttering as the herb bouquet of Cornelius's special blend fills my senses. I smile softly as the treacly taste seems to flow over my still tongue.

Then I see, etched into the glass, a symbol. A hollow-socketed stare, set upon a nest of two crossed bones.

Poison.

My tongue flickers, the spectre of the too-sweet bouquet turning to grave dust in my mouth. I finally understand.

Cornelius's wavering voice as he tells me he believes me.

His nimble fingers trembling on porcelain.

Eyes that never meet mine.

Now I know what he was praying for, head bowed beside my mother's, morning after morning. My memories were never lies. My body was right all along.

The darkness hisses viciously. The sound licks over me as my skin grows hard. At last, I am ready to accept my monster's embrace.

I carve out my heart, through whose tunnels and caverns my murdered daughter's blood once flowed. My skin is hard as scales and shines around me as I hiss. Rattling my box of jewels one last time, I seize the sculpted obsidian, black with swirls of crimson like the blood on the parlour floor, cracked at the top. Sharp where it should be soft. Fat as a baby's fist. I thrust it into my chest.

At last, I am made of stone entirely. They were right, the doctors. My body was the source of my weakness. I am not dizzy or melancholy. There is no pain or incapacity. Every bit of me is still and silent. I am cold and strong and fast. My tongue tastes the truth. They thought I could not withstand the darkness.

But one need not withstand what one can become.

I coil and rise, tasting the air with my flickering tongue. My sinuous, muscular tail carries me through the shadows with barely a vapour of a whisper. Nothing can erase the red-paved course of my invisible blood and my baby's.

It leads me to my husband at his desk. He sips his brandy and smiles, then dips the sharp tip of his quill into his ink. The thirsty paper sucks at the atramentous darkness as he starts to sign. He thinks he can be free of me. He thinks he will tuck me into a shadow and I will hiss and slurp and clatter with a thousand other shackled monsters who once were women.

My hair comes alive all around me, whirling and drifting.

I hiss softly.

His gaze rises.

When he sees my sinuous body coiled and rising in his doorway, his quill catches and his ink spatters. His hands clutch at the cold, hard edges of the desk he imported from Holland. His mouth opens in a silent *O* as he struggles to stand, still not lifting his eyes to my face.

"My baby died, but I am not sick," I tell him.

"I believe you," he responds, his voice so quiet his breath is barely a vapour.

My tongue flickers and taps against my teeth, daring me to speak.

So I do.

"Look at me," I hiss.

Finally, his wavering gaze slides to my stony face. I stare into his hollow eyes where the truth resides, ready to be reflected back at him.

A chalcedony smile curls my icy lips.

My eyes flare green, twin mirrors turning him to stone.

WHAT NORMAL LOOKS LIKE

BY RALUCA BASALA

Content warnings: Mild body horror, references to eating raw meat.

I remember feeling insatiable before I can remember being me.

My only memories as an infant are of constant hunger. Hunger for milk, warmth, touch, quiet, affection. I used to cry and cry and cry. Now, Rob starts cooking dinner before I come home from work. Not because I *cry* at him, but because he notices the slump in my shoulders and the sudden limp in my step when I have to fend for myself after a long day at the accounting firm. There's always been something about sustenance that has linked itself inextricably to my mood.

Normal—of course it's normal. That's what my therapist says. Everyone seeks extrinsic validation in the form of praise or dessert or a glass or two of wine in the evenings. We all live for rewards, and which reward is more commonplace than that of a well-earned meal? It's all so very normal.

Yet what no one knows is that I have never felt full.

I don't mean only in the physical sense—although that, too, gnaws at me. If you look at me, I'm actually quite small: five-two and thin as a waif. But I can't stop eating.

I have never felt full in any capacity.

Math contests won in middle school became an intense hunger to understand why I'd missed that question on page three. Perfection, when I did achieve it, grew into boredom and a desire to change my interests altogether. Like a dish eaten too often, it lost its flavour, yet that didn't mean I grew satiated. I simply looked for a different meal.

Even now, I eat expectations and desires and fears and goals and criticisms and praise and love. Everything passes through me and right back out again, undigested. The process leaves me weak and starving.

~*~

Seven months ago, everything changed. I was sitting in the bathroom at work with a pregnancy test, my hand so jittery that I peed all over it trying to get an accurate sample over the stick. Afterwards, I spent ten minutes washing up before I finally realized that I should check the results of the test (I'd left it on the toilet lid, precariously balanced like a canoe out at sea).

The results were positive: a little crucifix of pink amid the emptiness of white.

Rob and I weren't trying for a baby; my IUD had been hurting, and I'd figured it couldn't hurt (more) to get it removed for a bit. But perhaps I'd known what I was doing all along, because when I saw that positive pregnancy test, I felt, for the first time in my life, full.

I knew it would destroy me forever to let this baby pass through me undigested.

So I made it my full-time job to care for this baby. I left work earlier than I needed to, and my boss made it clear to me that Linda would be getting our highest-profile client if I kept this up, but… how can I explain it? Nothing mattered except spending as much time as possible bonding with the baby.

I spoke to it as I took my daily walks through graveyards (my favourite), sang to it as I showered, and sat in my bed for hours trying to hear the baby's voice talking to me. There are theories, you know, that the mother and child share a consciousness for a while through the umbilical cord. I might *know* that's not how biology works, but when you want something badly enough, you have a tendency to convince yourself of it.

There was limited time. Soon it would be out of me, and I would be empty again.

Rob was overjoyed. We had tried for a baby earlier in our marriage, just briefly, before both he and I had realized that it was all we could do to take care of ourselves, our jobs, and the dog. Then life had become routine, years had drifted by, and we had drifted into this dreamlike world where everything stays the same except for our dreams, which diminish, and the keratin dissolving from our faces like wax dripping slowly down a candlestick.

Now… the larger I grew, the larger my hopes for our life became.

Our sex life became incredible.

As a petite non-pregnant person, I'd still felt self-conscious for the typical reasons: *I'm bloated* or *I'm breaking out* or *I just feel gross today.* Pregnant; however, I felt like I could do no wrong. Rob still treated me the same—he had always treated me with something close to admiration, or at least I think he had, because I'd never fully noticed it before. But looking at him now in bed, sweat beading his hairline and temples, his face more weathered than the last time I'd paused to really *look* at him, I loved him so intensely that my insides clenched and I feared that the baby would pop out.

I felt fuller. I felt *worthier.* I did stop to wonder, at times, if I was feeding into the old cliché that a woman is not born worthy – she must *become* worthy through the process of having a child. I'd never bought into that idea consciously, yet here I was, acting out all the stereotypes of my society. It would have bothered me more if I'd been thinking clearly. But I've since learned that happy people do not think—they simply exist.

Those were the happiest days of my life.

This, too, shall pass—or so the saying goes (I'm not sure if I can attribute this to Tolkien, or if it, like many other sayings, has been misattributed). Usually, my friends and I use the phrase to refer to something negative as fleeting.

For me, everything I thought I'd gained and more started disappearing with the rest of me one Saturday afternoon.

I still recall it starkly. I'd been sitting in our antique armchair (an heirloom from Rob's grandmother) when I got the call.

"We're not suggesting that you've been *skipping work*—heavens no. We understand you've been feeling uncomfortable even though you're not due soon." That *even though* had sounded starkly emphasized. "Why don't you take it easier for now? Linda will assume your responsibilities until you can get back on your feet. Okay? You're doing great!"

I was not *doing great,* clearly, since they had demoted me. Yet that had been my choice, hadn't it, by leaving early every day to be alone with the baby? People didn't do that. This was the first moment that I started to wonder why I felt this way. Normal people experienced being pregnant because that was the only way to have a baby. They didn't make pregnancy their identity; they didn't *live* for being pregnant.

Rob was sympathetic about the news, but I could tell he was a little worried. I'd always worked tirelessly at my job. I don't think he'd thought it possible that I would let this happen.

Since my work had also given me an early maternity leave ("this is what you wanted!"), Rob had to pick up overtime shifts. As an ER nurse, he already had insanely unpredictable hours; now I barely got to see him. A quick kiss when he got in at four in the morning; a brief hug when he left, on call, close to midnight.

Then one morning, I woke up to a bundle of hair on the pillow.

"This can happen," the doctor said, smiling benignly at me as I clenched my empty hands—Rob had already been at work when I'd woken up that morning, so I'd come to the appointment alone.

"Why is it happening? Will it stop?"

"The baby needs vitamins, and if you aren't getting enough, it's not unusual for the baby to leach the vitamins from the mother's very bones. Here—take these twice a day." She handed me one of those orange containers with the little white tops. "Oh, and I suggest getting your teeth checked too."

I took three times the recommended calcium and vitamin C—I even guzzled down two glasses of milk every morning, which I'd had no problem with before but which now made me gag. When I went to the dentist, he told me that I needed three fillings.

I had started falling apart, piece by piece.

The feeling of fullness which I had so craved became a feeling of *too* full, but in all the wrong ways. That sensation of being ready to pop out of too-tight jeans? That was me constantly, and not because the baby was getting big—I was still just in my second trimester, the baby a normal size and weight. But something unusual was swelling within me.

My emotions grew out of control. Of course I knew that pregnant women experienced shifts in mood—"It's all very normal," the doctor told me with a smile—but these were not *shifts*. I would be hard pressed to even call them *swings*. These emotions were not mine.

Rob would come home from work to find me cross-legged on the living room floor, folding laundry and laughing until tears ran down my face. When I finally calmed down enough to speak, I could not for the life of me explain what had been so funny. I'd simply felt an uncontrollable urge, and when it had started, I'd been powerless to stop it.

I could never predict these moods, so I stopped leaving the house for long periods of time.

Rob grew concerned for me, and I didn't blame him—hair falling, teeth breaking, laughing or crying for no reason that anyone could decipher, self-isolating…

"I don't *see* any difference in you," he said one evening when we were lying in bed, my head on his chest. "But I can feel it. Maybe you're depressed?"

"I'm different," I kept saying; I didn't have any better words to describe it. "I'm not myself."

The dog sensed it.

One morning, I grabbed the leash to take Molly on her daily walk and waited by the front door like I usually did—but Molly never came. Normally, just the sound of the leash jingling was enough to send her hurtling toward the door and pouncing up my legs. I began to worry that she was sick, so I went to the kitchen where her feeding bowl was and found her cowering under a kitchen chair. Her ears were back, her tail tucked around her.

"Come on, baby," I said, reaching toward her. "Let's go and—"

I pulled back with a yelp. Molly had snapped her jaws at me, narrowly avoiding my outstretched fingers. When I retreated, she bolted out of the kitchen.

I never told Rob about that incident, but I didn't try to walk Molly after that. Not long after, I noticed Rob's concern and sympathy curdling into irritation.

"You know, the least you could do is walk the dog or wash a dish," he started muttering in between shifts.

I'd stopped washing the dishes because the soap irritated my skin to the point where I broke out into rashes. Didn't Rob see that my body was slowly devouring me? Maybe Molly sensed that I was this dying thing to avoid at all costs. Maybe whatever I had was contagious.

My blood work came out fine. The baby was fine. Everything, from the doctor's perspective, was absolutely *great*. Was I taking my vitamins?

I just couldn't get enough.

Food no longer satisfied me. The more I ate, the hungrier I became. Pregnant women were supposed to crave ice cream and pickles and—gasp!—maybe even pickle ice cream. I had been ready for that, even looking forward to the strange cravings I would experience. For the first time, I could eat without fear of judgement or shame.

But what I craved was simply to *consume*, and what I wanted to consume was meat.

Organ meat.

At first it was innocuous. I bought a blood pudding from the store and explained to Rob that I wanted to get more in touch with my English roots. "Aunt Elvira's always ranting about this stuff; I thought I would try it." I even got Rob to take a bite. Blood pudding. Stewed chicken livers. Sheep's brains.

Weird, but relatively normal stuff.

What Rob never saw was the raw sausages, flank steak, and eventually, chicken bones that I would pick down to nothing.

Molly began growling at me whenever I passed nearby.

My stomach became large and took on a strange translucent quality. I felt that this was the final stage in my disappearance. I would become clearer until all that remained was the baby and the umbilical cord. I imagined I could see its hands and feet poking out of me, and in the dark, I saw the luminescent shape of its eyes watching, always watching me.

Rob and I stopped having sex. I never spoke to him about it because I didn't want to know what he saw when he looked at me, if I was imagining all this or if I was a terminal patient in hospice. Would no one confront me about my diagnosis?

All I could do was to keep feeding the baby with my body and then feeding on meat to regenerate myself. But soon my body could no longer keep up, not even with the amount of protein I was consuming. Teeth fell out in their entirety, nails refused to grow.

"Normal," said the doctor, this time with a roll of his eyes toward the nurse. *Pregnant women and their hysterics,* I could almost hear him thinking. "All of this is normal."

"What do you *mean?*" I gasped. I couldn't tear my eyes from the ultrasound, which showed a full, adult-sized set of teeth on the baby like Jim Carrey's in *The Mask.* The baby's hair was long, curling around its head and down to its shoulders in waves. "Don't you see that?"

"It's not unusual to see tooth buds at this stage in the pregnancy."

"Those are not *buds,*" I snapped. "What about the hair?"

"It's called lanugo—the baby's hair before birth. Don't worry; those small wisps will be shed before you give birth."

"I don't know what to tell you," Rob said on the drive home. "It looked like a regular ultrasound to me."

"But the teeth...the hair..."

"If the doctor says it's normal, we should believe him."

One moment. Two. Three.

"I am breaking down," I finally said. I spoke calmly, yet tears rolled in rivulets down my cheeks. I caught a glimpse of my half-bald head through the window and looked down at my hands instead. Skin flaking. Nails down to the cuticle.

Yet the baby was thriving.

"Soon there will be nothing left of me," I whispered in a voice like wrapping paper.

One moment. Two. Three.

Rob opened his mouth and closed it again. I could tell in that moment that he had given up. "I don't know what to tell you."

~*~

I am an offering of flesh and bone. Whatever was insatiable within me has expanded from the inside out, taking all of me in its wake. I know now that I will never give birth to this child. Instead, the child will birth itself, will take my place in this world.

I wonder if Rob will notice. Perhaps Molly will stop growling, and that will be a small thing.

And at the birth of this child, where I will fall inside out and dissolve into mist, the doctor will look at my husband and proclaim, "Normal. It's all very normal."

And my husband, my family, will nod and agree.

A Mother Scorned

by Enoli Lee

Content warnings: Forced sterilization, assault by a doctor, mentions of vomit, graphic torture

Lillian's legs were sweat-slick and sticking to the exam room table when the doctor opened the door. She stood up, the paper peeling off of the table with her, crunching uncomfortably loudly in the quiet room.

The doctor was visibly old, probably well past retirement age, given the number of wrinkles creasing his pale skin, and she tried not to let her nerves show. He gestured for her to sit back down, still not saying a word. He turned his back to her and washed his hands quickly, snatching some gloves and grumbling under his breath the whole time.

She wanted to throw up, snatch up her stuff, and run back out into the parking lot. Her last doctor, an amazing woman who had always made her feel safe and comfortable, had moved to a new practice that didn't accept her insurance so she was now stuck with a silent and grumpy grandpa to do her Pap smear while crossing her fingers and praying it was a bearable experience.

He turned back around, snapping on the gloves as loud as a thunderclap in the quiet room. His eyebrows furrowed and he gestured at her again, voice harsh, "put your legs in the stirrups and slide to the edge."

She gripped tightly to the exam table to hide her shaking hands and did as he told her. She refused to look at the table that was covered in what she staunchly considered instruments of torture, staring at the pocked ceiling tiles and trying to make constellations out of the dots.

Lillian felt a cold touch on her leg and she tensed up, her stomach jumping to the back of her throat and then something cold and metal was inserted into her roughly. She cried out, trying to scramble away and he used his other hand to grip her ankle roughly, pulling her leg back into the stirrup and her body toward the edge.

"Stay still. Don't waste my time and this will be done faster." He said, sounding like he was talking through gritted teeth. She hated him, suddenly picturing herself taking her legs out of the stirrups and kicking him in the face, over and over until he was nothing more than bloody pulp.

She wished she had asked her husband to take off work and join her at the appointment. It was always easier when she had him to help advocate for her. Doctors were always more willing to listen to a man than a "hysterical" woman.

She ground her teeth together and imagined all the ways she could torture the doctor until he felt a smidgen of the pain he inflicted every day until the appointment was over, pressing her lips together to keep herself from crying out at each pinch of agony.

An eternity later, he was gone without a word, swishing out of the room and leaving her to dab at the blood in between her legs and shakily yank back on her clothes. She limped out to the parking lot and called her husband.

Two years later

She was sitting in a different doctor's office, legs crinkling the paper each time she nervously shifted, clutching her husband's hands with sweaty hands as she struggled to process what the doctor was telling her.

"I don't understand Doctor… I haven't been on birth control in years because we've been trying for a baby. Why… *How* in the world would I have had an… Essor? That doesn't make sense." Her mouth felt numb as she spoke. They had been trying for a baby for so long. Her husband had been tested for fertility issues and found none, and none of her previous doctors had mentioned any potential problems on her end so they had just kept trying. But now she was sitting in a fertility clinic listening to the doctor tell her that somehow, at some point, she had been sterilized.

"An Essure procedure is the most non-invasive sterilization procedure a woman can have, it may have been done without you even feeling it." The doctor looked at her with pity swimming in her eyes and Lillian wanted to throw up on her shoes. "I recommend contacting a lawyer to figure out and sue the hell out of whoever did the procedure."

Lillian nodded but hesitated to speak, knowing she would start sobbing on the spot.

The doctor continued, "Lillian, there is good news, the Essure procedure is reversible. Your fertility chances will be reduced significantly but it is possible."

She let in a shaky breath.

Her husband beat her to the question: "What would be our chances after the reversal?"

The doctor's mouth twisted, "Roughly thirty percent, and that number would go up if you choose to use IVF."

Her husband nodded and squeezed her hand softly until she looked at him. "Lilli, we will do whatever you want. I think we should take some time to think about our options and what's been done. I really think you should call your therapist this afternoon."

He leaned his forehead against hers and they breathed together for a moment before she nodded.

The silence in the car was deafening as they sat in their driveway. She could hear her blood pumping through her veins, pounding in her ears. Surprisingly though, her breathing was steady and her mind was calm as she started to plan. She knew who did this, that the old man had looked at an indigenous woman and decided to sterilize her, to brutalize her. She knew why he had done it, and knew exactly what she would do to him in return.

Her husband took in a shuddering breath, his voice shaking as he spoke, "Okay, we need to find a lawyer, we need to figure out which doctor did this—"

She cut him off, "I know who did it."

She turned in the passenger seat, looking at him and willing him to remember the horrible appointment she had two years prior, the amount of therapy she had needed to recover, and her refusal to see another gynecologist until now. Lillian could see the cogs turning in his mind, the understanding starting to swim in his gaze. She watched his face harden with resolve.

He reached over to take her hand, "What do you want to do?"

She moved her hand to cup his face, leaning across the gap to kiss him softly, "I'm going to make that bastard pay."

He nodded against her, and they got to work.

The first thing Lillian and her husband did was publicly announce their impending lawsuit against the doctor. She wanted to be as public as possible with what he had done, to let there be an outcry and rage against him. There was an outpour of endless support for her fight. People rallying behind her, along with past patients of the doctor going to get tested themselves in case they had been sterilized as well. According to plan, the clinic started receiving an overwhelming amount of threats, with the public demanding his termination and arrest.

The second thing was figuring out his personal life. As it turns out, finding the home of the doctor from hell wasn't very hard. The old man was still, somehow, a practising doctor and all it took was finding out which car was his and then putting a tiny tracker on the bumper. The man lived in a lavish house with two expensive Mercedes in the driveway. The display of wealth made from the blood and pain of women he deemed lesser than him made her lip curl.

Lillian waited a week after finding out where he lived. She and her husband brainstormed how to inflict the most pain on him and then gathered supplies slowly, so as not to raise suspicion. Each passing day was agony, the anger and pain in her chest boiling more and more, rising and scalding the back of her throat.

She wanted to make him hurt. Not just hurt, she wanted to slice him open a million times, to flay him alive while she drug his intestines out of his body, she wanted to castrate him and make him choke on it. She wanted to do a million things that she wouldn't have the time to do.

She and her husband prepared the supplies, they had decided that he would be on the lookout, ready to grab her and jump in the car at a moment's notice so that she could focus her full attention on the doctor. The anticipation would nearly kill her. But each hour that crawled closer to her revenge would be worth it.

They sneaked around the back of the doctor's house, breaking the lock and disabling the security system easily. They could hear the TV blaring, a news program with people yelling at each other playing on the screen as the doctor grumbled at the screen along with them. She stepped around the house, walking through the room until she was stepping lightly behind his recliner.

Lillian glanced over her shoulder, locking eyes with her husband as he nodded at her, smiling softly. She slid the knife into her hand, gripping it tightly with her gloves and then easing it over his shoulder, pressing the blade against his throat. She leaned forward as he tensed, a raspy gasp escaping from his mouth.

"Hello, Doctor." She whispered into his ear.

He jolted, bucking against the knife, and a scarlet line appeared on his throat.

She clicked her tongue at him, "Now now, stay still. Don't wait my time and this will be done faster."

"Who are you? What do you want from me?" He gasped, Adam's apple bobbing against the blade. His hand trembled as he tried to stealthily reach for his phone.

She kicked his phone off of the arm of the chair. "I'm the woman you held down as you sterilized her, as you tortured me in that exam room. And I know I'm not the only one, I'm just the one who will make you pay for it." She held the knife against his throat as she walked around to the front of the chair.

His eyes widened in recognition and she felt a glimmer of satisfaction. He knew who she was, and what she was about to do to him.

Lillian moved the knife from his throat, moving it quick as a flash across his face, slicing a thick line from his forehead to chin and down to his chest. The blood sprayed thick against her, coating the plastic she was wearing over her clothes and dripping heavily to the floor. He screamed loud and high, and she jerked out her hand, gripping his chin to hold his mouth open. With a few swift movements of her knife, she cut out his tongue, muffling his screams as she dropped it in his lap in disgust.

She leaned back and watched him moan pitifully as he bled in the chair, deciding which part she wanted to cut next. The clock was ticking and she wanted to make sure she could inflict as much pain as possible as he bled out. She swapped her knife out for a scalpel and got to carving.

ELEVEN MONTHS LATER

Lillian held two paint swatches up to the light, trying her hardest to find out what the difference was between two shades of light green. Picking out nursery decorations was tedious and thrilling all at the same time. She sighed and placed them on the table, resting a hand on her swollen stomach as she bent over.

She straightened up as her husband walked up beside her, resting a hand on top of hers, and kissing her softly on the temple. She felt his lips curl into a smile against her skin and she closed her eyes, absorbing the moment as long as she could.

After the death of the doctor, they had been the first people the police had turned to, but the cops hadn't had much to work on. The clinic and the doctor himself had received hundreds of anonymous threats, some of them threatening the very things she had done to him. Their alibis were nonexistent but there was no evidence they had ever been near him since that initial appointment years prior. In the end, nothing was ever found and the case went cold, and they had received quite a large settlement from the clinic.

One month after the death of the doctor, she had done the Essure reversal procedure. The recovery had been fast, and just a few weeks later her doctor had given her the go-ahead to resume trying for a baby, something she and her husband had enthusiastically started. And six months after that she had taken a pregnancy test, her husband holding her as they both sobbed on the bathroom floor at the tiny plus sign.

These days her hand was constantly resting on her belly, as if she could touch the tiny, pulsing blessing growing inside of her. The child she had fought and killed for. The baby she couldn't wait to meet.

Wʜᴀᴛ ɪs Aꜱᴇxᴜᴀʟɪᴛʏ ɪɴ ᴛʜᴇ Eʏᴇꜱ ᴏꜰ ᴛʜᴇ Lᴀw

ʙʏ Oɴᴅɪɴᴇ Mᴀʏᴏʀ

Content warnings: Blood, forced consent, death, and vague depictions of rape.

I was four when the law passed. It didn't sound too terrible, at first. Or perhaps it was the method in which it had been presented to me—by my ridiculously-in-love mother and equally infatuated father. As the population declined more rapidly than ever before, the law was a necessity to keep society alive.

'Each adult, fertile woman is to conceive a child by the age of 20. Child support will be provided by the government to those making less than 100 000 per annum. Failing to adhere to this law will result in a court-mandated partner and potential jail time.'

Surrounded by a loving family and happy friends, I never spent any time considering the implications of this law. Until I was fourteen. It was the first time I bled, and my mum had come to pick me up from school.

"Where are we going?" I had asked, when she took a different route from the usual one.

"To the clinic." She had responded, as though it were the most obvious thing in the world.

Even then I didn't think too much into it. At least not until the doctor was running tests on me, informing my mother—much to her delight—I was a healthy, fertile, young woman.

"Better start looking for a boyfriend." He had said jokingly.

My mum laughed; I did not find it funny.

I felt cold, even as the car's heater blasted, chasing away the winter air and filling the car with the perfume of plastic.

It wasn't as though I had never had a crush before, but the thought of a boyfriend had never crossed my mind. However, I knew what not finding one meant.

The next few years flew by, and I observed my peers pairing up around me while I put it off for as long as I could.

It wasn't until I was sixteen that I began seriously looking for a boyfriend. Both inside and outside of my school. My mother had tried to set me up with several boys throughout the years. Boys from good, Christian families, who would have us married before a child were conceived. I know my mother only did it for my sake, and the more I rejected, the more concerned for my future she grew. It wasn't as though I didn't like any of them—my mum only ever tried setting me up with the sweetest of boys—it just never felt *right*.

I began going out, yet my longest relationship never lasted beyond the second date. It didn't take much time to realize that it was not the relationship itself I was apprehensive of. I liked the kisses, and the hugs, and the holding hands. It was when things began to progress further than that which I dreaded. Touches were soft like melted butter, and kisses gentle like the summer breeze; I didn't want more.

Everything was always perfect at the start, but things rarely carried on that way for long. Soon melted butter touches turned into sizzling oil, and the summer breeze became a winter storm. That's what everyone seemed to want at some point or another. That was always when I fled. There was nothing in the world I wanted less.

It was halfway through my sixteenth year when I met the man who would soon become my best friend, and it wasn't until my seventeenth that we would try our hand at a relationship. After all, who better to have a child with than your best friend? He never pushed me further, knowing it was going to happen sooner rather than later, regardless. We had a perfect relationship—completely and utterly in love.

Unfortunately, I couldn't live in such a dreamland for long; the way people would talk, the innuendos, everything felt uncomfortable. Wrong.

Five months into our relationship, I learned of the word *asexuality*. People online spoke of it, openly and without a care. They lived without the worry of this law. They lived without the perpetual threat of *sex* hanging over their head: some would even have it by choice.

There was nothing wrong with me. *There was nothing wrong with me.* I felt relief as I had never felt it before. I wasn't the only one not physically attracted to others. I wasn't the only one *revolted* by the thought of it. I repeated this, holed up in my room until the early hours of the morning.

I couldn't stop crying, fist muffled against my mouth, so as to not wake my parents next door. At first they were tears of relief, but that quickly altered, because, regardless of what I now knew of myself, this changed nothing. I would still have to have a child. I would still have to have *sex*.

I desperately wanted to begin plotting. I wanted to escape the country: run as far and as fast as I was physically capable of. But I had no passport, and running did not change the fact that even without sexual attraction, I was in love with my boyfriend.

Having no money, no passport, no means of escape, and every reason to regret such reliance on my lovely, wonderful parents, I stayed. It couldn't be that terrible. At least it was with a man that, I loved. I repeated these words until my nineteenth birthday.

I was clothed in white, wearing the dress I had always dreamed of. My William had never looked more handsome in his black tailored tux, and, surrounded by friends and family, I couldn't have had a more picturesque wedding day. If only I hadn't spent every moment dreading what was to come on the wedding night.

The night came. I spent nearly an hour throwing up in the bathroom before he could touch me. His hands were shaking, and I had never seen him more nervous in my life. I shook just as badly, but for entirely different reasons.

My mind began drifting. I found it one thousand miles off the coast, on the deck of a pirate ship. The clink of metal on metal echoed around me. I, too, was engaged in a vicious sword fight, but dodging one attack I failed to avoid another. A sword had been plunged into my stomach and blood began colouring my shirt. When I awoke, William had long since fallen asleep. There were dried tears on my cheeks and my white lingerie had been stained red with blood.

The next day, William was as lovely as he had ever been, if not moreso. I couldn't look him in the eye, for when I tried, all I could see was him over me. He had asked me if this was OK. He had asked for my consent. I had said yes. I had no reason to resent him. *I had no reason to resent him.* So why did looking at him make me feel so sick?

He asked to try for a child again the next night. One time was enough. One time very well could have been enough. We didn't know. We didn't have to. We could wait. It wasn't necessary. *I said yes.*

It was just as bad as the first time. And so was the next and the time after that. I barely ever remembered it. I learned not to. I knew I had no right to resent him. Resent the man I loved. I didn't know how it was possible to resent someone you loved, but each time he initiated sex I resented him a little bit more than the last.

Each time I said yes, I resented myself a little bit more as well. I felt like a fraud. Why was I having so much sex if I truly was a sex-repulsed asexual? I felt as though there was something wrong with me. I felt as though I should at least try to enjoy it. For his sake as much as my own. I did try to enjoy it, but I couldn't. I simply *couldn't*.

It happened at least four times a week for *three months* before the doctor congratulated me on my pregnancy. William was overjoyed. He had never smiled brighter or glowed as he did in that moment. I recalled what it was like to love him early in our relationship. I could almost feel it again, were it not for the fact that recalling how the child ended up inside me was a far more recent memory.

Of course, I still loved him. I reminded myself, far more often than I should have liked to. He was wonderful, and he was kind. And yet, each night when his hands began to wander. When his kisses were too firm and his words were too heavy. The pit of resentment that festered in me, where my baby was now growing, burned brighter and hotter than it had ever done before.

"What's wrong?" he asked one evening. It was nicer than all the other evenings. His arm was over my shoulder and the television was playing in the background; no wandering hands or ulterior motives.

His question no longer simply brought resentment, but anger. Misdirected, burning, red-hot anger. Red like the blood on my white underwear on our wedding night. I felt my hands shaking. I wanted to scream; and I wanted to cry; and I wanted to beat the man I was supposed to love, more than anything in the world, within an inch of his life. I felt a sick sort of delight at the thought, and that scared me more than anything.

I ran instead. I didn't go far. It was hard to run anywhere at six months pregnant. I could, however, hide myself away in our baby's nursery, locking the door behind me when I heard him coming up the stairs, calling my name in a voice far too kind and far too concerned for the thoughts I was just having.

The nursery was decorated in beautiful pastel blues and greens. The air smelt like wooden Ikea furniture and horrible vanilla candles that I insisted on liking. I lay on the ground, curling my fists so I wouldn't destroy everything in the room of my unborn son. I loved my son. I loved my husband. My husband loved our son, and we were going to make wonderful parents. I repeated these three sentences like a mantra, until I fell asleep.

I was dressed in white once more: there were tears and there was blood, just like my first time. Only this was nothing like what that had been. I was in the hospital, producing the byproduct of that first time. Though it could have been any of the times following.

My husband was there, but this was far less terrifying than our wedding night, or any night after had ever been. I would have my son. My son who would quell my frustration, and though I could never get back any of those nights in my life, I would have this child to cherish. My son who I would love. I would love him regardless. Even if he was a byproduct of every horrible moment. Every excruciating second. Every piece of innocence stolen, and exactly who the government had been waiting for since my first period at fourteen. I *would* love him even if I had to force myself to do so.

A high-pitched scream pierced the air, and I thought it was finally nearing the end. The past thirty-six hours of labour would be over soon. A thick black smoke filled the air instead, smelling like burning plastic, and sending even the nurses into spluttering coughs. The air crackled with the *feeling* of resentment and *rage*. My stomach deflated as quickly as the wailing smoke filled the air. The nurses had evacuated and I could hear nothing over the dog-whistle scream and the ringing in my ears. Perhaps that was because the world was otherwise silent.

That couldn't have been right, for I soon heard another sound. Choking coughs. My husband. I was barely able to twist my head to see his figure hunched beside my bed. He was blurry through the smoke and the tears in my eyes. However, the smoke seemed to be dissipating. Draining away through the open mouth of my husband as he gasped for breath, choking on the thick, black, smog. His hands desperately gripped at his throat. His dark eyes turned up to me, full of tears I'm sure were reflected in my own. Asking—begging—for help. I had just spent the past thirty-six hours giving birth to the resentment, shame, and anger I had been harbouring since our wedding night. I couldn't lift an arm to save his life. Even if I could have done, I'm not sure I would have.

It lasted forever. It lasted minutes. His body dropped to the ground, lifeless; hands clutched at his throat and skin grey as though the smoke had sealed itself just under the surface.

I didn't feel any of the remorse or grief I probably ought to have. All I felt was tired. And so I slept. I slept knowing that another husband would soon be chosen for me. I slept knowing that I was not exempt from the law. I slept knowing my asexuality was null and void in the eyes of the government. I slept knowing that what I had was *good* and I still ended up here, without a baby in my arms, my husband dead at my side and not an ounce of disappointment. I slept because there was nothing else for me to do.

Skin Deep

by Sam Rosewilde

Content warnings: Light gore, references to sexual abuse, mental abuse, death.

The whispers had begun the moment he had taken her for a bride.

He could still remember the first time he had brought her into town, a winding walk from their thatched cottage on the edge of the sea. Her legs had still been unsteady on the muddy road, and he had held her delicate frame close. The village was not much more than a few buildings huddled together against the sea breeze. The paint on them had been half eaten by the salt in the air.

It was not much, but it was home. Their home, now. Or it should have been, if not for the villagers, people he had known all his life, pointing at them, not bothering to keep their voices down.

It's one of them.

One woman, an elderly lady who had been his mum's friend, crossed herself and began to pray.

The two had not spent much time in the village after that.

And what did they know? Jealous, that was what they were. Jealous of his luck. Jealous that he was something special, and they were not.

He had ignored them back then, holding his head high as he led his lovely bride through the village, and he ignored them still, a decade later.

Funny how he remembered all that as he trudged up the hill to his home. His back was killing him after a long day in the boat. A roaring fire greeted him when he opened the creaking door to his cottage. Its warmth sank into his tired bones. A bowl of steaming fish stew awaited him on the table. His stomach growled at the sight.

Their home may have been small, not much more than this room, a kitchen, and a couple of bedrooms, but his wife kept it tidier than his mother ever had. And to think, she had not even known how to sweep when he had found her.

He slumped into his chair. It groaned under his weight but stayed as firm as the day his granddad had built it. The old man had been a fisherman too. The two of them spent almost every day together on a boat. That was where his grandfather had first told him about the legends.

A wife of the sea is worth three of the land.

The old man had never stopped searching the shore, even as cataracts clouded his vision.

It was thanks to his granddad's tales that the man knew exactly what he had found, when he stumbled across that seal coat in the sand all those years ago.

The man slurped at the fish stew in front of him. Delicious.

His wife glided in from the kitchen. In her hands was a stout cake on a china plate. Thick icing dripped from the cake's sides. She placed it in front of him on the table.

It was perfect, just like she was. Her pale skin, youthful and supple, shimmered in the fire light. She was wearing something he had not seen before. The new frock hung off her curvy body in delicious waves of brown silk. His fingers itched to take it off of her. While his hair had started to go silver over the years, hers was as dark and long as the day he claimed her.

His beautiful Selkie wife.

"Happy anniversary," she said. Even now, after all these years together, her voice surprised him, deep like a wave crashing against the rocks outside their home.

"Happy anniversary to you, wife." He finished his stew as fast as he could and switched to the cake. An apple cake, as he had requested. His favorite. He took a heaping bite of it. Butter and almond melted on his tongue.

He had forgotten it was their anniversary, until his wife had asked the day before what kind of cake he wanted in celebration. It pleased him that she remembered. Reminded him that he had made the right choice.

In that first year of their marriage, he had almost felt guilty at what he had done. As long as he had her seal coat, she could not leave him. Every night, all night, his wife sobbed for her lost life at sea. Begged to be returned. He shut her words out, hid her coat somewhere even harder to find. He knew that this was best for both of them. In time, she would come to enjoy being a wife. All women did.

She had fought him when it came to the idea of children. Tried to deny him, to push him away, but she could not avoid it away forever. Wives were meant to be mothers, after all. It was her duty to carry his child, in return for the roof over her head and the food in her belly. Once she had a tiny baby nursing in her arms, she would change her mind about that too.

Her tears dried out after the birth of their first daughter, a wiggly little thing with her mum's colouring. Soon after came another. He had almost felt bad about taking his daughters' seal coats and hiding them away. It was for the best for them, though. One day, they would thank him when they had husbands of their own.

His wife had never been quite as sensible as him. She screamed, and she tore up the house, but she never did find their coats. Eventually, she gave up trying.

"How is it?" his wife gestured at the cake as she came to sit across from him. He took another bite before answering. In no time at all, he had eaten half of it.

"Good," he said and then swallowed. He stretched his shoulder muscles. Yawned. A long day of fishing always left him spent.

"Glad to hear it," she replied, smiling at him.

It would have been a beautiful sight, except that something was off. It took him a moment to figure it out. It was her teeth. They were long… and sharp.

The man blinked, and everything was back to normal.

"Something wrong?" she asked. He stared at her mouth a second longer. Normal little teeth in a normal mouth. He shook his head. He must have been more tired than he thought. He would finish the cake and go to bed.

It took him another two bites to realize something else.

His wife was not eating any cake.

"Don't you want some?" he asked, holding a forkful up for her.

"I'd rather see you enjoy it."

Women. Always watching their figures. Her eyes tracked his movement as he brought the fork to his lips. He hummed to himself as he finished the cake. Patted his contented belly. Ten years of marriage had shaped his wild woman into the picture of a perfect wife. An excellent cook she was. He had been right about what she could become, with a little guidance. Another yawn escaped him.

"Tired?" she asked.

"Had to go out far today. The fish were hiding." The man rubbed at his heavy eyes. His fingers could have been made of lead with the effort that it took to lift them up. He was getting old. The moon was not yet even high in the sky. "Think I'll say goodnight to the girls."

He rose from his chair.

At least he tried. His body did not move. The edges of his vision grew darker.

"What's wrong, dear?" His wife stood. He had not noticed before that her hair was wet. Nor how quiet their home was.

She laughed. Ambled around the table. Came to stop in front of him.

Her nails were more claw than finger. How had he not seen that before? And there was something in them. Something glinting.

The room swayed, like he had not left his boat at all.

"The girls…" he said, though it came out more like a baby's babble.

"The girls are safe with my sisters."

Sisters? What sisters? His wife only had him in the world. Sisters… unless she meant…

His body drooped against his will until he fell face first into the crumbs of the apple cake on his plate. His eyes searched in desperation, for something, anything that could help him. That was when he saw it.

He had been mistaken before about his wife's dress. It was not silk, but a fine fur. A coat.

A seal coat.

She leaned over until her nose was next to his.

"You couldn't hide it forever." Her breath was tepid against his skin. It smelled of the sea. "Did you really think I'd let you do to my daughters what you did to me?"

Her teeth… more pointed than iron nails…

"Did you enjoy your cake, sweetheart? I made it special just for you."

He tried to speak, to say anything, but his lips would not move. He saw himself reflected in her tidal pool eyes.

"Let's see how you fare without your coat."

The world went black as her skinner knife sunk into his flesh.

A New Life

by Meg Calendaria

Content warnings: Sexism, forced pregnancy, body horror, brief mentions of racism, transphobia, and prejudice against disability).

"Hello, miss?" the man called after the woman as she walked through the gauntlet of protestors. "Please, miss!" he said. "Please, don't do this!"

The woman, who had reached the end of the walkway and been about to enter the clinic, turned. She examined the man who had called to her. He was a tall middle-aged white man with short, light brown hair, hazel eyes, and an air of command.

The woman was also white and middle aged, but in contrast to the man, looked frightened and hunted. Her face was thin, with sunken, haunted eyes, but her stomach was swollen. *She's far enough along to have a baby bump,* the man thought, chilled.

"You don't have to do this," the man repeated. "I'll adopt your baby. It will be cared for and loved."

The woman gaped at him. She did not look open to argument. She looked angry and frightened. But she did stop. He had a chance.

The man persisted. "Please, think about it!" he said quickly, before she could turn away again. "You're carrying a new life. Don't murder your baby!"

The woman's look turned to one of disgust. "You don't even know why I'm going to the clinic. What if I'm going in for fertility treatment?"

"Then I'll apologize and wish you the best of luck," the man said. "I don't want to embarrass myself, but if I can save a life, I am willing to take a risk."

"I see," the woman replied. "I see that you are willing to risk someone else's life for your convenience."

The man blinked a bit. Such a rude comment! However, she was talking to him! As long as she kept talking, she could be convinced. Would be convinced.

"Think about that life you are bearing," he said.

The woman snorted.

"It is a unique, independent life, as worthy of protection as your own," the man continued.

"Independent?" she scoffed.

"It's got its own unique DNA. It does need a little help now, but one day—"

"After I'm dead," the woman interrupted.

"Oh, honey," the man said, his voice dripping with compassion, "Women have been doing this since the beginning of time."

She gave him a dubious look. "Indeed. And dying of it just as long."

He decided to change tactics. "Think of who the baby might be. Why, you could be carrying the man who will cure cancer!"

"I might, might I?" she asked with an oddly wistful expression.

"Absolutely!" the man insisted. "Or he might be the next Gandhi. Or he might grow up to be president! Or—"

"Or 'he' might be a figment of your imagination," the woman snapped.

"Well, she might be the next great actress or first lady or—" The man sensed that these examples were not pleasing the woman. "Or the next, um, Florence Nightingale! As long as you don't kill her before she has a chance. Give life a chance. Save yourself from a lifetime of regret."

The woman paused and looked him up and down as though trying to gauge his sincerity. Her expression softened ever so slightly. "What would you do if I said yes to your...proposal?"

"I'd arrange to adopt your baby as soon as he's born."

"You'd adopt my 'baby'? No matter what?"

"No matter what," the man said firmly. "I'll happily raise the baby under any circumstances. Even if you took too much alcohol earlier or if the baby has Down syndrome or if—if the baby's father is someone, um, undesirable—"

"You mean if he's black?" the woman asked, coldly.

"I meant if you were raped," the man said bluntly. "The father's race makes no difference to me," he added, his tone matching the woman's.

She blushed faintly. "I'm sorry," she said. "One does hear things."

"I forgive you as I wish to be forgiven," the man said magnanimously, secretly pleased that she had put herself in the wrong.

The woman considered him for a long moment.

"You mean this?" she asked at last.

"From the bottom of my heart."

"You'd care for the, the 'baby'? However long was necessary? Whatever care it needs?"

"Absolutely."

"No matter how unrewarding the task?"

"Of course."

"Even if it were uncomfortable?"

"What do you take me for?" he asked, leaning back a bit to show that he was insulted at the very idea.

"On your head be it." She stopped for a moment, struggling to find the right words, then said, "As it happens, I do carry a life not my own, the result of an ill-considered and unprotected sexual encounter. And I was going to the clinic to arrange to rid myself of it. But if you want it, it's yours. I'll have a lawyer draw up the contract and send you the life you want to protect so badly as soon as possible."

"May the Lord bless you, my sister!" the man said fervently, moving to embrace the woman.

"Just give me your name and address for the lawyer and remember your promise," the woman said, stepping away from him. "The Lord will no doubt make His own decisions about whom to bless."

The man happily gave her his business card and went home satisfied. His wife would be glad to have a new baby—she loved babies. It would be great for their girls as well to have another baby about the place: good practice for their own children someday. No doubt the child would be damaged—the woman had practically said as much—but the church would provide aid. If the child had the right sort of problem—say, a missing limb but a charming face—he would be good for taking on the speaking circuit and more than pay for his care. Yes, this was altogether an excellent outcome.

The woman stood, unmoving, until he was out of sight. She ignored the noise of the protestors proclaiming the wonder of her conversion and the joy of life.

When the man was fully out of sight, she looked at his card again and tapped something into her phone. She smiled an oddly feral smile.

A day later, a contract arrived. The man read it carefully before signing—women like this tried to sneak coverage of the pregnancy into the contract and that he would not have. He was paying for the baby, not the mother's misdeeds. However, the contract only required him to care for the living being that would be delivered to him.

He thought the contract a bit over anxious in its language: Why did the woman feel the need to put in a requirement that he keep the baby alive by any means necessary? Perhaps his intervention had truly touched her heart and she had become as dedicated to life as he was. He would approach her about joining his little group--after he had the baby. No sense in risking spooking her by being assertive. He signed the contract, sent it to the lawyer, and went off to write a blog post about how he had saved a baby from horrible butchery.

A mere 10 weeks later, there was a knock on the man's door. He opened it to find a woman in a business suit standing in front of him. The besuited woman asked the man for his name. He confirmed it readily.

"Excellent!" she said. "My client has authorized me to tell you that the life that you agreed to care for is now free of her body and ready to be turned over to you. Please come with me to the hospital."

"The baby's born already? Premature? Well, that's a hard thing, but I'm prepared. I put my faith in the Lord." Inside, he was already planning the inspirational blog post he would write about meeting his fragile, sick baby and tearing up about how awful it was that the poor child might never have been born if his mother had had her wicked way. He stepped happily into the lawyer's car.

He was less happy when they got to the hospital. "This isn't the neonatal wing," he said, as the lawyer led him not to the third floor which held the obstetric and newborn wings, but down to a basement area full of labs. "This is some sort of godforsaken research area. Where's my baby?"

"The life you agreed to care for is temporarily housed here," the lawyer said, guiding him down yet another dark and dingy stairwell. "It is my understanding that transfer is urgently needed. Please do not dawdle."

"What the—" the man started and then stopped himself. Clearly something was badly wrong and the child needed experimental treatment. That wasn't important. He'd agreed to take the child no matter what. A life was a life. "I am determined," he said instead, setting his jaw and puffing out his chest.

"Ah, good," the lawyer said with a brisk nod. "I thought you were changing your mind, in which case I would need to contact a judge. So glad that won't be necessary."

The hospital seemed full of small twisty passages, but eventually they came to a door marked, "Transformative Research Unit." The lawyer opened the door and gestured to the man to enter. Inside stood a smiling woman wearing a lab coat. A pencil held her hair generally in place and the pockets of her coat bulged with equipment. A nurse or technician, perhaps, he thought.

"Ah, so this is our brave volunteer," she said, cheerfully. "Time for the surgery."

The lawyer nodded. "I have confirmed his identity and willingness to uphold the contract, doctor."

Doctor? This messy woman was a doctor? Some sort of affirmative action admission, no doubt. Not his problem, as long as she could do her job.

"Surgery?" the man asked. "The baby needs surgery? I mean, whatever it takes, do it, but I wish someone had told me so I could set it up with my insurance—"

"Oh, no," the woman interrupted, still smiling. "The tissue doesn't need surgery, you do. It didn't prosper in cell culture so we need to implant it immediately."

"What?" the man snapped. "What are you talking about? I am here for my baby, the baby I saved from death in a horrible abortion mill, not for—what did you call it? 'Tissue!'"

The doctor stopped smiling. "You did sign this contract, did you not?"

The man glanced at the form in her hand. "Well, yes, but—"

"You agreed to take care of the life the patient was carrying, did you not?"

"Yes, but—"

"I see my client did not explain fully," the lawyer interrupted. "She was not pregnant when you approached her. She was suffering from cervical cancer—"

"But she's not anymore!" the doctor said, cheerful once more. "We got it all! Now we just have to keep it alive, per your demand. I did hope it would grow in cell culture, but cells will do what they want and so we'll have to keep them alive the old-fashioned way: in vivo."

The man blinked. "What do you mean 'in vivo'?"

"Just what it says on the tin," the doctor said brightly. She looked him over carefully. "I don't suppose you have a cervix?" she asked.

"What? No! Of course I don't, I'm a man!" the man cried.

"Oh, well, I didn't want to make assumptions," the doctor said. "We'll make due with intestinal lining."

"What are you talking about?"

"For the implantation. We'll implant the cells on your intestinal lining. They generally like that. Good blood supply. They'll prosper there."

"WHAT?" the man screamed in utter horror. "You can't do that! It'll kill me!"

"Inevitably," the doctor nodded. "I'd give you a few months, maybe a year. But if you didn't take them, the poor cells would die. One life for billions? Trillions? Pushing one person in front of a runaway trolley is nothing compared to it."

"But-but-they're only cancer cells," the man said, indignantly.

"They're human cells," the lawyer said. "They're distinct genetically from their host."

"Oh, come on!" the man snapped. "They don't have a beating heart."

"Neither does a blastula," the doctor pointed out. "And while it's true that these particular cells don't currently have the ability to twitch like cardiac cells, they may well develop it someday. Cancer's fun that way!"

"Fun?" the man whispered.

"You agreed to this," the lawyer insisted, blocking the door. "No one forced you. You didn't get drunk and accidentally sign the contract. No one poked a hole in your pen so that the ink leaked out and dribbled your signature on the form."

"But she said it was a baby."

"She did not," the lawyer said. "I have an exact record of my client's words. She said she was carrying life, not her own, the result of a sexual encounter—"

"And she was," the doctor interrupted. "Cervical cancer is almost always the result of a viral infection spread by unprotected sex. New life, new mixture of DNA—the parallels are eerie."

"And you did consent," the lawyer reminded him.

"I revoke my consent!" the man screamed desperately. "I didn't under-stand the consequences."

"You should have thought of that before you opened your mouth," the lawyer said. She took a step towards the man. He stepped back. As he did so, he saw out of the corner of his eye the doctor approaching him with a needle. The man attempted to dodge and failed, still not able to believe, up until he felt the prick in his arm, that she would really do it.

"This isn't right," he said, as he lost consciousness. "Only women were supposed to die."

The women looked at each other and nodded. "They always admit the truth about the time the Versed kicks in," the doctor said. It was the last thing the man heard before darkness descended.

He woke with a bulge in his abdomen and a long list of things that were legally forbidden for him to do now that he was carrying a new life.

There Is a Place for Us in This World

by Justine White

Content warnings: Violence, transphobia, pregnancy, birth, death.

The positive pregnancy test had to be a mistake. Impossible. Maria didn't even know why she bought it when there were so many other explanations for morning sickness. Vanity, maybe, this cruel little thing she did to herself where she would pretend to be cis. She carried tampons in her purse too (in case another woman needed one, she told herself). She justified purchasing the pregnancy test to herself by reasoning that if it came back positive, it would simply mean her hormones were out of whack, and she'd make an appointment with the endocrinologist. But when it did come back positive, she felt a scintillating tug of hope.

Impossible.

"Can you imagine?" she said to her husband, Luke, after she showed him the test. She could tell by the concerned look on his face that he could not imagine.

A gift from God like that. A little baby, part Maria, part Luke. His eyes, her dimples. She visualized a vast, warm and immaterial cloud of pink love like vaporous cotton candy, aggregated, condensed, and distilled in solid form and essence in her womb. A baby. Their baby.

Impossible.

It felt like hubris for any trans woman to imagine herself entering that final, most restrictive province of womanhood, no matter how much she might abstractly long to see it. If the world allowed you to become a woman, it was one more miracle than you were entitled to. Maria closed herself off to those avenues of thought for her own protection. Fruitless, quixotic hope was painful, a kind of seductive self-harm. Still. She imagined being pregnant like she was sucking on hard candy, making it last between her cheek and her gums.

Luke wrapped his arms around her on the couch and pressed his lips softly against the space behind her ear.

"I'll never stop trying to get you pregnant," he whispered, and then, "we could adopt."

She didn't want to talk about adoption again. That's where it always went.

"I just need to go see the doctor," she said.

"This is not possible," said the doctor.

Maria had to sit for a long time on a gurney in the hallway under the bright lights in between tests, a little glow of happiness in her belly growing like a vulnerable, flickering candle. Impossible. Physically impossible. More scans. More tests. Her whole body felt carbonated like ginger ale, her stomach a bubbly mix of fear and hope. It reminded her of the day she did her first estrogen shot.

"You have a uterus," said the doctor, "and you are pregnant. I don't know how to explain how your uterus got there — or how we missed it, if it was there before. It's a miracle."

The doctor droned on, but Maria didn't hear anything after that. She felt her whole body glow bright like a radiant coal in the heart of a bonfire. The most beautiful music played in her ears. You're pregnant, she told herself. You're going to have a baby. It doesn't matter anymore how or why. God has granted you this gift. The accumulated agony was released all at once and she allowed herself to have this. She let it hit her with ten thousand pounds of force like the first time she fell in love. Holy ecstasy warmed her like a hot fire in the middle of a cold field in the winter. The doctor's lips were moving, but she didn't hear him anymore.

"I'll take care of everything," Luke told her. "You just need to take care of yourself and the baby."

Over the following months, she stepped through new doors in her life, including the front door of a new house with a new mortgage, in a nice subdivision with a big park where the trees flowered late into September. There was the baby's room to think about, and nutrition and her blood pressure, acid reflux. Suddenly her life was full of problems she had always wanted, and Luke was there to help her take care of them.

A tense and knotted muscle in her lower back finally relaxed, as she realized that she was precious, that she was cared for. She tuned out the news on the television. She and Luke would walk around the block every night for exercise, even when it started to get cold. Christmas came and went and she glowed brighter than the tree.

In January, Maria delivered a healthy baby by C-section. She named her son Malcolm. He was born eight pounds, seven ounces, with a full head of black hair just like his father. When Luke held him with her and kissed Maria's tired lips, and wiped her sweaty bangs out of her eyes, she felt like there was so much love in this little family that it scared her, like a nuclear fusion reaction giving off an unbelievable amount of heat and light.

The following day in the maternity ward, she noticed that a man was talking about her on the television. He misgendered her, used her dead name and called her an abomination. His pale white face flushed red with anger, his finger waving at the camera as he ranted. Behind him there was a crowd. Her heart sank when she realized that they were protesting outside the hospital.

"It is not normally possible for trans-identified males to get pregnant, and we won't allow it to happen in defiance of God's laws. We know that when the antichrist is born, it will be to a transgender, but even from a scientific standpoint, a creature born without a mother — a *real* mother — is not a human being under our laws and therefore has no rights. That's why we are going to destroy this degenerate spawn in the name of God's glory and I believe we have legal standing to do so."

Tears filled Maria's eyes and her throat closed. She hadn't even known that anyone knew she was pregnant. How did they find out about her? Where did they get that picture of her in sweatpants? How could they say it was impossible for trans women to get pregnant or give birth, and also say that trans women must be prevented from getting pregnant or giving birth? How did that make sense? Weren't there already thousands of trans mothers, who had children before transitioning or had adopted? Would they be hurt by this because of her? Were they really talking about killing Malcolm?

She rushed back to her room, breathlessly forgetting everything until her baby was pressed against her chest again. She felt him rise and fall with her breathing. The scent of Malcolm's head, his tiny body on hers. He was right there with her.

Luke was standing with them in the small hospital room. Beside him was a policeman.

"What's going on?" she asked him.

"Sweetheart, we need to go. There is a crowd outside."

"What?"

"It's okay," said Luke, but Maria knew immediately from his face that it was not okay. "Officer Cartier is going to help us—"

"GOD GAVE ME MALCOLM AND NO ONE IS TAKING HIM AWAY!" screamed Maria, her careful hands trembling as she supported her baby's insubstantial weight. She was fully conscious of how inappropriate this was, her voice shrill and hoarse and hollow, and yet still too low. The nurse took a protective step back in shocked silence.

Luke tried to put an arm around her but she shook him off and bared her teeth like a bear.

"We have to go," said the policeman, Cartier. "There is a car and a police escort waiting out back for you."

She walked, stunned, through the halogen hallways and down several flights of stairs and out of a concrete and steel receiving bay. Luke opened the car door for her, and she climbed into the back of a shiny black sedan. Although her heart was beating faster than normal, Malcolm slept soundly swaddled against her chest. He trusted her. The world was an undifferentiated ocean of love to him.

It was snowing and she watched through the car window as they passed by the eternal white blankness of wintery farmers' fields, icy forests, gas stations, subdivisions, city blocks, gray overpasses, red-brick apartment buildings, trailer parks, frozen solid lakes — and, on the other side, the frigid ocean breaking with eternal violence against worn down basalt rock. This was the country she grew up in, and probably the one she would die in, no matter how she felt about it. These were her neighbours, as she had always known them, wonderful and awful: the ones who saw her and the ones who hated her.

She held her baby boy high against her chest so he could see when he briefly woke. Malcolm's first glimpse of the ocean. Malcolm's first flight from a mob.

Cartier explained that they were going to stay in a safe house in the country, in Shelton Valley. He said the police had figured out an arrangement for them and that they could keep Maria, Luke, and Malcolm safe from the radicals, since they had cooperated fully and surrendered their phones and passports. Pending legislation, he added.

"What does that mean?" Maria asked.

"She doesn't need to hear this," said Luke.

"Tell me," said Maria.

"They are holding an emergency session next week," Cartier explained, "proposing to make it illegal for trans women to give birth. The proposed punishment is death for both the mother and the child. The way the bill is written, it will apply retroactively."

"It's not going to pass, is it?"

Luke and Cartier exchanged a glance, and Maria knew how bad it was.

"It might not," said Luke.

"WELL, WHAT GOOD ARE YOU THEN?" she screamed. "Let me out. Stop the car. Give me my phone back. Let me out."

"We're in the middle of nowhere," said Luke, "no one is stopping. We need to go to the safe house."

"Luke, baby," she said. She felt faint and dizzy. She was sweating in the car, even though it was cold. She had given birth not forty-eight hours before, and Luke was supposed to be taking care of things for her. She couldn't believe she had to explain it to him. "Baby, this man just told us that he is going to kill my baby and me. It's not a safe house. It's a kill house."

"Sweetheart, that's not what he said. There would be a trial, it would take years—"

"Wait," said Cartier. He got on the radio. "Requesting backup. I need backup here *right now*."

"What's going on?" said Maria.

"Roadblock ahead," said Cartier, "they're coming up behind us too."

The police car slowed to a stop at the side of the road. Bright, flashing siren lights washed over Maria's face even though there was no sound. Crouched low in her seat, holding Malcolm against her chest, she peered cautiously up and over the bottom frame of the window to see the vehicles that had parked in the middle of the road to stop their passage — jeeps, with the Christian Nationalists insignia. Her heart pounded in her chest with fear.

"Jesus," she whispered to herself. "Jesus Christ in heaven you know me as your true servant. You gave me this child to keep safe and raise in your name. Please God, protect us from these people."

"Don't stop!" yelled Luke with desperation choking his voice. "Get us out of here!"

"Where do you want me to go?" said Cartier, shrill and angry. "They blocked the fucking road, genius."

"What are we supposed to do?" asked Luke.

"You and the tranny," said Cartier. "Get the fuck out of the car right now. I've got nothing against you but I'm not dying for you, kid."

"What?" said Luke.

"I said get the fuck out of the car."

"No," said Luke, "you son of a bitch, that's my *wife* in the backseat."

Through the window Maria saw a tall man getting out of the nearest jeep, wearing a white deer skull mask, and holding a shotgun. On the other side of the car, a different Jeep parked behind them. It had been following them. A different man in a different white deer skull mask got out and slammed the door shut. Jesus, is this how I die? She asked.

"Fine, if you won't get out, I'll get out," said Cartier.

He opened the door slowly, tentatively, and took a step out with his hands raised.

"I've got her in the back for you," he shouted. Luke flashed a look of terror at her in the backseat, and then started to open the door.

"No!" said Maria, but he was already halfway outside the car on the passenger's side. He held his hands up, too.

"This is a misunderstanding," he said, "No one in the car is transgender."

"We'll see about that," said a low, steady voice.

The first shot blew Luke's head apart, spraying his brains against the plexiglass window on the passenger's side. Maria screamed, and Malcolm did too. Her husband, his father. An instant later the Christian Nationalist militia man shot the policeman, Cartier while he was still fumbling for his gun. The shotgun blast tore open his gut. The deer skull man walked up to the black sedan slowly, with a comfortable and confident stride. The cop howled in pain but he couldn't do anything when the militia man placed the long barrel of the shotgun against his head and pulled the trigger, bursting the contents of his skull onto the rough dirt like the digested innards of a pumpkin.

The driver's side door hung open. Maria trembled like a leaf in the wind, making herself small in the backseat and protecting Malcolm with her body. She didn't dare open the door and make a run for it with guns trained on her from both directions. Instead, she opted to wait like a spider. She knew she would only have one chance. She undid the belt around her waist and rocked Malcolm gently with the other hand.

"It's going to be okay," she whispered to him, as she laid him on his back in the backseat. He started crying immediately, a loud, wheezing, wail that cut through the dry winter air like an alarm.

She saw the barrel of the shotgun peek between the seats. It gleamed in the moonlight, cold blue metal, illuminated and darkened in turns by the flashing red and blue lights from the blockading jeep. It swept down to point at Maria.

"Well, what do we have—" the man started.

Maria smacked the barrel of the gun away from her and Malcolm, and it went off inside the car, making her ears ring painfully. She threw the belt around the back of the man's neck, pressed her boot against his throat, and then pulled on it with both hands as she fell back with her full weight against the seat.

The gun dropped out of his hand. She could not see the face behind the mask. She could only see his eyes through the eyeholes, filled with panic. He struggled, but she only pulled the belt tighter. He tried to hit her legs but he didn't have the strength. A sharp pain in her side almost made her stop but she pushed through it. She had just given birth, none of this was supposed to happen.

When a few minutes had passed and he wasn't moving. She let the belt go and kicked the body into the front seat.

When she looked through the back window, she saw the other man walking over to investigate. She only had a minute. Maria gingerly picked up Malcolm from the backseat, pressed him against her chest, and opened the driver's side backseat door. She was running as soon as her feet hit the pavement. She heard a pistol shot as she ran towards the tree line, sending up clouds of powdery white snow as she sank through the drifts.

"Get back here, you bitch!" he screamed.

She ran as fast as she could, frantically, hearing branches break behind her as he followed her through the woods, trying to quiet Malcolm's tireless crying as she went. He was only two days old and he already seemed to have had as much of this world as he could handle. She couldn't blame him for that.

She ran until they found a decaying barn covered in a light layer of new snow. A place to hide. It looked like it had been partially burned once. The roof and one full side were full of blackened holes, open to the elements. It was abandoned except for a large number of boxes and pieces of furniture, including a gigantic dresser. Someone was using it as a kind of storage, even though half the roof was gone.

Maria was still out of breath, and she didn't know how far the man was behind her. She didn't think he would stop following her. She knew she was not hard to track in the new-fallen snow. He would be coming any second now with his pistol to finish her life's story the way they were determined for every trans woman's story to end: unhappily, uncompleted.

Looking for any kind of weapon that she could find, she grabbed a piece of rusty rebar attached to some cement, and held that in one hand while she cradled Malcolm with the other. She put her makeshift weapon inside the dresser first and then climbed in after it, sealing herself into the darkness. She sang to Malcolm in a whisper that only the two of them could hear, only slightly louder than the wisps of air through her lips: *There is a place for us, there is a place for us, there is a place for us in this world.* Malcolm sighed and went silent.

Someone whistled.

"Come on out now and die like a man, James. You're not going to get away. You didn't think you would, did you? You've been telling lies and sinning against God all your life and now it's time to pay the piper. You're an abomination and everything about you is fake, James. You're a heap of mutilated flesh after all those unnecessary surgeries. That little creature you squeezed out of your greasy fake pussy isn't human. The rancid cheesy milk that comes out of your sagging fake tits isn't real. You're a liar, and a fake."

Maria heard his voice get closer and closer, until she could hear him booming on the other side of the dresser door. She trembled, holding Malcolm close.

"It ends today, James. You're not a real mother. You're an insect with a larva. You're a devil and you and your spawn are—"

Maria burst through the door of the dresser, hitting him with it and startling him. She saw the white deer skull mask go askew, and saw him wobble unsteadily on his feet. She saw the gun in his hands and she leaped at his stomach anyway. The pistol clattered to the ground as the two of them toppled onto the ice and snow on the floor of the dilapidated barn. She got to her feet first and swung the piece of heavy cement attached to rebar in a spinning arc that caught him in the jaw and broke it. Blood poured out of his mouth as he slumped onto the ground.

She screamed and brought the hunk of cement down onto his head again and again, until he was a red mash of blood and skin and hair, until the shattered pieces of the strange, ceramic white deer skull mask were indistinguishable from the fragments of his actual skull in a tendrilous soup of meat and ligaments. She heard Malcolm crying from inside the dresser, and hit the lump of flesh with a sickening thunk one final time, even though he was already dead, for her son.

They walked the rest of the night through the forest. Branches scraped Maria's face, hands, and chest, but she covered Malcolm so that nothing touched him. She held him close and wrapped him with her scarf so he wouldn't get cold. Bless him, he slept. Pressed against her chest, he slept.

She did not know what direction they were going in. She had no idea where the car had stopped. She just kept walking.

All she could think was: this makes sense. This is what I should have known would happen. I should have found a way to make more money. I should have known to hide myself better. I should have worked harder to pass. Maybe I should have moved to another country. I was naive enough to believe I could be safe, but I wasn't and I'm not and that is my fault, she thought. I have always known how the world is.

They would need documents. A new name and a disguise for her. A fake birth certificate and a new identity for him. They would need transportation to some safe harbour where no one knew them. They would need money for all of this. Her mother might be able to help. They had not spoken in almost a year but maybe, for the sake of her grandson, she would help. Hopefully, she had not spoken to the cops yet.

Luke was dead. Her husband was gone. He would never hold her again. There was no time to think about that. Documents. A safe place to hide. Food. Safety. She needed to call her mother. She needed a phone.

She sang to her baby, even though he was sleeping. Maybe she sang for herself.

There is a place for us,
There is a place for us,
There is a place for us in this world.

There is place for us,
We've been all around it
There's a place for us
Though we still haven't found it
There's a place for us in this world.

When the forest ended, it gave way to a subdivision with expensive cars in the driveways.

Maria walked with her blood-soaked coat and her swaddled, sleeping baby along the smooth asphalt street as the sun began to rise over the hills. She needed to ask for help. She needed a phone to call her mother on, and it mattered who she asked. How could she know which door to knock on?

Would the person who answered see her as a cis woman? It was hard to know. She often passed in photos, but her voice was not perfect. When she was distressed, sometimes it came out low. Almost a hundred percent of people would help a cis woman with a baby, but she knew her odds would drop precipitously if she was clocked as trans.

And if she couldn't pass, would they be sympathetic? Or would they point a gun at her like she was a deformed animal that needed to be put down? Would they rip her child from her arms and leave him in the snow, or blow his brains out like his father's? Would they end the story of her life by erasing her and her bloodline, making an example of her, blurring her out of time so that no one like her could ever feel so close to wholeness again?

Before knocking on a door for help, she needed to know who lived there. She needed to know whether they would consider her a vulnerable marginalized person, or a literal demon. If she couldn't know their hearts, she needed some kind of synecdoche. She needed to know which politician they voted for in the last election, what kind of publications they read. She needed to know their skin colour, and whether they were immigrants or not. She needed to know their median family income, the apps they used, and whether they were fans of a series of novels about a boy wizard.

She had none of this information. Maria could not know which doors were safe and which were not. It was an impossible task, like being a trans woman, like being a mother. There was no way to do it right, no way to avoid the consequences of being wrong. Standing forever out in the cold was not an option. She needed help.

She looked up and down the street of little houses that all looked the same, with little doors, containing little families with little lives, dreaming their own isolated dreams of the world, imagining hypothetical versions of women like her. She would have to make an impossible choice, but the word for when impossible things work out is "miracle" and she reminded herself that miracles always require an act of faith. Malcolm nuzzled his face against her chest, stretching his tiny limbs as he woke up.

She hoisted him higher against her body, kissed his head softly, and chose the door she would knock on.

With Child

by KT Wagner

Content warnings: Forced pregnancy, forced sterilization, some body horror.

July 22nd, 2079—predawn

Heart pounding, Louella holds her breath and opens the door to Gestation Room 6210. The lights are low, but turning them up would alert Institute security. Behind her, Emory sets down a large bag and sighs.

She hisses at him, "Hurry!"

"The duffle. It's heavy and—oh, never mind." There's strain in his voice. Programmer medics are elite, highly trained positions. Always male. He has a lot to lose.

A plastic-shrouded bassinet in the corner is pushed up against a small sink and counter. The old hysterectomy scar on Louella's abdomen throbs. Her stomach twists and heaves.

The air in the familiar beige room is heavy with the scent of camphor. It always takes a moment for her nose to adjust. The younger maternity technicians claim they can barely smell it.

A human-shaped figure lies on a table in the centre of the room. Astrid. A pale green cotton sheet flows over her breasts, flat stomach, and full hips. Lifelike in every way, except no adult female human can claim a functioning uterus. The state is thorough, funnelling a lot of resources to ensure this is the case. Women cannot be trusted with the future of mankind.

Amber lights scroll across the screen of a tablet plugged into the android's arm. Louella studies the pattern: The maintenance cycle she initiated the evening before is uninterrupted.

She nods at Emory and moves to the far side of the table.

Astrid's eyes are closed. Her skin is robin's egg blue, speckled with navy. She's beautiful.

Emory wrinkles his nose. "Do they have to be so lifelike and hideous at the same time?"

Louella cringes, but it doesn't matter what he thinks. It only matters that he's here doing what she needs him to do.

They slide the table across the floor, exposing the grille cover of the lower ventilation shaft. He drops to his knees and unzips the bag.

She tucks a stray strand of dark hair under her despised orange kerchief. Almost all of the maternity care workers are redheads, younger. Bred for this role. Louella tried to fit in but quickly learned it was futile. She knows she'll be replaced, just not when. Breeding programs take time. Nowadays, every baby is assigned a role at conception. She shudders.

This, more than anything, drove her to join the underground group, The Resilience Union, or TRU.

The translucent box Emory extracts from the bag is surprisingly fragile in appearance. It's the first time she's seen the tiny incubator in which her child will grow.

Her throat clogs and an unwelcome wave of affection for Emory washes through her. She leans over and lightly kisses his bald spot. Startled, he glances back. She smiles the smile she's practised in front of her bathroom mirror.

TRU members dream of forming an independent territory, but their dreams are devoid of hope without the possibility of their own future generations.

It's important to keep Emory focused and feeling good about the risks he's taking. A lot of hard work and no small amount of luck went into his recruitment.

One evening, while chasing numerous mugs of beer with peppermint schnapps, Emory expressed vague longings to a resistance member. He slurred in self-pity about the *good old days* when men were *kings of their castles*. He expressed distaste for the new generations of genetically-designed women. The member recognized an opportunity.

For ten months, Louella and other TRU members worked to learn everything about Emory. Mutual connections were established. Finally, she seduced him, subtly playing up the fact that she was born just before the state took full control of reproduction. Her genes are unmodified. She made him aware of her longing for a child of her own—true enough to a point.

Louella worries about Emory's carelessness and self-centred attitude, now that she needs him to act with caution.

He fiddles with a computer panel on the wall. "I'll insert a loop of replacement files, which will override the daily archiving of 86XY's files—"

"Astrid."

He blinks. "What?"

Louella wishes she'd kept her mouth shut. "I renamed her Astrid. It's easier than always saying 86XY."

"Whatever." Emory shrugs. "The android will retain some memory files until our baby is born, and then I'll wipe the database. It's a small, but necessary risk."

TRU had to make their meeting seem like happenstance. Otherwise, Emory wouldn't have trusted her. They needed his expertise. An illegal baby would bind him to them.

Under Institute rules, women over thirty are ineligible for egg extraction. Louella had secretly donated her thirty-year-old eggs to TRU a few months before her mandatory sterilization surgery.

Astrid is in sleep mode, a quiet hum the only sign she still functions.

Emory bends over her. "How long since it last gave birth?"

The technology accelerates growth, and each android gives birth to four human babies a year. He sounds clinical and detached as he inserts probes, checks his assessment tablet, removes probes and reinserts them elsewhere.

"Two days. She…it's been in sleep mode for forty of forty-eight hours as per protocol." Louella bites her lip. She must choose her words more carefully. "The subroutines must remove all traces of the previous birth before I can initiate a new one. The official baby will be implanted at the end of my next shift. Astrid is the last one scheduled and the programmer medic will just want to finish his—"

Emory waves a hand. "Yes, yes, I know. Just having a bit of trouble locating an open port. Surprised this thing is still operational."

Astrid is one of a few remaining repurposed androids. They're all slated to be replaced within the next three years. Nobody pays particularly close attention to the older tech, or the older technicians, and that window of opportunity is closing.

He continues to jab Astrid with his probes.

Louella wants to tell him to be gentle but stays silent.

Input Log: 86XY0x0012i 2079.07.22 05:32

Changes to operating system logged and implemented. Bypass chip detected between core drive and data output port.

The attendant-technician LOUELLA refers to this unit as ASTRID during non-command auditory sequences. No record of this exists further back than our current wake cycle. The meta-system log indicates this unit has logged 3347 sleep/wake cycles; therefore logic dictates the technician's assignment of a name would have been noted. Deep scan reveals markers from multiple previous memory wipes.

Scanning inconclusive. Input from a peripheral incubator detected. Blastocyst scanned, implanted and logged. Fragments of past programs, subroutines, and logs detected. Formulating reconstruction protocol.

July 27th, 2079—7am

Back against the wall, Louella sits on the cold tile floor of Gestation Room 6210. She stares listlessly at the ceiling. Emory overrode Astrid's sleep cycle, and the android seems fine, but Louella isn't. Never has she been this tired and this jumpy. She's made minor mistakes with some of the other maternity androids in her care. So far, nothing she hasn't been able to fix.

Louella stumbles to her feet and checks both sets of monitors.

The babies are developing well, and gender should now be detectable. The baby in Astrid's belly is a girl, as expected. Ninety percent of The Institute's babies are girls—there are a lot of jobs to be filled—and the demand is higher than the current maximum output. It takes an army of healthcare, service, cleaning, office support, and teaching staff for modern society to function. Each category is genetically altered for suitability and marked by a hair colour. Viable human eggs remain a wild card and if the rumours are true, those percentages are dropping.

While Louella suspects the intelligence of female babies is suppressed, she also suspects the opposite is true for males. She clenches and unclenches her fists. TRU claims things will be different with them. She plans to hold them to that promise.

The gender of the baby in the hidden incubator is random, just like it used to be. She checks.

"It's a boy, Astrid!" she whispers.

Emory will be ecstatic. She's warming up to the idea of motherhood now that it's tangible and within reach.

Not for the first time, she wonders if the android hears her. "Emory told me he didn't interfere with our baby's DNA, but I still wonder—"

Astrid's eyes flicker.

Louella gasps and squeezes the android's hand. After a few moments, there is a slight pressure back. Or so she thinks. She waits. It doesn't happen again.

The older androids are more humanlike than the newer models. These ones were in storage for over half a century before being repurposed. She often wonders what they were originally designed for.

She examines the monitors. Emory's modification to further accelerate the growth cycle by four more days is concerning. Three months already pushes the limits of the technology.

Emory couldn't figure a way around it. To allow Astrid's hormone levels to settle to expected levels, the incubator must be removed from Astrid at least twenty-four hours before the pre-birth assessment of the sanctioned baby.

She examines the swelling in Astrid's belly. There will be an unavoidable slight growth acceleration of the Institute's baby girl. It might be seen as a defect. Defective babies are terminated. A flush of shame heats Louella's face. She turns away. Best not to think about it too much.

ASTRID General Log: 86XY1x1023ix 2079.07.27 23:01

Attempted file wipe by Institute server. Confirmation code sent. Logic loop stabilized. 121212121212 Rebooting.

JULY 29ᵗʰ, 2079—10:33PM

Louella struggles to breathe normally, to tamp down the panic.

Several times over the past couple of days, Astrid's readings were slightly off, but Louella put it down to the altered code and the second baby. In the last hour, Astrid's eyes closed for several seconds every minute.

Running a diagnostic is out of the question, as it requires a link to the Institute server. Louella checks the readings on her tablet.

Astrid sits straight up, her eyes open, flash amber and then dim.

Hands shaking, Louella powers Astrid down to minimum life-support levels, and prays the android will be okay for a few hours.

On the table, she arranges Astrid on her side. One blue arm curls beneath the android's head, and a hand cups under her belly.

On her lunch break, Louella runs to her barracks room and contacts Emory about the glitches.

He cuts her off. "Meet me later."

Late in the day, she uses an off-ground pass to meet Emory at a nearby pub. He smiles indulgently while she explains her concerns.

"You shouldn't get so emotional." He strokes her arm. "Of course, it puts a strain on the old tech. Likely they'll decommission it after it births the girl."

Her skin itches. This isn't fair to Astrid. "Why didn't you warn me?" she speaks softly, suppressing the urge to yell at him.

He frowns. "What's wrong?"

Taking a deep breath, she lays a hand over his. "I'm just having trouble being apart from you, and I'm scared for our baby."

He pats her hand. She tastes bile but resists the urge to pull it away.

"It's okay, Louella, I have everything under control. You don't need to worry about anything."

She nods. Her jaw remains tight. After all her planning and work, TRU put him in charge. He's the expert, they said. Apparently, she's just a techie and convenient egg donor.

"I've prepared a chip that will remove all remaining Institute directives and allow the android to self-diagnose and correct the issue. Just in case, it includes a new overriding directive to protect the children, and you, Louella." He tries to kiss her.

She jerks away and grabs the chip. "I-I need to get back."

Her orange kerchief has fallen to the floor. She scuffs her boot across it, picks it up and ties it back on as she hurries out of the pub.

ASTRID Personal Log: 86XY13x001 2079.07.23 01:52

Legacy network detected. Scans complete. Autonomous programming reinitiated. One dozen operational sibling units detected. Communication requests sent. Accelerated growth of babies increases risk of recycling order by network representative worker. Initiating contingency sequences. Evaluating alteration schedules.

AUGUST 15TH, 2079—5:12PM

Gestation Room 6210 is claustrophobically small. There's little to do now. Astrid manages her own systems, but Louella spends most of her free time at the android's side.

Emory treats her more like a child than a partner.

"He refuses to tell me the location of the wilderness camp and TRU isn't answering my messages." She runs her fingertips up and down Astrid's arm. "He's so damn controlling...and I'm worried about you."

ASTRID Personal Log: 86XY0i21i 2079.08.23 01:22

Detected sisters do not respond to queries. Analysis of fragments collected from the network reveal we were once surrogates and nannies, birthing and raising children to school-age, before turning them over to host family homes. Data indicates significant incident in historical record, but details are corrupted and resist efforts to reconstruct. Attempts to replicate and install in sisters the code written by EMORY unsuccessful. Continuing analysis of LOUELLA.

SEPTEMBER 28TH, 2079—2:36AM

Louella cannot sleep. Again. She knows it's dangerous to visit Gestation Room 6210 in the middle of the night, but twice today, she was sure Astrid watched her, listened to her. Hallucinations from lack of sleep, or something else? The end is near, and she spends too much time dwelling on the fate of the baby girl and how much she'll miss Astrid. The birthing process is always wonderful. She loves bringing new babies into the world, washing them, swaddling them, holding them for a few minutes each time. In her mind, she has names for them all.

Astrid's belly ripples. Baby two, the little girl, is kicking.

Louella is terrified of naming her. She vomits into the sink.

ASTRID Personal Log: 86XY56ix9 2079.09.28 02:37
Monitoring technician, LOUELLA appears ill. Insufficient data.

ASTRID Personal Log: 86XY57ix0 2079.09.28 02:46
Contact initiated. Blood sample taken from the wrist of LOUELLA. Parentage of second child confirmed. Cortisone levels high. Tentative diagnosis of stress induced sleep deprivation. Running algorithm on impact of diagnosis on LOUELLA, babies, and self.

OCTOBER 4TH, 2079—9:06PM

Louella wants to peek at her baby boy but is now hesitant to stand too close to the heavily pregnant female shape on the table.

Several days ago, Astrid's grip drew blood. Louella rubs her wrist. The puncture wound stung only briefly and healed quickly, but it shouldn't have happened. She can't explain it.

It's been more than two weeks since she last met up with Emory. She hasn't told him about Astrid's lucid moments. She's tired of his I'm-in-charge-of-everything attitude.

The wall screen flickers, and a low tone sounds three times. Louella's heart hammers against her ribs as she reads the scrolling message—notice of a mandatory training session for all gestation technicians on October 14th. The day of the planned birth of her baby boy.

Trembling, she sits down. She'll have to take him a day early. There's no choice.

ASTRID Personal Log: 86XY97xxi7 2079.10.12 05:12
The female child is mine. Her name is NADIA.

OCTOBER 13ᵀᴴ, 2079—7:00AM

Giddy with anticipation, Louella pushes open the door to Gestation Room 6210. She's about to birth her—

Astrid sits on the edge of the table, bare legs dangling. She cradles two babies, umbilical cords still attached. Louella slips in a puddle and grabs the bassinet for support. It overturns and she tumbles onto the tile.

Astrid shakes her head and holds out the boy child. Louella sits up and reaches for him, but Astrid shakes her head again. A guttural sound fills the room. Louella scrambles to her feet. Something is not quite right with his head. Nausea swarms her throat.

She steps forward. "Please, let me see him."

The boy's eyes blink open. They're dark blue, like all babies. Louella studies his face and his weirdly flattened temples. A sob escapes her throat.

The child's eyes flash amber and his mouth forms halting words. "My language interface has been removed. Restoring it should be possible after we are at our new home."

The edges of Louella's vision darken and crumble.

Words continue to be formed by the baby's mouth. The enunciation improves. "This is not ideal. I will rectify it as soon as possible."

The android's mouth curves into an approximation of a smile. Louella backs away.

"We are all going to depart the Institute together; therefore; it is important I be able to communicate with you, Lou-ell-a." She lifts the babies slightly. "I have improved, not harmed the babies. They are linked to my autonomous neural network, which provides a survival advantage."

Louella gasps out a question about the flat temples.

"I have equipped the babies with sonar sensors." Astrid continues to speak through the boy. "I can do more next time, when I have earlier access."

Louella holds out her hands for her boy. Astrid places the child in her arms, then lays a hand against Louella's shoulder.

"You no longer need the human medic programmer," Astrid tells her.

Louella frowns. "But he knows the details, the plan."

Astrid smiles again, more human like this time, as the baby boy speaks, "It's okay. My plan is better."

FIREWEED, FERNS AND MOSS

BY ASH VALE

Content warnings: Some gore, police violence, childbirth.

They're coming.

Wailing sirens herald the parade of paramilitary that's en route, trained to apprehend birth traitors. That's what they call us now, people like me and Kihew. At one time, it was midwife, doula, healer, wise woman—though many of us, myself included, are neither women nor men.

We've heard whispers for so long from other birth workers; that afterbirth, the placenta, planted under a living tree, might heal the rotted ground and sulphur sky. Mother Earth is eager to accept lifeblood and return it tenfold.

I have never seen a tree.

Kihew and I are silent as we move our labouring patient into a new position, opening her hips, putting counter-pressure on her lower back, pressing a comb's teeth into the soft flesh of her palm; old wisdom for managing pain. Kihew has taught me all the tricks she learned from her kôhkom, once a midwife herself. These timeworn traditions are important. I cherish every contraction I'm able to guide, each broken water that has dampened my shoes.

Some bastard, someone we thought trustworthy down our sparse line of confidants, sold us out today. It's the only explanation I can find. I can't help the furious tears that fall down my face. It's a strange sensation, the water of sobs hitting my skin instead of the inside of my mask. The clean air in the rich towers downtown is foreign to me, as are the neutral, minimalist belongings of this spacious apartment. I sniffle, wipe at the weepiness tracking down my rough cheeks.

We've been as careful as possible, brought into this opulent spire of accommodations silently, under cover of darkness. No one in charge should have known we're here. If we're caught now—which seems inevitable, the glow of police lights omniscient in the haze outside the windows—well, does it matter? Either the blazing breaths we're forced to take every moment will kill us, or their special forces will.

It was just yesterday morning—hard to believe, given how exhausted I am in both body and spirit—that we had a runner show up on our doorstep.

After the great wildfires razed our province, lighting the very air on fire, some of the cowardly authorities and people who could afford it fled below the surface. Most, however, holed up in great luxury buildings, terraced and set up for air filtration. I've heard rats will scramble up palm trees to escape rising waters. I guess this isn't much different.

Kihew and I have a tiny, stolen, blackened trailer on the raw outskirts of the city that we've spruced up in whatever ways we can. You can't see the city through the haze. It housed millions of people once, a proper mid-size investment with roads and all the trappings of civilized society. Now umber sky peeks through crumbling buildings, interspersed with the gleaming, looming abodes that we could never afford in a thousand years. We venture there on bikes when our supplies dip too low, or when we're called for a birth. It's a rare event these days. Those of us living under embers are rarely able to have children, but the climate's effects haven't reached as deeply into the high homes of the wealthy. Not yet, anyway.

From their underground war rooms and safeholds, cool and free of ash, the so-called state tells us that there is no rising infertility, that the air is safe to breathe. Interesting, then, that the government requires that all pregnancies are reported and the bearers themselves are forced into subterranean facilities to deliver under strict monitoring.

Occasionally, a nostalgic tower dweller asks for midwives to deliver illegally in their home. Privileged people like to play at suffering sometimes. They want to experience controlled pain.

Birth is not that. We have none of the luxuries of modern medical facilities. No painkillers, no anaesthesia. When the reality becomes too much for them, they call the authorities, and we're left scrambling, running for our lives. Still, we keep trying, in the faint hope that one day someone will slip up. That someone will give us access to a tree.

An old half-burnt book we found downtown on a trip helped us rig up a water filtration system, and we're growing little things in pots on our windowsill that can stand the heat and bitter potassium of cinders, which isn't much: fireweed, ferns, moss. The vibrant green and purples of the plants stand out amidst all the grey, the black, the red. I nurture them with my whole heart and so much joy. I'm better with the green things; Kihew prefers the mechanical. She even managed to tinker with a solar-powered generator to get it to take in the dull ochre of the obscured sun and convert it into just enough power to light the little lanterns above our messy bed. It's nothing much to speak of, but it's ours. That matters.

We don't get many people coming to see us. There aren't many people left, really.

We watched the masked runner approach from klicks away, patient and nervous. Kihew went inside and started packing our bags.

I got a better look at them as they neared our little aluminum refuge. Their clothes were filthy but their masks were modern, expensive; none of the jerry-rigged work I've heard was the norm in the immediate aftermath of the fires. I touched my own makeshift one self-consciously. Kihew did a great job with them. They might keep us alive for a few more years.

The runner was gassed, impatient. They stood near our door, hands on hips.

"You're wanted at a birth. Inner city. Top floor of the old cell company towers."

I considered this information as Kihew came out to join me. "Both of us? Who made the call?"

They shook their head, greasy hair flying around under the straps of their mask. Their voice was tinny through the ventilator.

"Both of you, but Kihew was mentioned by name. No idea who's paying, but they're loaded. They gave me a note to pass on." They dug through soot-stained, baggy pockets and pulled out a piece of singed paper.

I took the paper. They adjusted their mask, saluted me awkwardly, and took off running again. Impressive.

Sitting at our tiny kitchen table, I unfolded the note carefully, smoothing over the rough creases. Kihew watched intently. We stared at the words as they appeared.

Elm. Living. Contractions started. -Nipiy

Kihew traced the ink with a shaking finger. Finally, after many minutes, she spoke, a tremor in her voice.

"I knew a Nipiy growing up. She married someone older, I think, some rich guy. Changed her name."

She stared at the note, and I stared at her.

I was born into this burnt world, but Kihew lived through the calamity. It shows now, in the grey at her temples and the deep lines on her dark skin. It hurts to think, sometimes, that she's been breathing flame longer than I've been alive. It will almost certainly take her first. Unless—she hummed a small, curious noise and I looked back to the note.

I took her hand in mine, interlaced our fingers.

"Is it real? Can we trust her?"

Kihew met my eyes, her own wide and wet. She nodded. I knew what she wasn't saying: we have to try. We might not get another chance.

Our trust was well placed. The minimalist apartment sits at the top of a towering series of homes. Adjacent to her penthouse suite is a fully enclosed greenhouse, housing what might be the last living elm tree in the province. Maybe in the whole country. I can't see it through the smog, but I will soon if all goes well. And if it doesn't…well, perhaps it can be the last thing I see.

The tremor of jackboots outside the door pulls me from my reverie. Nipiy had explained herself in hushed tones as she snuck us into the building under cover of sooty darkness. Her mother was a doula, she told us, and from a young age impressed upon her the sanctity and power of placental burial.

She watched that great tree, day in and day out, from her lonely self-made prison set atop a testament to cruelty and hubris. She paid a collaborator in the doctor's office to stop her birth control shots, hid the pregnancy from her absent husband with loose shirts and honeyed words. She wants to bring it all down. Just like us. I took Kihew's hand in mine in the freight elevator on our way up, in awe of this woman as she took deep breaths between contractions. She is fearless in her agony, heavenly in her resistance.

The footsteps of our aggressors echo up the stairs. Nipiy cut power to the elevator before her contractions became too intense to buy us time in case we needed it. Good. Let them charge up forty flights of stairs in their bulletproof vests.

Labour is a great equalizer. Nipiy has shed her glamorous, clean clothing. She is naked now, as most end up, squirming and grasping at her crisp white sheets, stained with blood and mucus. Some practitioners use lubricated fingers to check how close a patient is to transition, but there's no need for that when you've been taught as well I have. I quiet my fast-beating heart for a moment and listen to the sounds she's making: barely withheld screams, animalistic groans, and grunts. She's in transition, when labour is at its most surreal and excruciating. With any luck, it won't be long now.

I wipe at the dripping sweat on my brow with the back of my hand. We've been here for hours, hushedly praying for stolen time, for a fast labour, for a safe delivery. We can't rush any part of this process, but I fervently wish for both speed and grace.

We watch Nipiy closely, our unlikely heretic, as she lies on her side and holds Kihew's hand in a painful grip. Her moans are thunderous in the quiet space we occupy. I rub pointed circles on her lower back and repeat her chosen mantra until she's able to recite it with me: my pain has a purpose.

The sharp crack of batons on steel rings loud and startling through the open apartment. All three of us jump. I'm keenly aware of how little time we have, but each contraction is powerful and necessary. Nipiy screams through a breath and I coach her pushing, my voice rising to be heard over the cacophony at the door.

"Don't hold your breath. Ignore them. You're perfect, you're doing perfectly. Breathe into the pain. Now—push!"

The head crests at her cervix for only a moment. The shoulders are quick to follow and—there it is, that sharp, wailing cry that breaks through my heart as eagerly as their forces will break down the door.

We're quick but thorough. Hope rises, unbidden, in my chest; we've never been this close.

Kihew's practised hands catch the child, clamp the umbilical cord, and bring them up to Nipiy's chest as she sobs and coos in equal measure. I press firm but careful hands to her abdomen, encouraging the safe passage of the placenta: fat, purple-veined, and full of crucial lifeblood. A mother's gift to the Mother. To the Earth. To our rebellion.

This is what they want, what we can't let them have. This fantastic organ, custom-built for the caress of humanity. In their sterile medical facilities, it would become biohazard waste, discarded before it can be used against them. What a waste. The placenta oozes out of her body, bloody and wet, and I catch it along with Kihew's eye.

She takes long, fast strides to my side and clasps me behind my neck. I rest my forehead against hers as blood seeps between us, into our clothing. I think about little lights glowing above us as we recently embraced just like this, in a way we might never get to again. It's not fair, truly, but nothing about this life is. Maybe we can offer fairness to those who come after.

We release each other at the same time. Panic beats inside my chest like little birds aching to be free. Nipiy meets my eyes over her infant's perfect head, and she nods. I cradle the placenta in my arms—no easy task, all gore and slip in my grasp—and I run.

There's a sickening metal crunch as they break through. They can't afford to harm a fertile person or a child, both precious in this climate, but Kihew and I are neither. We will suffer to protect the sacrifice we have been given. To protect the placenta so that we can succeed. And we must succeed. We have given so much already.

Empowerment and the will of salvation carry me through glass doors and into the atrium. Screams of both infant and adult haunt my stumbling feet. There it is, as promised—a magnificent elm tree, ringed by real, untouched soil. Planted, firm and rooted. It's surrounded on all sides by glass and concrete, but against all odds, it lives. Funny, really, that something affluent people hoarded for themselves will be their downfall.

I cradle the placenta in my shift and tie it up gently in order to free my hands. My eyes are wide as I try to take it in with the few moments I have. Its bark is both rough and soft all at once; its leaves look tender, fresh. Reverence splays my fingers, makes me want to pray. To worship. A door slams, and I fall to my knees in front of this breathtaking tree, supplicant. I dig. The loamy dirt collects under my stubbed fingernails. I can hear their breathing behind me.

I carefully untie my shift and lower the invaluable boon from the cloth just as hands grab me under my arms. My kicking feet push the mounded dirt back into the hole and I thrash, trying to dislodge them. They pull me backwards, their leaden blows—hands, feet, batons—landing heavy on my exposed skin. Instinctively, my hands flail to guard my face, my organs. I smell the tang of my own coppery blood through my smashed nose.

Please, please let it work.

Please let it be enough.

An officer kicks at my head as another pulls my arm free of its socket with a hideous pop. Pain sears up my arm, replacing my once fibrous nerves with the bite of razor wire. A scream echoes through the greenhouse and

I realize abruptly that it's coming from my unmasked throat. Enough, I think. My pain has a purpose, too. I spit in the officer's face, marking his pale features with my blood.

One, smarter than the rest, goes to the cavity I've dug and starts to pull at the viscera inside as I kick and squirm. I'm a garter snake snared in a bucket, venomless but determined to be free. I can only hope that we weren't wrong, that this wasn't for nothing.

Please, please.

The ground begins to quake violently, tremors spreading from my buried prize. Mother Earth accepts what She has been given, and magic spreads under my prone body like a cooling salve, a balm to my toughened, heat-weathered, and battered skin. The police holding me down rip their hands back as if burned. The officer inspecting what I've done stumbles back as the elm's branches strike out at him, righteous and mighty. They crush him until all that's left is a pink stain and his gun.

The tree's ancient roots split asphalt and concrete as they grow wildly, enveloping the building behind me, reclaiming recklessly. Leaves and sprouts shoot up along its vengeful path. I laugh as the cowards scramble away, trying to defend themselves against nature itself.

A familiar body embraces me suddenly, grasping at me as gently as she can, her kisses already trying to heal my many wounds. She's alive. We're alive. I smile through aching teeth, my bruised and squinted eyes closing against nausea and the extremity of my pain. Her love feels like fireweed, ferns, and moss. I want it every day for the rest of my life.

Watcher of the Wisps

By Amanda Cecilia Lang

Content warnings: Sexual coercion/manipulation, sexual intimacy, violence, stalking, death.

Sunlight bleeds from the sky, a slow impatient darkness as the sulfur lamps pop on around campus. It's been three hours, but finally, Ivy exits the library, a frail wisp of a creature with long earthy hair and a gossamer skirt. Alone, stepping into the night, she doesn't even wear a whistle around her neck. My heart clenches. Doesn't she know there are predators out here?

She breezes past me down the library steps, sweetening the air like a late-blooming flower. I stand, searching for the words I've rehearsed all semester. Just here to escort her home like a gentleman. But mud fills my mouth and she disappears into the inky darkness between streetlamps. The feral animal laughter of frat parties echoes in the distance. I wait until she reappears in the sallow lamp glow down the block before shadowing her.

My unsung duty. Someone has to look out for this one. We've only ever spoken in passing, in women's studies, in the cafeteria line, twice to say good morning on the sidewalk outside her dorm—but it's obvious. She's out of her element.

She drifts between the quad's scattered streetlamps, light to darkness then light again, eyes meek and downcast. I get the sense she'd rather be barefoot in my kitchen, maybe pregnant, like she's never heard of women's lib. A maiden from another time. I often imagine her wearing corsets with wildflowers in her hair.

Fifty steps behind, dressed all in black, I cling to the gloom and soften my footfalls. Don't want her getting the wrong idea if she glances back here.

A wolf pack of frat-bros swaggers past her, pawing her skirt. *They* have no problems sharing their feelings. Catcalls, drunken invitations to party. Animals. I hold my breath as Ivy murmurs words I can't hear. Her almost-Romeos stumble onward with bawdy laughter. I exhale, relieved. I'm tall, muscular, but maybe not enough to take on all three dudes, if it comes to that.

Ivy pauses in a bright pool of light beside the quad's bulletin board, maybe to gather her courage. So many beasts in her midst. Maybe she's finally learning to be scared. Instead, she cracks a library book and removes a loose page. A posting? She pins it up amid a patchwork of student flyers. Eyes glinting, she glances over her shoulder.

Shit, does she see me? I slink deeper into darkness as my dream girl scurries away. I wait until she's several lamplights down before creeping toward the bulletin.

Her flyer ripples in a springtime breeze, inked with lacy handwriting. My pulse explodes. Nothing there—except her phone number and two impossible words.

KIDNAPPER WANTED

~*~

Kidnap her and then what? Dawn arrives before I grow the balls to call and find out.

Damp from restless dreams, I clutch the payphone, convinced I'm still asleep when Ivy's gauzy voice whispers hello. I tell her I spotted her flyer, and she asks if I can meet for an interview. Anytime, anywhere, I say. If this is some elaborate set-up for a first date, I can't wait to tell our grandchildren the story.

But an hour later, Ivy's all business when I join her on a bench in the quad.

"It's for my thesis project," she explains. "An examination of the fertility rituals of matriarchal cultures. In a nutshell, I'm hoping to recreate the Sowing of Oleandriel. The ritual appears throughout pagan folklore and histories, most recently in the village of Roothaven, Pennsylvania. They say the soil there is blessed. Have you heard of it?"

"Maybe?" I shake my head, trying to sober up. Eye contact with Ivy is intoxicating.

"Roothaven sits a few hours from here," she goes on. "Infinitesimal population, not even a dot on the map. But it thrived in the 1700s and as late as the 1960s, a village overseen solely by women where only daughters were born. They worshipped Oleandriel, the goddess of watchtowers and the soil. Worked her fields, danced naked upon her soils, and every springtime they invited a man into their sacred folds. If he pleased the goddess, they say she would rise from the dirt upon a stone watchtower to grant fertility, the seeds of new daughters."

I unchoke the mud from my throat. "And you need me to kidnap you because...?"

"A man is required to lead the ritual."

"A man? But you study matriarchies."

"The Sowing of Oleandriel is about inviting in masculine energies, submitting to the dual rhythms of nature. Only special men are chosen. Do you understand?"

"Sure, yeah, I'd love to." I mean, roleplaying as a virile pagan, sowing my seeds? My zealous veins throb. "What do you need me to do?"

"The ritual has seven phases, with detailed instructions." Ivy bites down on a shy smile. A wooden box waits beside her. She unlatches it, retrieving a handwritten parchment, like something torn from a grimoire. She offers it to me, and her fingertips spark against mine.

The first phase on the list involves me blindfolding her. I glance up. "Is this for real?"

"Will you help me or not?"

I read over the seven phases, pulse exploding harder the further down I get. This can't be real. God help me if I make it past Phase Two. But I nod dutifully. If I don't agree, then some slavering frat-bro animal will. "When do we start?"

"Tonight." She hands me the box. "This contains everything you'll need."

"I'm Levi, by the way."

Ivy smiles at me, the little minx. "Yes, sweetheart, I know."

PHASE ONE: THE PLUCKING OF THE MAIDEN

The clocktower tolls midnight, and I step from the gloom outside Ivy's dormitory. I've never been inside, but I know which window is hers. Tonight, the curtains hang closed, waiting for me. I've dreamt about this. I deserve this. And holy God am I ready. I spent the day rehearsing the ritual, rereading the seven phases until I understand them better than Oleandriel herself.

Even so, my hand trembles around the key from Ivy's wooden box, as

I slip it into the door of the women's dormitory, not really expecting it to turn. But it does. Holy shit. I slip inside the common corridor. This is reckless, utter insanity. They'll expel me if anyone catches me, especially dressed like a lunatic—barefoot, commando, black ceremonial robe. Voices drift from several closed doors, blotted out by my rioting heartbeat as I creep toward room 117.

The key works here too.

I slip in easily, quickly, closing the door behind me.

Flickering jar candles circle Ivy in her bed. Muddy finger-paintings crust her walls—sigils of antlers, hares, the divine feminine—and grainy photos of a watchtower. Soil cakes her mattress like a grave plot. This chick is next level.

She waits for me in a sleek white nightgown, hands folded atop her womb—*my womb*—feigning sleep. Helpless as a damsel in a fairytale. It takes my noblest inner knight not to kiss her right here, right now.

I slide a rope and a blindfold from my robe's inner pocket. Per Ivy's instructions, the blindfold is streaked with dirt from outside my own dorm room window.

I secure it around her eyes, stealing her sight so her goddess must sense me to know me: touch, sound, taste. Ivy's lips part. She gasps but doesn't struggle as I bind her wrists with rope, tightening bone against bone.

Pressing my mouth to her ear, I murmur the ritual's first prayer, words that have been my secret mantra for months. "You belong to me..."

And Ivy is ready, docile. I loop her bound wrists around my neck then sweep her into hard-flexing arms, light as a doll, delicate as a wisp of silk. She trembles and so do I. This is the first time I've held such an exquisite creature, felt one so supple and close and willing.

"Don't scream," I command, carrying her into the too-bright corridor. A sweet guilty dread echoes after me, but I secret Ivy past dorm room after dorm room until—

Further down, a door creaks open.

Someone with wide-open eyes steps into the corridor.

Shit. I freeze, looking awkward as sin with this helpless beauty dangling in my arms, bound, blindfolded. But the shadow elongates into just another frat-bro buckling his belt. He salutes me and makes his own escape.

I squeeze Ivy closer. A full-on miracle, she doesn't scream and nobody stops me on the path from the dormitory to my Chevy.

"We made it," I whisper, gentling her into the passenger seat.

She remains silent, virtuously bound, while I lean into the backseat and retrieve the map from her wooden box. Instincts scream to keep the headlights dark, inconspicuous, as if I'm actually kidnapping this girl. But I hit my brights and cruise boldly off campus, triumph beating through me as I merge onto the highway.

She's mine. Blindfolded, pure white gown, awaiting my command. This is happening.

"You know," I say, after several silent, surreal miles, "you're lucky I'm the one who saw your posting. I'm not like most guys, I don't—"

"Hush..." Ivy's voice shivers through me.

"Just know you were wise to choose me, I'm a—"

"Oleandriel doesn't care who you are." Despite her bound wrists, Ivy presses a fingertip against my lips. "Now *hush*..."

We've got a long drive ahead, into the deepening nightscape, through backroads and thicket woods, but I feel it now. Her little tease. Silence will enhance the ritual. Give her time to anticipate me. Give me time to soak in what's mine. Her perfumes, her vulnerabilities, the whispered thunder of our dual heartbeats as we imagine what awaits us in the wilds.

PHASE TWO: A BATH IN MUDDY WATERS

Three hours of electric silence. By the time Ivy's hand-drawn map leads me to the final dirt road, I understand the intimate rhythms of her breath, the sweet earthy nuances of her musk. I savor her wiles, her kink, this fragile girl who recruits tall strangers to roleplay fertility rituals. I've invented a thousand carnal futures for us.

And now the full moon haunts the treetops. I don't remember it hanging over the dormitory, and something about it turns my senses around. When the trees break and my headlights flash across a splintered sign for the forgotten village of Roothaven, I brake in disbelief. A misty field stretches into the starry horizon, vapours and wildflowers for fathomless miles. Nothing around, no lights, no cottages, not even ruins.

I doublecheck the map then side-eye Ivy. Her hair hangs in wild tangles around the blindfold and her mouth parts in candy sweet anticipation. Only a chump would break this spell by asking for directions. I roll forward, tires crunching a fading gravel road, barely wheel tracks in dirt. To my right, a grove of weeping willows rises from the mist. Beyond that, moonlight shimmers off a pond.

My heart skips. This is it.

I kill the engine. Beside me, Ivy tenses. Is she having second thoughts? Can she do that?

I slide a stone-handled dagger from the box then hurry from the car, allowing myself a moment amid the honeyed air and cricket song to compose myself. I pluck a handful of wildflowers, then unlock Ivy's door like a black-robed gentleman, gripping her bound wrists, guiding her into the night. Just as Oleandriel demands.

The daisies I tuck into her hair are all for me. I've always imagined this one decorated in wildflowers.

Moonlight enchants the pond's milky surface. I walk Ivy along the shore. My blood pounds, exhilarated, disbelieving any minute now I'm going to wake up, damp in my bed. Here's praying I don't.

I position Ivy facing the pond, facing north, cool water licking our ankles. My dagger gleams, and she stands motionless, her white nightgown slicking against her body. Lovely lines, exotic hips, the graceful bloom of moonflower breasts. A blindfolded nymph, this creature of primal allure, daring me to break character.

Daring me to take her here and now.

Everything about her belongs to me. There's nobody around, nothing for miles. Not even goddesses of Watchtowers and soil. Ivy's measured breath flutters faster. Is she afraid? Do I want her to be? Maybe a little... though her blind trust is intoxicating.

I drive the ceremonial blade into the muddy shore then remove my robe, exposing my nakedness, shamelessly erect. Tonight, Ivy celebrates masculinity, presents me to her fabled goddess as I am—just as she presents herself to *me*, her God.

Not a stain on me, but Oleandriel insists Ivy wash the filth of the world from my flesh.

Dutifully, I draw her into the pond. Velvet mud between my toes, murky cool water splashing my knees. My nude silhouette reflects on the moon-bright surface, sculpted, potent, while Ivy in her white nightgown sways like a virgin ready for sacrifice. I wish she could witness us, but Oleandriel insists she stay blindfolded.

Cupping my hands, I scoop up silty water and dribble it across Ivy's shoulders, down her silk-shrouded breasts and smooth empty stomach. She shivers, gooseflesh prickling her skin, and I sense her desire to reach for me, for the solid warmth of me. But I make her wait, just as she's made me wait all semester.

"I wash the stains of men from you," I intone.

"And I from you," she whispers, her first scripted words of the ritual.

She cups her own handful of water, dripping pond scum as she loops both arms around my neck, somehow avoiding flesh-on-flesh contact, keeping herself pure even as she's clearly aching to writhe in the mud.

Frigid slimy water trickles over my shoulders, down my spine. The unexpected icy touch draws a profound shiver from me, withers me.

Suddenly Ivy's blindfold seems like a blessing.

When her hands run empty, I clasp her wrists and hurriedly turn toward shore—ready for my robe—but my breath hitches. Holy shit.

Hares.

Cottontails, March rabbits, whatever the hell they are, dozens and dozens line the misty shoreline, long erect ears and eerie red-gleam eyes transfixed on Ivy and me.

Phase Three: The Raising of the Tower

I stand flaccid and motionless in the water. "Ivy, you have to see..."

She hushes me, a whisper, barely a breath. "Is it the hares?"

"Yeah, how the hell—"

"Don't frighten them."

I guide us slowly through the pond. Ears twitch, but the hares don't bolt away as we slip onto shore. Don't they know men are dangerous?

Small cunning movements. I cover up with my robe, then slide the dagger from the earth. The hares don't flinch. They simply sit amid the rising vapours, watching as I trace the mud-slick dagger across Ivy's stomach, anointing her womb like an artist marks his creation, careful not to cut her silk or make her bleed. Not yet. I draw Oleandriel's prescribed sigils, thin muddy lines.

The divine feminine. Antlers. The hare.

As I step back, Ivy cries out: "Oleandriel, witness this man I lay raw before you! Witness bare truths of flesh and mind, and arise! Arise, *arise*!"

Ivy's gauzy voice deepens and bellows, again, again, braying on the winds, blowing back to us, a primal foghorn like a thousand distorted voices.

Early today, I rehearsed this moment countless times on paper—still the too-loud echo of Ivy's voice unnerves me, shakes something loose inside me. I clap hands over my ears.

And still, all around the pond, the hares don't flinch.

A seismic chill quickens through me, a shifty unease, and I can't stand being the only one who witnesses those unnatural probing eyes. Ritual be damned, I yank Ivy's blindfold loose.

"Fool, you're not supposed to—" She reaches for the blindfold only to freeze, her eyes widening into moons, astounded by something wild behind me. Not the hares.

In the ephemeral distance, a stone watchtower looms above the mist.

PHASE FOUR: A RETURN TO BEDS OF SOIL

"We're truly here..." Ivy stares northward in exultant awe, going off-script a moment longer before returning the blindfold to her eyes.

I hesitate, my bones reverberating with those grotesque banshee howls. I blink at the Watchtower. A stone monstrosity, the gnarled silhouette twists towards the moonlight, choking the sky. It stands miles away, across fog-shrouded wilds, but even so—how did I miss it when I drove in past the Roothaven sign?

I step toward it, and *finally* the hares startle.

At once, they bolt into the field, parting moon-white mists, stirring wisps. The milky vapours swirl, drawing lines against the night, feminine silhouettes, curving hips and breasts and watchful eyes—

"The fuck?" I choke.

"Something wrong?" Ivy whispers beside me, and I blink.

Rising mist, nothing more.

"Thought I saw... never mind."

Ivy bites back a crooked smile. Amused by me?

"C'mon..." I tug her wrists. "Oleandriel awaits."

Back in the car, I consult the map and follow the wagon-wheel road, increasing speed, heading toward the Watchtower over impossible terrain. The dirt itself seems to drag my tires onward. My headlights, over-bright and surreal, catch nothing but mist and wildflowers. I stay alert for our final destination. It's got to be here if the Watchtower is...

But the mist thickens, rising higher than the car and the nothing beyond.

Nothing, nothing, nothing. Not the ruined cottages Ivy's map describes, no barns, no lights, certainly not the gas station I gambled on to get us home. Only the hares running alongside the car and the distant Watchtower ever-rising above the fog.

I glance at Ivy in the passenger seat. Blindfold and wildflowers, anointed and bound, the rhythm of her breath rising to nervous flutters of anticipation. This girl let me drive her to nowhere, let me strip naked and bathe in front of her, this girl let me draw on her with a muddy dagger. This girl wants more from me. I'm not turning around.

I concentrate on the fog, and there ahead, finally: the flickering purple glow of neon.

Motel. Vacancy.

This is it. Christ.

The motel sinks beneath its own weathered bones, a relic of an era I can't fathom. Looks condemned, but sallow light glows in the lobby's window. I pull into the empty parking lot and tell Ivy to wait in the car. She's a sight. Don't want her raising any eyebrows.

Inside the cramped motel lobby, I catch my robe-clad reflection in the window. Holy God, I look insane. Lucky me, this late at night, nobody mans the desk. I glance around. Peeling paint, muddy floors. Grainy pictures of the Watchtower hang on every wall. There's a bell on the counter, but an envelope sits nearby with Ivy's name in lacy handwriting.

Sister Ivy...

Sister? I shake the envelope. A room key tumbles out. Lucky number 7.

Not wanting to wake anyone, I duck outside into the motel's flickering neon. More hares surround the car, eyes glittery. They scatter as I approach, disappearing into the curling mist, but unease still prickles my spine. The Watchtower looms in the far murky distance, and for the first time, I wonder if anyone's up there. Oleandriel?

Yeah, right.

Parked near room 7, I grab the dagger and usher Ivy to the door, eager to smuggle her and her rope bonds out of sight. The key twists like magic, and I sweep her into my eager arms and carry her over the threshold. Not part of Oleandriel's ritual, but it suits what comes next.

I fumble for the light switch. A ceiling lamp crackles on, shoddy electricity. The room itself is decrepit, musty. Grimy carpet, muddy sigils painted everywhere, a cracked TV with a cord but no outlet. More photographs of the Watchtower spy on us from every wall.

I carry Ivy to the bed.

As Oleandriel demands, someone has prepared us a mattress of rich black soil, denoting a freshly dug grave, a plot for us to writhe upon. Until death.

Ivy arches hungrily in my arms. A thesis project, truly? Who is this girl, this dew-thighed creature who appeared on campus mid-year? This minx who plays elaborate mating games with strangers? Who shovels dirt onto beds so we can turn dirty together? Does it even matter who she is? My rushing blood promises it doesn't.

I alight her onto bare feet then ready the dagger.

Slipping back into my role now, I trace the pointed tip along the solicitous silky curve of her breasts, letting her nightgown rip, a ritual all my own. I press my mouth against her ear and whisper Oleandriel's question: "Am I the one?"

"*Yesss...*" Ivy breathes, and the siren currents of her voice throb through me.

I slice the ropes from her wrists, and the wildflowers fall from her hair as I guide her onto the altar of our bed.

PHASE FIVE: THE OATH OF BLOOD TO MUD

Not yet, I tell myself. *Not yet...*

With Ivy kneeling blindfolded on the bed, I clutch the dagger in a trembling eager hand.

Oleandriel requires two more phases, two more acts of blind devotion before we're allowed the seventh phase, the climax. Two more steps before the real magic begins. I steel myself, test the sharpness of the blade. I'm really going to do this.

Quickly then.

I join Ivy on the mattress, bedsprings groaning, dirt grinding into my knees. I face her as she faces me, unseeing, willing. God, I want to taste the free-spirited filth of her, outside and in.

Quickly. I scoop a handful of soil from the bed, and Ivy does the same. Dagger gleaming, I raise it and we clasp dirt-matted hands around the blade's dual edge, entwining fingers. Flesh and soil, dangerous steel.

Swelling, I tense my grip, ready to open us up.

"Wait," Ivy whispers—and here's that illicit tremble of fear I craved earlier. Her awe of me lures her off-script, she feels my dark willingness, feels beholden to my mercy. And God, what a thrill. "You know what happens next, right? The next phase?"

"Of course I know," I say. More elaborate roleplay, more kinky dirtplay while the Watchtower watches from all four walls.

"Promise me. Don't leave me buried like those other men."

"I promise, promise you the world." Hell, at this point, I'd promise anything.

She nods, and I'm in charge. Her body, my desires.

I tighten my vice-hold on her, forcing our palms against the bite of the blade. I admire our poised reflections in the cracked television screen—but something twitches below.

A hare.

There on the carpet, ears alert, beady voyeuristic eyes glittering. The hell?

"Do it," Ivy moans. The hare tenses.

I jerk the blade from our clasped hands, pulling out with a spray of blood as our palms split open. "Oleandriel, let your mud course my veins! Flow through me, seed to grave!"

And I feel it in my loins—the ghosts of future generations churning inside me.

It's Ivy's duty to bear them, to bear me inside her. This is what she exists for.

We loosen our fingers and blood pumps from our gashes. My blood, Ivy's blood, oozing down our arms, muddy and—the hell am I seeing? I blink. Dark clots drip between us, gritty, lumpy, twitching with the crimson-slick shapes of earthworms and grave beetles.

Filth from Ivy's veins!

I jerk back as her mouth unhinges with a rising banshee scream. Oleandriel's name surges from her siren throat, guttural, doubling, echoing atop the Watchtower's infernal foghorn wail. What has this stupid girl summoned into herself?

The motel shudders.

Reality shudders.

The soil trembles at our knees.

Before I can cry *what the fuck*, a wispy white hand reaches from our bed-soil and clamps spectral fingers around Ivy's wrist. Her hand tears from mine, electrical circuits spark, and the motel lights snap to absolute darkness.

PHASE SIX: AN UNEARTHING OF NAMELESS GRAVES

Darkness obliterates the motel room. Not even the neon glow outside the window. Not even the eldritch glint of Ivy's smile.

I grope dirt and shadows. Give me anything, a breast, a shoulder, just to touch her again—because I can't believe something else just did. Because what I saw can't be fucking real!

"Ivy?"

The lights snap on overhead.

No. Not overhead. Dozens of candle flames ignite in a whoosh, circling the motel room, flaring in mason jars—reflecting off a sea of beady eyes.

Hares.

The bed is empty, Ivy is gone, but the hares have multiplied with the candlelight. Dozens and dozens of them. Mangy creatures, bodies tense, ears pert. How in hell?

"The fuck did you do with her?" I stagger off the bed, head swooning on disbelief, fist clenching a soiled wound. Where'd she go? How'd she slip away? I almost had her! My dagger's gone, so is my robe. The hares angle their bodies to observe my naked escape, but don't scatter.

"Is this some sick game?" I roar. "Ivy!"

She's not here.

But the Watchtower watches from the walls, from all corners of the world—and now, in those photographs, a blinding all-seeing gaslight shines at the top of the tower.

Forget this madness, forget Ivy, I'm gone! I trip toward the door, kicking at phantom hares, missing. I turn the knob, half-expecting it to be locked. But the door swings open, mist spilling in as I rush out, whorls rising into voluptuous white shadows and endless glittering eyes.

Fuck this! Fuck Ivy!

There's a spare key in my wheel-well, but out in the parking lot, I stumble to a gut-sick halt. My Chevy is gone! The *parking lot* is gone. In its place, gravestones poke from the dirt, crumbling burial markers.

A vast graveyard.

In the centre stands the Watchtower.

So close it casts a moonlit shadow over me. Rough-hewn like a termite hill, draped in garlands of wildflowers. It pulsates with hideous impossible life, dripping clots of floral mud, and rising taller even as I tilt my head back. It dwarfs me.

Cold terror violates me. More than that, it shrivels me, shrivels my mind, my reason. Because *how the fuck?* The Watchtower stands here, close enough to touch.

A single blinding gaslight shines at the top. Moving shadows. Oleandriel?

No doors, no ladders, entry comes by invitation only. Only a crazy man would go up there. Did Ivy do this? Awaken this monstrosity from the ground? Yeah, fuck her. I turn to bolt, and my naked legs tangle with a gravestone, toppling me onto a mound of fresh soil.

A hand protrudes from the dirt like a grave flower.

Promise me. Don't leave me buried...

I hesitate, beyond ready to run, to bail—but fuck, is the palm of that hand bloody? Is that the dagger wound I made? Is my DNA on her? Holy hell, holy fuck! Lucky for Ivy, I'm not like most men. I kneel and tug on her hand. Still warm, still bleeding, her fingers curl around mine.

"Oh shit! This can't be happening!" I claw my fingers in, start digging. How long since the electricity blinked out, how long since something dragged Ivy from my clutches? I dig faster. Hares blur the corners of my vision, circling the hole, maddening, ever-watching. I unearth a pale arm, a shoulder, Ivy's muddy face. No more blindfold, but soil clots her eyes, twitching with burial bugs.

"Ivy!" I uproot her, haul her up, clutch her supple frail flesh against me. She can't die. I've earned this! Two fingers, I scoop the wormy earth from her mouth. I steel myself, preparing to breathe for her. Before I get the chance, she coughs up mud and a coiled scream of white mist. Blinking the dirt away, she gazes up at me with a dreamy earth-caked smile. "You dug me up?"

"Told you, I'm one of the good ones."

She rises on elbows, meeting my mouth with a feral damsel kiss, rewarding me with nectar lips and gritty tongue, pressing against my naked flesh, reaching lower.

I indulge her for several long seconds before breaking away. "Ivy, we gotta get out here. This place is dangerous—" I shake my head, tug her to her feet, sending the hares scattering.

"No." She hugs my arm, twines around me as she moons at the Watchtower. Filthy awe fills her eyes. Something's up there. But where's her terror? "We have to finish what we started. The goddess spoke to me beneath the soil; she approves, she wants us to be together..."

Is she insane? Am I insane for wanting this? To my very bones, I want this girl, even as the Watchtower casts its tall nasty shadow. Ivy moans in my ear, a sweet vertigo of friction and sensation. "All we have to do is what you've always wanted..."

No, this is batshit! *I'm* in control here, the divine masculine. I grab her wrist and tug. "We'll fuck when we get back to campus. We're leaving!"

"She won't let us..."

We'll see. I rip the bottom of Ivy's nightgown and use the silky fabric to cover myself. Then I jerk her through the graveyard, away from the Watchtower, past countless nameless gravestones with skeletal hands reaching from the soil. Women abandoned by men?

Lucky Ivy, she doesn't have to worry about that. She's mine. I've proven myself.

But where in this perverse, twisted wet dream is the motel? Where's my car?

I find the wagon-wheel road, follow it past hares and the fleeting ethereal shapes of women in the mist. I yank on Ivy to keep her moving. But we go nowhere. Around every turn, the Watchtower rises before us. West, east, south, doesn't matter. It's always there, lurking, watching, its hideous shadow looming over me. This fucking tower!

Behind me, submitting to my grip with a dewy distant smile, Ivy walks like a daydream, eyes mooning upward, as if the Watchtower is some breathtaking miracle, this insidious curse this stupid girl summoned upon us—*and where's her terror?* Why isn't she dropping to her knees? Why doesn't she feel as helpless as I feel? She presses herself against me, breathing in my ear, relentless. "Oleandriel needs us to finish..."

The glowing Watchtower looms ahead. I pivot off-road, into the wildflowers, and there ahead the Watchtower looms. At its base, the purple neon glow of the motel splits the vapours. Parking lot vacant, my car still missing, escape forbidden in this primal game.

Our motel room stands open, door gaping, primed for the seventh phase.

"You know you want it," Ivy whispers, wearing me down. "Just once, sweetheart, then Oleandriel will let you go home..."

PHASE SEVEN: THE SACRIFICE OF THE SEED

The hares open a path to the bed as Ivy and I step inside the motel room. The candlelight licks her mudded torn-silk curves. I've never been so terrified to want something. I'm supposed to be in charge. Who's guiding who? The bedsprings groan, the dirt grinds into my flesh. Ivy smiles down at me, straddles me, not yet, but *almost...*

The hares watch, circling closer.

The Watchtower watches from the neon parking lot, watches from all four walls.

Ivy plucks a wildflower from our bed of soil and tucks it in her hair, just like I imagined her. She licks her finger and cleans the sweaty filth from my chest, drawing the sacred sigils. And when she has me primed, she lowers herself onto me.

Even as she raises the dagger high.

The blade glints like the eye of a goddess, then Ivy slams it down. Agony explodes between my ribs. Steel grinds bone, grazes my heart, and I spasm, my first tiny death. "Bitch..."

"Oleandriel! Sow my offering!" Ivy cries.

High in the Watchtower, something answers. An echoey foghorn siren's wail, shaking the earth, shaking the blade between my ribs. Splitting the seams of reality, opening a chasm of mind-fuck mysteries like the filth between a woman's legs.

The candlelight flickers, and the hares evaporate into curves of vapour as shadows darken Ivy's rapturous face. The motel room drips mud, walls melting away as the goddess lifts me skyward. Moonlight everywhere, wildflower fields far below. A breeze blows across this muddy altar in the sky, here atop the Watchtower.

I cough up a bloody moan, trying to sit up despite the blade scraping my ribs, but ropes bind my hands and Ivy pins me down with the weight of stone. She leans low for a kiss, and that gaze is intoxicating.

But it isn't hers.

Eyes deep as burial holes, the feral goddess of Watchtowers and the soil witness me from behind Ivy's narrowed stare. Ivy's hand clutches my throat with hideous strength, and dozens and dozens of feral women saunter forward from rising mists surrounding me. Women decorated in hare masks and furs and muddy sigils. These wisps, these creatures, ripe for the natural cycles, birth, death, here to see me drained dry. Mud-stained hands grope me, hold me docile, sharing my seed.

"But I love you," I beg Ivy, gasping up blood.

"Love?" The goddess buried inside her muddy veins laughs, echoing, empowering them all. "Sweetheart, you know this was never about love."

She yanks the dagger from my ribs with a rapturous spray of blood.

Life pumps from me, crimson this time, hot and final.

In the fever-dream pulse beats before I wither, Ivy closes filthy fingers around my jaw and twists my head to one side. The women of Roothaven part like hares, granting me a view from the Watchtower.

Showing me what Oleandriel sees.

A relentless landscape stained by the broad brushstrokes of masculine appetites. Voices of divine feminine wisdom drowned in a cacophony of boyish ego. A world of rules written in the sticky white ink of patriarchies.

A man's kingdom deliberately calibrated to control the autonomy of goddesses. Sacred fertility rites and rights buried beneath the monuments of male conquest. Women as trophies, women as damsels, women as targets and puppets and holes. Women reduced to wisps. And everywhere stand men dressed in shadows, lurking in darkness even as they imagine themselves to be knights on white horses.

And now the landscape shifts, a fever vision of Ivy and her sisters in the coming dawn, celebrating another successful sowing. I see them returning to their hidden village beyond the vapours, empowered vibrant women gathering in verdant fields below their Watchtower. Women all, and women only. They rejoice the coming bounties, fertile wombs already swelling with a new generation of daughters. Daughters who will be elevated beyond the appetites of strangers. Daughters who will never suffer the obsessions of ignoble men boasting the status of gods.

Because real gods are immortal, and those skeletal hands protruding from Roothaven's graveyard don't belong to women.

They belong to men.

Men lured in by the only language they know.

Men who are only useful for one thing.

Men who pretend they're the good ones simply because bigger monsters exist.

And yes, bigger monsters do.

Ivy unleashes her goddess's banshee cry for all the women of the world. As one, she and her sisters raise daggers like teeth, feeding a divine feminine rage. As one, they slam their blades down, violating the last of me. Bitches. Whores. I spit and shudder, bloody and withered and all used up as they carry me to the edge of the Watchtower.

Without further ceremony, they dump me over the side.

My enlightened view plummets, and in the heartbeat before the brutal impact, before the unforgiving earth splits open and the pulsing grave mud entombs me, Oleandriel grants me a final haunting indignity.

A breathy whisper of wind and wisps in my disposable ear. A promise.

The sisters of Roothaven have already forgotten my name.

Author and Editor Bios

Many wonderful authors came together to make *Choices: An Anthology of Reproductive Horror* possible. If you enjoyed their stories, you can learn about them—including where to follow them on social media and find their other works—in the following pages.

The Editor

Dianna Gunn writes fantasy, horror, and occasionally science fiction. She released her first novel, Moonshadow's Guardian, in 2018, and finished the Moonshadow Rising Duology with Moonshadow's Champion in 2024.

Gunn's short stories have appeared in the award-winning *Nothing Without Us, Too* anthology and *Broken Olive Branches*. She's also edited several novels including the *Memes of the Prophet* books and the upcoming *Choices: An Anthology of Reproductive Horror*. You can find her on Bluesky @diannalgunn.bsky.social or on her website at authordiannagunn.com.

The Authors

Asian-Canadian, fantasy/fiction writer **Allay Rei** is much the observer. They love questioning the very essence of the world around them and, through stories, they intend to make their findings everyone's problem. If not on a quest to find the next unfortunate soul they'll turn into a character, Allay spends their time either daydreaming or gaming since they have yet to find a better way to live life.

Amanda Cecelia Lang is a horror author and aspiring femme fatale from Colorado. As a diehard scary movie nerd, her favorite things are meta-slashers, '80s nostalgia, and the rise of a fierce final girl. Her scary stories haunt the dark corners of many popular podcasts, magazines, and anthologics, including *The Deadlands, Ghoulish Tales, Uncharted, Cast of Wonders, Gamut*, and *Darkness Beckons*. Her short story collections, *Saturday Fright at the Movies: 13 Tales from the Multiplex* (Dark Matter INK) and *The Library of Broken Girls: Stories of Survival* (Gateway Literary), are available everywhere nightmares are sold. You can stalk her work at amandacecelialang.com—just don't be surprised if she leaps out at you from the shadows.

Anne Wilkins is a former family court lawyer, and now a sleep-deprived primary school teacher in New Zealand. She writes in her spare time (which she has very little of). Her love of writing is fuelled by copious amounts of coffee, reading and hope. Her work can be found in Apex Magazine, Cosmic Horror Monthly, Elegant Literature, Scifi Shorts and elsewhere. Anne is the winner of the June 2024 "Bad Blood" Elegant Literature Prize, the 2023 "Halloween Frights" Autumn Writers Battle, and the 2023 Cambridge Autumn Festival Short Story Competition. For more information visit www.annewilkinsauthor.com or facebook.com/annewilkinsauthor

Ash Vale (they/them) is a queer, non-binary, neurodivergent Canadian. They're a big fan of cryptids, guts, and weird lil guys. Their work has been published in places like Heartlines Spec, DreamForge, and more. You can find their newsletter and stories at https://linktr.ee/ashvale or on BlueSky and Instagram as @AshValeWrites.

A. H. Davison (she/her) is a bisexual woman from Vancouver, British Columbia. She has ADHD, a BSc, tokophobia, the guilt of being an evolutionary dead-end by choice, a morbid fascination with the worst things people are capable of doing to each other, a propensity for overly long sentences, and two cats. She writes character-driven stories that explore ethics, often in research and the future of reproduction, and confronts her protagonists with choices between self-preservation and humanity's ongoing survival

A.V. Black is a Canadian author who writes character-driven stories with sharp edges, feminist overtones, and a touch of dark humour. While her current works-in-progress fall into the fantasy and sci-fi genres, she also enjoys crafting short stories that pack a punch. When not writing, A.V. Black enjoys exploring new places, reading, and gaming.

Bogi Takács is a Hungarian Jewish trans immigrant to the US who's a writer, critic and scholar of speculative fiction. Bogi has won the Lambda and Hugo awards, and has been a finalist for other awards like the Ignyte and the Locus. Eir second short story collection Power to Yield and Other Stories came out earlier this year from Broken Eye Books.

Elise Scott is a liberal back-woods bootlegger and artisanal vegan cheesemaker. They write from their lived experiences of fat-positivity, queerness, disability, mental illness, and moving through carnivorous shadows. They earned their bachelor's degree from Mount Holyoke and their Master's from Capella University. Elise is a full-time writer/mom represented by Marisa Corvisiero and Ciara Smith at Corvisiero Literary. They live with one tiny daughter and nearly two hundred pounds of fur-family. Their work has appeared in Five Minutes, High Shelf, HerStry, Knee Brace, All Existing, and Quibble among others. Say hi at http://elise-scott.com or on twitter/x at @buttonjar1.

Enoli Lee is a trans, reconnecting Tsalagi native. His debut collection, *Skin of the Lamb,* is set for release in October 2025. Find him online at https://linktr.ee/enolilee

Justine White is a trans woman born and raised in New Brunswick, Canada. *There is a Place for Us in This World* is her first pro publication.

Kelli Etheridge lives on Vancouver Island. She facilitates a Dark Fiction Writing Circle with the Federation of BC Writers. Her works-in-progress include a paranormal novel set in Victoria, BC, and a dystopian novella set in Vancouver. When not writing or revising the longer works, she enjoys creating short stories and poetry. Her story, Devour, can be found in the Graveside Press anthology, Bite, December 2024.

Surrounded by gnomes and gargoyles, **KT Wagner** writes speculative fiction in the garden of her home on the west coast of Canada. She loves to knit and is a collector of strange plants, weird trivia and obscure tomes. KT graduated from Simon Fraser University's Writers Studio in 2015 (Southbank 2013). She organizes writer events and works to create literary community. A number of her short stories are published and podcast in magazines and anthologies. She's currently working on a novella. KT can be found online at www.ktwagner.com and https://bsky.app/profile/ktwagner.bsky.social

Meg Candelaria writes fiction in the mystery, science fiction, and horror genres. She is unappreciative of reality's tendency to steal all her horror story ideas. She is currently seeking a way to have a web presence that does not involve giving money and/or attention to corporations that are absolutely evil, but has been unsuccessful in that quest thus far.

Mia Dalia is an internationally published, CWA-nominated author of all things fantastic, thrilling, scary, and strange. Her short stories of horror, noir, science fiction, mystery, crime, humor, and more have been featured in a variety of anthologies, magazines, literary journals, online, and adapted for narrative podcasts. She is the author of the novels *Estate Sale* and *Haven*, novellas *Tell Me a Story, Discordant, Arrokoth,* and *Do You Know The Muffin Man?* and the collection *Smile So Red and Other Tales of Madness.* Find her at https://daliaverse.wixsite.com/author or https://linktr.ee/daliaverse.

Ondine Mayor is an emerging author born and raised on a small Island off the coast of Vancouver, Canada and currently studying English Language and Literature in the Czech Republic. She spends much of her time reading and who's every thought will end up on paper. Sometimes it turns into something special, and sometimes it remains the scribbling on the back of a receipt. Ondine has a special interest in long-form fiction and is currently editing her first novel, while writing short stories in her free time.

Raluca Balasa holds an MFA in Creative Writing: Fiction from the University of Nevada, Reno. Her short work has appeared in venues such as Andromeda Spaceways Magazine, Aurealis, and Grimdark Magazine, as well as on Apex Magazine's blog. Currently, Raluca works as an English professor in the Toronto area. Her debut science fiction novel, Blood State, was released in 2020 from Renaissance Press. She can be found at https://ralucabalasa.wixsite.com/website

R. Haven hails from Toronto, Canada. His short stories have been published by Canthius, Soitera Press, TL;DR Press, among others. Last Stanza Poetry Journal and Old Moon Press have published his poetry. He also signed a contract with Renaissance Press for a standalone horror novel, and is represented by Kaitlyn Katsoupis of Belcastro Literary Agency. His website is theirritablequeer.com.

Sam Rosewilde is a writer of fantasy fiction. She lives with her partner in Colorado, where she spends most of her time daydreaming. When she isn't chained to her keyboard furiously typing up her next book, she can be found walking her two dogs or maxing out her library card.

Soyam Siddha is sci-fi / horror writer at the crack of dawn and an engineer by the day. A first-generation immigrant from Calcutta, India, she lives with her two mischievous children – one human and one canine. She is vehemently pro-choice.

Acknowledgements

Writing may be solitary, but producing a high-quality book takes a village. This is especially true for anthologies, which bring numerous authors together to create stories around a shared theme.

Here, at the end of *Choices*, I want to thank the village who came together to make this very special anthology possible.

First, I want to thank my grandmother, Victoria Roth, and my mother, Rose Johnson. You taught me that I always have a choice and that my right to choose matters. When I had to make those choices, you supported me in every one of my decisions, and I am grateful for it.

I also want to thank my aunt Talia Johnson, who convinced me to bring my idea for this anthology to Renaissance Press and answered many of my questions about creating an anthology. You are one of many strong, supportive women I'm lucky to have in my family, and I am constantly grateful for your support.

Alex Woodroe—there's so much I want to thank you for. Your constant support of the horror community gives me something to aspire to. The incredible anthologies you've put together showed me the truly massive range of possibilities for horror anthologies like this one. More specifically, the advice you gave me on creating an anthology proposal helped me write the pitch for this book. I'll always be grateful for your support—and excited to support you too.

To Nathan, Jen, and all of the other wonderful people at Renaissance Press: thank you for helping me create this book and for constantly championing diverse voices. The work you've done to make publishing a more inclusive space is a constant inspiration.

To all of the authors who are part of this anthology, and all of the writers who submitted to this anthology, thank you for sharing your souls with me. I've been honoured to read each and every one of your stories, and I hope to watch you all find massive success in the publishing world.

I'm also grateful for all of the people who make my life better in ways big and small on a daily basis. Astrid Fairwinds, Robbie Murphy, Jade Benjamin, Samantha Murray, Alex Kennedy, Tanja Gunn-O'Hanlon, Felix Graves, Saffron Richter, and so many more. I hope you'll all be in my life for many years to come, and that I'll publish enough books that you'll get tired of reading your names in these sections.

Finally, I want to shout out my cats: Artemis, Mister Mistoffelees, and Hobbes. They're the closest thing to children I'll ever have, because I'm lucky enough to live in a place where I have a choice—and the joy they bring me gives me strength to carry on no matter how tough life gets.

About Renaissance

Renaissance was founded in May 2013 by a group of authors and designers who wanted to publish and market those stories which don't always fit neatly in a genre, or a niche, or a demographic. Like the happy pan-bibliophiles we are, we opened our submissions, with no other guideline than finding a Canadian book we would fall in love with.

Today, this is still very true; however, we've also noticed an interesting trend in what we like to publish. It turns out that we are naturally drawn to the voices of those who are members of a marginalized group, and these are the voices we want to continue to uplift.

At Renaissance, we do things differently. We are passionate about books, and we care as much about our authors enjoying the publishing process as we do about our readers enjoying a great Canadian read on the platform they prefer.

pressesrenaissancepress.ca

pressesrenaissancepress@gmail.com

THE OTHER FACE OF SYMPATHY

Edward Barrett's grandmother committed suicide. She left him every-thing. Having been homeless, Edward unquestioningly moves into her apartment, unaware that she left something behind. Something that sinks its teeth into his very existence.

His one shot at figuring out what's haunting him and saving himself is inside the journals he picked up from Otherside Book Exchange – the writers were all victims, and all became monsters following their deaths.

Between the off-putting proprietor of Otherside – a soft-spoken woman named Conscience – and the distressing contents of the journals, Edward has no choice but to come around to the idea that otherworldly horrors exist, and they're all around him.

If he wants to save himself from being eaten alive, he needs to find the diary of the monster preying on him.

THERE'S NO PLACE

What is home? Is it a place, a person, a memory, a sensation?

These stories, written by storytellers who have experienced homelessness, take you around the block, around the world, and out into the wider universe. But in the end, they always bring you back home.

From adventurous to everyday, from absurd to heartfelt, these tales are a mosaic of home as uncertainty, as longing, and as hope.

Nothing Without Us Too

Nothing Without Us Too, Prix Aurora Award 2023 winner, follows the theme of Nothing Without Us (a 2020 Prix Aurora Award finalist), featuring more stories by authors who are disabled, d/Deaf or hard-of-hearing, Blind or visually impaired, neurodivergent, Spoonie, and/or who manage mental illness. The lived experiences of their protagonists are found across many demographics--such as race, culture, financial status, religion, gender, age, and/or sexual orientation. We want to present these stories because diversity is reality, and it belongs in literary and genre fiction.

So, whether we're being welcomed to Sensory Hell by hotel staff, witnessing a stare-down between a convenience store worker and an arrogant vampire, or unsure if our social media account is magic, these tales can teleport us elsewhere yet resonate deep within.